DEATH AT HUNGERFORD STAIRS

DEATH AT HUNGERFORD STAIRS

CHARLES DICKENS &
SUPERINTENDENT JONES INVESTIGATE

J.C. BRIGGS

PRAISE FOR

THE MURDER OF PATIENCE BROOKE:
CHARLES DICKENS & SUPERINTENDENT JONES
INVESTIGATE

'This is a well-written and engaging novel …The pages keep turning, and the evocation of foggy Victorian London is excellent'

The Historical Novel Society

'[An] aspect of this novel that adds to its enjoyability is the fact that it feels very much like a traditional gaslight mystery, with footsteps in the fog, an unseen person with sinister voice singing a well-known tune … Put all these elements together and it creates just the right amount of suspense'

5-Star Review, Crime Fiction Lover

'From the first few pages you are captured by this fast paced, descriptively brilliant yarn, which sweeps its reader away into the tangible world of dark, damp, foul-smelling Victorian London'

5-Star Review, Dickens the Sleuth, Amazon

'… he had quite exceptionally bright and active eyes that were always darting about like brilliant birds to pick up all the tiny things of which he made more, perhaps, than any other novelist has done; for he was a sort of poetical Sherlock Holmes.'

Charles Dickens by G.K. Chesterton

Do ye hear the children weeping, O my brothers,
Ere the sorrow comes with years? …

And may well the children weep before you!
They are weary ere they run;
They have never seen the sunshine, nor the glory
Which is brighter than the sun.
They know the grief of man, without its wisdom;
They sink in man's despair, without its calm, –
Are slaves without the liberty in Christdom, –
Are martyrs, by the pang without the palm, –
Are worn as if with age, yet unretrievingly
The harvest of its memories cannot reap, –
Are orphans of the earthly love and heavenly.
Let them weep! let them weep!

From *The Cry of the Children* by Elizabeth Barrett Browning

For Tom

'Tom was the idol of her life … always to be believed in, and done homage to with the whole faith of her heart.'

David Copperfield

Original cover photograph ©iStockphoto.com

First published 2015

The Mystery Press is an imprint of The History Press
The Mill, Brimscombe Port
Stroud, Gloucestershire, GL5 2QG
www.thehistorypress.co.uk

© J.C. Briggs, 2015

The right of J.C. Briggs to be identified as the Author
of this work has been asserted in accordance with the
Copyright, Designs and Patents Act 1988.

British Library Cataloguing in Publication Data.
A catalogue record for this book is available from the British Library.

ISBN 978 0 7509 6417 3

Typesetting and origination by The History Press
Printed in Great Britain

CONTENTS

1

REMEMBERING

He remembered the rats. And how they had swarmed in the cellars of the crazy, tumbledown warehouse; sometimes in the grey shadows he had seen hundreds of eyes glittering like little red lamps, and then there would be a skittering of claws as they vanished down holes and into corners. Mary Weller, a servant at his childhood home in Chatham, had scared him half to death with the tale of Chips, a sailor and his talking rat which had gnawed at the seaman's ship and Chips, too. He had been haunted by them, imagining them curled up on his pillow, nestling in his blankets, darting across his counterpane. When he worked at the blacking factory at Hungerford Stairs, he had hurried up the rotten staircase, trembling, in case they pursued him. He was twelve then, at work, pasting the labels on to the bottles of blacking, twelve hours a day for six shillings a week. He had never forgotten the dark, wainscoted room, the damp, rotting floors, the dirt and decay, and the heave and slap of the river at the walls when the black tide was in.

Now, Charles Dickens stood outside for the first time in twenty-five years. He had avoided the place as if it were plague-stricken. He could hardly believe it was still standing. The ancient wooden balcony had almost slipped into the thick mud into which his feet were sinking and the poles that had once held up the balcony leaned at drunken angles. The upper storeys tottered over the lower and half the roof had fallen in, though there was still a casement window open in the part that remained. It looked like a wrecked ship, though, he wagered, the rats would not have deserted it. The door had gone but rotting planks had been put in its place. They had been pushed aside to make an entrance. By this, a police constable stood waiting for them.

Dickens and Superintendent Sam Jones had received the message from Inspector Harker of Scotland Yard. From Bow Street they had hurried along the Strand, turning through the market which stank of rotting fish. A few traders still lingered, but by this time of a late, cold afternoon in November most business had been done, and the boats which had brought the sprats, the herrings and the oysters, packed close in their barrels, had sailed away. The two men had gone down Hungerford Stairs to the bank where the brown river formed scummy pools in the muddy sludge, and from where Brunel's pedestrian bridge crossed to the south bank. They had not spoken. The message had been about a dead boy found in the old blacking factory. And Dickens and Jones were looking for a boy – a boy gone missing. And a dog. Inspector Harker had known of their search which was why he had sent word. A dog had barked, and a man, alerted by the noise, had gone into the old warehouse where he had found the boy. That was all they knew.

Superintendent Jones looked at Dickens's strained face, knowing what he was thinking. He saw his lips moving and knew that he was saying, 'Let it not be Scrap. Let it not be Poll.' The same desperate words fluttered on his own lips. Dickens glanced at him as if he had heard them though Sam had not spoken. Each man's fearful eyes told the same story.

As they turned at the bottom of the steps, Dickens was face to face with the detested place. He would not have come here were it not for Scrap, the boy they knew. Inspector Harker, thickset and full of purpose, came through the black hole and crossed to meet them.

'The dog,' said Dickens. His urgency was so intense that he could not even greet the inspector. 'Is the dog here?'

'No,' said Inspector Harker. 'It had disappeared when the man who found the body came out.'

It could not be Poll then. Poll would not leave Scrap. She would have stayed with him. Dickens thought this, but Sam Jones had to ask.

'Did he say anything about it?'

'Just a dog – a little thing, he said.' Dickens looked at Sam. Poll was a little dog. He looked along the bank. Was she there? Cowering and afraid. But there was no dog to be seen.

Inspector Harker followed his gaze and turned back to Sam. 'I'm sorry. The man heard it barking by the hole there and thought someone might be trapped inside the building – what's left of it – so he went to have a look. The body is just inside – dumped there, I think.'

'We'll have a look then. Charles, do you want to stay outside?' Jones thought it might be too much for him – if it were Scrap, perhaps it was better that he did not see.

Dickens shook his head. 'I'll come.' He had to go in and see for himself. He could not wait here in the bleak November afternoon. He followed Inspector Harker and the superintendent, their boots squelching in the ooze. He felt a leaden dread lodged in his stomach. Sam Jones glanced back at him, his grey eyes troubled, but he said nothing.

They pushed through the old doorway to find themselves standing on wet, sticky earth in the murky light of the old room. The floor had rotted away, but Dickens saw in the gloom that the staircase still went up to the room where he had laboured over his pots of blacking. There was a scuttling on the stairs and an old grey-headed rat, as large as a cat, sat and stared at him as if to say, 'I know you – what do you do here?' It was gone in a second, the gristly tail vanishing through a crack. ·

Inspector Harker held up his bull's-eye lamp to show the boy lying face down in the dirt. He was encased in grey mud which had dried, almost set round the corpse as if he were in his coffin already. The face was buried in the mud; you could see how the hair had stiffened into spikes, and how the clothes had crumpled into dried ripples, not fabric but moulded clay. The arms were stretched above the head, the fingers splayed out, sculpted from mud. He did not look real. The impression was that he had been thrown there, so much waste from the river. Flotsam, thought Dickens, a piece of cargo from the wrecked ship. Let it not be Scrap.

The constable turned him over and the mud flaked away, revealing the thin lad who was real, had been alive, had been a boy, had played with his dog, perhaps, on the oozing shore, had grinned at its antics, had wondered at the passing ships, had dreamed, had longed for something. And now he was dead, here in this place that still smelt of the grave. They stared at the poor, gaunt corpse with its dirty, mud-encrusted face, as yet unrecognisable. Sam's lips moved — a prayer for the dead. He always did that. His faith was quiet and private yet, whenever a corpse was found, he murmured his prayer, this tall, strong man in the face of whose authority hardened wretches quailed.

The constable wiped the boy's face with surprising tenderness, using the handkerchief which the superintendent had handed him for the purpose. Dickens, who did not know that he had been holding his breath, exhaled, and felt as if his heart had restarted. It was not Scrap.

'No,' said Sam. 'He is not the boy we are looking for. We'll leave him to you, but let us know, will you, what you find out. He might belong to someone — someone, somewhere might be waiting for news of their boy.'

'I will,' said Inspector Harker. 'It looks as though he might have drowned — see the mud and weed round his mouth. The clothes

are dried out, but they look to be stained with water. I wonder if someone found him on the bank, couldn't be bothered to report it, and just dumped him in here. It happens – too often. Apart from you looking for a boy, I've had no reports of another one missing. But then, he might not belong to anyone. The man who found him didn't know him. There are always boys about, mudlarks, scraping a living here. Who knows?'

'Aye,' said the superintendent, 'I know – too many lost boys, and girls, too.'

Dickens and Jones turned to go. The superintendent began to push his way through the hole. Dickens made to follow but his attention was caught by some chalk markings on the wall.

'Sam, look here.'

The superintendent backed in again and, raising his lamp, regarded the marks. They formed a picture, the figure of a man, the face of which seemed to be a mask of some sort. He was reminded of a childhood horror – a figure chalked upon a door with a great long mouth and hands like two bunches of carrots. This was not the same at all, but he felt a similar revulsion, remembering how he had run from that figure. The mask here seemed so curiously out of place. Dickens thought there was something sinister about it – what was it doing here, and who had scrawled it? Was it, he wondered, some kind of message connected to the dead boy?

'It might be worth noting this,' Sam said to Inspector Harker, 'though of course, it might mean nothing at all.'

The inspector came over with his lamp. 'Could be the work of children – the place is not secure, as we have seen. It looks childish. Still, I won't forget it.'

Outside, there was a thin wind sneaking along the water. It was nearly dusk; the sun was setting over the river. The sky was a curious green, marbled with red, purple and orange lines like the cover of a book, and the brown river took on a greenish hue like poison. As they stood watching, the colours changed, the marble lines shifted, and the green began to change as the sun sank. The wind created ripples on the river and the colours there broke into splinters, the water darkening and moving restlessly under the sky.

'Ominous sky,' said Dickens, shivering as the wind reached them, and flecks of rain spat at them. 'I wonder if that sketch meant anything – it did not seem like a child's drawing to me – it looked sinister, somehow, deliberate.'

'I know what you mean – if it were the work of a child, one might expect more scrawls, more carelessness in the drawing, but there's not much we can do about it. The case belongs to Inspector Harker.'

'Poor lad. I wonder if he did drown.'

'Looks like it. It's not uncommon. These boys and girls, the mudlarks, take risks, go too far out, especially when they see something floating on the surface – might be a piece of wood, a cask, a piece of cloth – something unusual that they might be able to sell, and I have known it before – that the body is dumped somewhere because it's too much trouble to report it, and if there is no name, no parents, then who cares? Too often, no one.'

'We do – we care about Scrap – and we want him back. What do we do, Sam?'

'I don't know what we can do. I have Rogers and the other constables on the lookout in the alleys by Crown Street and over Holborn. He can't have gone too far. Where would he go? And why?'

'Unless he was taken – but, then, what has happened to Poll? He must have gone after her. He would, you know.'

'I know – and when he finds her, I'll bet he comes back.'

'And if he does not find her?'

Dickens's question hovered on the bleak wind which snatched it away, leaving them silent and miserable. There really were no answers to their questions. They would have to possess themselves in patience, and wait, and hope.

They turned away to go up the stairs. Dickens looked back at the warehouse rotting into the river. He thought about the lost boy who lay there in the mud. Had he drowned in that terrible water, sucked under by some freak eddy which whirled him to his death? Had he known that it was all over, and that he would never come up again into the light? His heart twisted with pity. What a place. The shadows were lengthening now; that curiously green sky had darkened as the thick clouds gathered like a threat; the cold was biting.

Superintendent Jones began to ascend with Dickens behind him when a man started to come down, an old white dog at his heels. They waited for him, the steps being narrow and slippery with weed and slime. As he approached, they saw that he looked like a seafaring man with his cap and pea coat, and his red belcher handkerchief round his neck. His hazel eyes were clouded with anxiety as he stopped to look at them.

'Do you know about the boy?' The question was urgent. 'I heard a dead boy has been found.'

'Yes,' said Sam. 'Do you know of a missing boy?'

'I do – my grandson is missing – I came to see – I hope –' He broke off, uncertain. It was clear he wanted to go and see. The dog looked up at his master, sensing his agitation.

'We are looking for a boy and a dog, but the boy there was not the one we seek. I hope he is not yours,' said Dickens.

'Thank you, sir. I hope you may find your boy – now I must –'

On impulse, Dickens handed him his card. There was something about the man which appealed to his sympathy. 'If you need help, you might wish to come to see me.'

The man took the card, and without looking at it, pushed it in his pocket. He nodded at them, and went away towards the old factory. The white dog followed closely at his heels. The man stopped and both looked out across the darkening river. They watched as the man squared his shoulders and then walked towards the black hole where the door had been.

Dickens and Jones turned to climb the steps which would take them into the passage by two inns, the *Old Fox* and the *Swan*. Dickens remembered how he and his fellow worker Bob Fagin would sometimes buy a glass of ale and bread and cheese from the miserable old *Swan*. He could see now in his mind's eye, Bob in his ragged apron and paper cap with his hand curled round his glass, the nails encrusted with the blacking, and he remembered scrubbing at his own hands trying to take away the stain. He had thought he would die and be buried in blacking.

As they passed the inns, a ragged boy, in the act of transferring a heel of grubby bread from hand to mouth, stared at them curiously before turning down a squalid alley where he vanished from sight. Another lost boy. Too many to count but two, at least, were wanted.

2

A DECISION

Dickens and Jones parted on the Strand, the superintendent bound for Bow Street and Dickens turning from Charing Cross to Regent Street, its vast linen-drapery establishments a world away from the rat-infested warehouse. He passed the plate-glass windows dressed with elaborate costumes, rich velvets, glistening silks, lace, golden fringes and tassels, and he could not help but think of the ragged boy with his chunk of dirty bread.

He crossed Oxford Street and made his way through Cavendish Square where he saw a well-dressed lady walking her dog, a little spaniel which made him think again of Poll, the dog who was lost and Scrap who might have gone to find her – and the Brim family, the children who owned Poll and loved her.

Mr Brim owned a stationer's shop; it was there that Dickens had first encountered Scrap, who had helped him pursue the man with the crooked face wanted in connection with a case on which he had worked with Superintendent Jones. Mr Brim had been very ill at the time – still was, though not so bad as then – and Scrap, the street boy, had become his children's unofficial protector before being promoted to delivery boy, for Mr Brim's business had flourished from the many customers Dickens had pointed his way. Elizabeth, the superintendent's wife, had looked after them all and still assisted in the shop when Mr Brim was sick. A most satisfactory outcome for all, Dickens had thought – until Scrap and

Poll the dog, had vanished. Where was Scrap? The question had tormented Dickens for three days now; Mr Brim's children, Eleanor and Tom, were inconsolable and Elizabeth Jones was equally upset. Dickens felt that he must restore all their happiness by finding Scrap and Poll. What he wanted was to appear at the shop door producing Poll from under his coat as he had once produced a guinea pig from a box of bran to delight his children.

He found himself in Wimpole Street just by number fifty, once the home of poet Elizabeth Barrett Browning, who had married his friend Robert Browning; they were in Italy now. He remembered meeting her outside this house, a slender woman with a shower of dark curls framing her face, large expressive eyes with thick lashes. Her spaniel, Flush, had been with her, and she had told Dickens that the beloved dog had been kidnapped three times – she had paid a ransom, despite her father's and Robert Browning's opposition. He remembered the dog, and how it had looked at her with eyes like her own, wise and loving – he would think about Flush when he invented Jip, Dora's dog.

Dickens stood stock still. Stolen! Poll had been stolen – that could be it. That must be it. Scrap would have gone after her. That was how the children had met Scrap – he had saved Poll from a thief. Soft you now, he told himself, let us think. Admittedly, Poll was not a pedigree like Flush – there was a trade in pedigree dogs; ransoms of as much as ten guineas had been paid, and there was profitable business in the export of stolen King Charles Spaniels to Holland and Belgium. But Poll had a collar – had some opportunist thief snatched her? If so, however, when would the demand for a ransom be made? Why not immediately? His questions died in his throat. It could be worse – dogs were often sold on at country fairs and markets, having been clipped, sometimes even dyed to disguise them. Many, and he shuddered for Poll at the thought, were killed for their skins. And his own dog, Timber, the small curly white-haired Havana spaniel that he had brought back from America all those years ago, had been stolen once from the kitchen at Devonshire Terrace. Timber had been brought back by the coachman, Topping, and a very large policeman. It happened – often.

Would he pay a ransom for Poll? Of course he would, just as he had been prepared to pay a ransom for Timber. He could not have borne the thought of loyal Timber tied up in some dank cellar. And a ransom for Scrap? Yes, and he would pay a ransom for any of his own children, for anyone he loved and who needed to be rescued from some dank cellar, for someone whose life might be set at naught. He knew the counter-arguments that in paying a ransom he would be encouraging the trade, increasing the wickedness, putting money in the hands of blackmailers. But he felt driven to his wits' end. And, what would Sam say? He, too, was distressed by the disappearance of Scrap and the dog, but he was a policeman; he could hardly be paying money to thieves. But this was Poll who had to be saved. Dickens thought he would have to do it without the superintendent, and without telling Elizabeth – he could not compromise her, a policeman's wife. But then, he checked his racing thoughts, how to find a dog thief?

Occy Grave! The very man. Occy, whom Dickens knew well, was the crossing sweeper whose pitch was at the junction of Drury Lane and Long Acre, convenient for the pedestrians coming and going from Lincoln's Inn, Bow Street Police Station and the magistrates' court. He had been there for twenty years, and knew everyone, even their cats and dogs which he returned to their owners if they had strayed. Sometimes he delivered letters and parcels to augment his earnings. He never forgot a face. He might have seen Scrap, Dickens thought; he might have seen Poll, and he would certainly know a dog thief – a dog thief in what might be called a small way. Dickens knew that there were those who were organisers in a big way; a certain Mr Taylor could be paid to get a dog back – no questions asked. Chelsea George was famed for his ingenious, if repulsive, method of dog capture; he smeared his hands with a paste of cooked liver and tincture of myrrh then seemed to caress the dog's nose and hey presto, he had a faithful follower. No, thought Dickens, Poll was not valuable enough for a Chelsea George.

It was too late now to see Occy – too dark. His business was finished for the day. Mornings were the best times. He made his way home out of Wimpole Street and on to Devonshire Terrace. It was quiet here behind the high brick wall but he could hear the hum of the teeming city. Dickens went through the iron gate and into the garden. The clouds had fled and he stood looking at a sky clear as black glass, cracked here and there with the splintering stars.

That restless night he dreamed a familiar dream, of a long staircase up which he went, feeling his way in the shadows to a landing where there were closed rooms. Somewhere a child was sobbing, but all the doors were locked. In the dream, a dog howled and he woke. He heard it again and went to the window to look out at the empty night, and into the garden where the bushes hunched like beggars, and the black trees reached down to them as if to pluck them from the dark. He heard the clip clop of a horse, and a hoarse cry suddenly shut off as if an unknown hand had stopped it. The night seemed threatening – out there, he thought, were terrors. Those living in the mansions and grand houses of York Gate and the elegant squares thought they were safe, but the alleys and courts were too near and out of them came menace – the sly thief, the mug-hunter with his cosh, the assassin with his garrotte and the dog stealer. Somewhere a dog howled again, the lonely, haunting, hollow sound of something bereft. *Where were they?*

3

OCCY GRAVE

The morning brought no news from Superintendent Jones, but there was a letter from Mrs Georgiana Morson, matron of Urania Cottage, the home for fallen women Dickens had established at Shepherd's Bush. She was reporting on the insubordination of a girl called Isabella Gordon and her partner in mischief, Anna-Maria Sesini who called herself Sesina. The rules of the Home were not harsh; the girls were allowed out, although always accompanied; they wore plain dresses in different colours rather than the institutional garb of the prisons, the workhouses or reformatories. They were taught to read and write, to cook and sew, because Dickens intended that these girls should be instructed to desire a better life. They would find new lives in Australia where he advised them they might marry and go on to lead useful lives. That was the plan; in most cases it succeeded, but there were some for whom any rule was chafing, and for whom a quiet and orderly life was stifling. One girl had simply vanished over the wall one day and another had been expelled for drunkenness.

Isabella Gordon was full of life, restless, witty, intelligent but rebellious. He had liked her, but had wondered very often whether she would last. When Sesina came, they formed an unholy alliance – Mrs Morson had suggested that their relationship might have been more than a girlish friendship, and that, he thought, was dangerous to the stability of the Home, but he could hardly have dismissed her on the suspicion that she was sexually involved with Sesina, and, in any case, Mrs Morson was not sure if their conduct were not just deliberately provocative, simply to get attention. Now, it seemed that they were conspiring against Mrs Morson, breaking the rules, fomenting dissatisfaction and quarrels. It was time for Isabella to go; perhaps Sesina would settle down without her friend. Dickens doubted it; he could well imagine them departing together in a flurry of indignation and accusation. He would have to go to Shepherd's Bush, and the committee would have to meet to deal with these two girls.

Time to find Occy Grave. He was up to date with his monthly instalment of *David Copperfield*; he thought it a smashing number, describing young David's first dissipation in which he gazed at himself in the looking-glass with vacant eyes and wondered how only his hair looked drunk, and in which he was indignant that someone had accused Copperfield of falling downstairs, realising that it might be true when he found himself on his back in the hall – Dickens had laughed when writing it, remembering his own youthful folly. The novel was, in effect, his autobiography – he had not needed to go back to the blacking factory to remember it – the memory was written on his heart.

He had not time to look at the other letters – he expected a sea of correspondence in response to the two letters he had written to *The Times* protesting against public hangings after he had seen the Mannings hanged for the murder of Mrs Mannings's lover. Dickens was so horrified by the brutal mirth and callousness of the watching crowd that he had thought it was like living in a city of devils; he argued that such sights must surely coarsen and harden the spectators and he did not believe in the idea of hanging as a deterrent. And he was haunted, too, by the dead shapes swinging from side to side on the gallows, the woman's skirts ballooning out so that she seemed not dead but doomed to swing there forever, enduring the yelling and whistling of the crowd. Murderess as she was, it had been better that she hang in private, he believed. He had been relieved when the murderer whom he and Jones had pursued in an earlier case had escaped the hangman. The man had been callous, selfish and depraved, but Dickens had not wanted to hunt him to the gallows to be baited with the rabble's curse. And that, he thought, was the moot point – it was all very well to bay for the murderer's death when another man put the noose round his neck. Well, he thought wryly, some of these letters would no doubt be protesting against his views but he could deal with them later. Out, out, he told himself – let us find Occy.

Dickens enjoyed walking – seventeen miles was nothing to him – so a ten-minute walk to Drury Lane was a mere step. Occy was there in his long coat and leather cap, sweeping a path for his customers with his habitual good cheer. For Dickens, Occy was a source of fascination. His past was quite remarkable – Dickens thought it as extraordinary as anything he might have written. Once, on a cold winter's day with a particularly insolent and insinuating wind, Dickens had taken the frozen man to a nearby chop house with a warm fire and even warmer rum punch, and Occy had told his tale.

His father had been a scholar, a man so immersed in books that in a fit of abstraction, he had married his kitchen maid, and, according to Occy, he could not have found a better Mrs Grave, though she was destined for an early one. It was by her economies that the family survived at all, their income being rather smaller than the outcome of their union which was nine children.

Septimus Grave was a student of the arcane; he had formed a lunatic scheme for the improvement of the family fortunes. Himself a seventh son, he determined that he should produce a seventh son, which prodigy would save them from ruin – if they could wait long enough for him to grow to man's estate. Before this madness set in, Septimus named his first two sons plainly: William and John, but the madness gained hold step by step through each succeeding child. Thus they were christened, in turn, Tertius, Quartus, Quintus, Sextus (who was followed, with a gnashing of teeth, the mother's in labour, the father's in baffled rage) by two daughters and then, at last, the longed-for Septimus – seventh son of a seventh son. But alas, Tertius, sickly from birth, died of a fever. The lunatic's confusion was alarming. In his derangement, he believed that now Septimus was only the sixth. Another child came – the exhausted mother assumed that he must be Octavius. Not so, he must be Septimus, and the others, by the ingenious calculation of the madman, should be renamed; Septimus should become Sextus and so step by step backwards to Quartus who filled the empty space left by Tertius. But before the accomplishment of this confusion, the madman died. There was just time to christen Occy as Octavius. The fever raged through the house again, taking off Mrs Grave, all her offspring bar Occy himself and one sister; they were taken in by Mrs Graves's sister, a cook, with no children of her own. Her husband was a crossing sweeper, and in time, Occy came into his inheritance – the broom.

Occy had told his story with remarkable cheerfulness. 'What,' he had asked, 'would have become of them all at the mercy of Septimus Grave?' They would have starved to death, that's what, he had argued. For himself, he had been happy in the care of Emmy Theed, the cook, and was grateful for his inheritance. What more should a man want than a regular job, a comfortable wife? Here he toasted Mrs Sally Grave, his own, and two good sons. They would not take the broom. 'Why, bless you, Mr Dickens,' Occy had said, 'with all this new traffic, omnibuses, cabs and the like, the days of the crossing sweeper are numbered.'

Dickens waited for Occy to come back to his side of the road. 'The George at twelve? I need some information.'

Occy signalled his assent with a wave of his broom before clearing the way for two pedestrians. Dickens had an hour to kill. He could not go to Bow Street without telling the superintendent what he was planning. He ought to go to the stationer's shop, but could not bear the thought of turning up empty-handed, nor could he bear the flare of optimism which would light up the children's eyes if he appeared at the door. They would think he had news. Dickens stood uncertainly on the pavement. What a curious thing – he was at a loss, somehow lonely, not knowing where to look for Scrap and Poll who might, for all they knew, be dead.

The traffic whirled past him, cabs and omnibuses wheeling by, the dust swirling in clouds; pedestrians buffeted him as they went by; a man with a basket balanced on his head jostled him and a woman poked at him with her umbrella as if he were a suspicious piece of meat – the stream of life that will not stop, pouring on, on, on, he thought. A blind violinist took up his place at the corner of Queen Street, his white eyes turned up to the troubled sky. He was dressed as if for some long-ago concert in a worn black tailcoat, once-white shirt, ragged tie and cracked patent shoes. As Dickens drew nearer, he could hear the strains of music which for a moment seemed to drown out the roaring world. Most blind musicians were not musicians at all – they got their money for pity, but this one seemed, with his uplifted eyes, not of this world, as if he played for some invisible audience seen only in his mind's eye. The sound was piercing in its sweetness, plaintive and infinitely sad. It spoke of loss and yearning, and no one listened but Dickens as if he and the ragged blind man were alone in the teeming city.

The spell broke when a crowd of sharp-faced, hard-eyed urchins jostled the player and yelled abuse. Dickens threw some coins away down the street and they scattered, shoving and pushing each other to claim their prize. The violinist bowed to Dickens. Perhaps he had sensed the unseen listener. Dickens placed some money in the battered top hat, and saw, for the first time, the little dog crouched at the man's feet. Not Poll. He walked away.

Time to take refuge in the warmth of the George, an ancient black and white inn just along Great Queen Street. Inside, the landlord greeted Dickens as an old friend, and Dickens was cheered by the sight of the fire and a hot rum punch.

'Wot's 'e up to, that Steerforth, Mr Dickens? No good, I 'spect. Is Little Em'ly in danger? – I thought it very queer, sir, when 'e spoke of the black shadow following 'er. 'E kep' lookin' after 'er, too. It's all very mysterious, that it is.'

Dickens said he must wait for the next instalment; he was pleased that Bill Sprigge, the landlord, had read so attentively. In truth *David Copperfield* had not sold as well as *Dombey and Son*, and he was disappointed because he had put so much of himself into it; the writing of it made him restless, in want of something never to be realised, though he did not know what, and the visit to Hungerford Stairs had brought his childhood misery back as vividly as when he had depicted David Copperfield in the bottle factory. He was haunted, he thought, by the phantoms of those days that seemed to follow him. He could never shake them off. The past seemed so often to be snatching at his coat tails, sometimes shoving him on, impelled to achieve greater and greater things, and sometimes dragging him back as yesterday to that dreadful wreck of a place where as a boy he had felt so hopeless and forlorn.

Occy Grave arrived punctually at twelve, having left his broom at the post where he swept – it would be safe, he said, as everyone knew whose it was. They settled themselves in the box by the first fireplace where, Occy had sagaciously pointed out last time, there wasn't a leg in the middle of the table which all the other tables had – very inconvenient, he had observed. He chose a pint of ale, a mutton pie and mash, in which Dickens joined him. They ate first and when the last morsel of meat and pastry was gone, and when Occy had downed a draught of his ale, he looked at Dickens.

'Very good pie, that. Thank you kindly. Information, sir?'

'I am looking for a boy – and a dog. The boy is called Scrap – black hair, about four foot eight – he does deliveries for the stationer's in Crown Street. You might have seen him going to Lincoln's Inn with his parcels. If you see him, you'll let me know?'

'I will, Mr Dickens. Can't say as I've noticed but there are a lot o' boys about.'

'Dog thieves – seen any?'

'Professionals or amateurs?'

'Amateurs, I should think – the dog in question is neither very big nor very valuable. A little terrier which belongs to some children I know. Missing for a few days. I want to get it back for them, if I can.'

'Boys take 'em sometimes – 'oping to get a bob or two from the professionals. Sometimes sell 'em for fightin'. There's meetins' at the King's Head in Compton Street. Yer know – settin' 'em on rats. Big money in that.'

Rats took Dickens back to Hungerford Stairs and the dead boy. He felt sick. Not Poll, he thought, oh no, not little Poll put to fight rats. A horrible business that was – fifty rats flung in a pit and the dog sent to kill as many as he could.

'Oh, Lord, I hadn't thought of that, Occy –'

Occy saw his face turn white. 'Not likely, Mr Dickens – don't yer fret none. A fancier'd only buy ones ter train up – your dog won't be ready for that yet. Now, I ain't seen any dog fanciers my way, but I know someone who might 'elp – sister's 'usband – second-hand clothes in Monmouth Street – Zeb Scruggs.'

'Zeb? With a Z?'

'Story there, Mr Dickens – if you wants to 'ear it.'

Dickens was delighted. What could equal the story of Septimus Grave?

'I do, and for the telling you ought to have another glass.'

'I'll not say no. Dusty work this morning.'

A grey-faced waiter in a greasy apron splashed with mutton gravy brought the ale. Occy drank deeply.

'Zeb,' he began.

'Let me guess – Zebedee – it has to be.'

Occy grinned. 'Worse than that.'

Dickens gave thought to his, admittedly, limited repertoire of names beginning with 'Z'. And there would have to be a 'B' to make sense of Zeb. Something from the Old Testament – wasn't there someone called Zobah or was that a place? Zeeb? No, he'd made that up, surely. He looked at Occy who was still grinning.

'No, I give up. Put me out of my misery.'

Occy took another swig of his ale. 'Zerubbabel.'

Dickens laughed out loud. 'No, no, I'll not believe it. No mother could …'

'She did! Mrs Scruggs was a mortal religious woman. Took to it like a man takes to drink. Which was the trouble – Mr Scruggs drank and Mrs took to the good book. Read 'an read for 'er child was coming an' she thought to save 'im from the wickedness of the world. An' a passage took 'er fancy from a prophet or some such body – Haggai – wot told this prince Zerubbabel that 'e 'ad to obey the Lord an' be strong. It seems 'e did an' was chosen by the Lord for something. I don't recall wot, but Mrs Scruggs wanted 'er lad to be obedient and strong so that must be 'is name. Mr Scruggs tried to stop 'er but chapel preacher was all for it. Zerubbabel it must be.'

Dickens tried, and failed, to imagine a babe in arms saddled with such a name. He shook his head.

'Tis true, Mr Dickens, though, o' course, no one could be bothered with all that babbling, not even Mrs Scruggs, so Zeb 'e became and Zeb 'e stays an' a good strong man 'e is an' a good 'usband to my sister.'

'And dare I ask if Septimus Grave bestowed a name on your sister?' Dickens remembered that Occy had not named either of the two girls born to his lunatic father.

''E did – as I told you, 'e was powerful disappointed when the girls came – paid no attention at all so my mother made the choice. First, there was Mary – she died with the rest, of the fever, as I told you, an' my sister –' Occy drank again. He was a born storyteller, knowing exactly when to heighten the suspense.

'Occy, the suspense is killing me. What is your sister's name?'

'Well,' Occy grinned, 'that's a story, too – you'd 'ardly credit it.'

'I think I might – after all you've told me.'

'As I said, old Septimus didn't pay attention when the girls was born an' 'e didn't seem to notice Mary at all, but 'e did, it seems, come to, as it were, when my sister was to be christened. My mother, a sensible body, had chosen Meg, but 'e, the lunatic, cries out that it was a servant's name not the name of a gentleman's daughter – not the name for a scholar's daughter – and so, at the church, when the reverend asks what the child's to be called, 'e cries out "Euphemia" – Greek apparently. Not that 'e ever spoke to the child after so 'e 'ad no occasion to use the name. Meg woulder done just as well. Anyways, she's Effie now, an' it suits 'er fine.'

'So Euphemia married Zerubbabel,' Dickens laughed, 'who became Effie and Zeb. Any children?'

'Mary, Gabriel, Michael and Peter! 'Ow about that! Now, I'll take you to see them and we can find out what 'e knows.'

Monmouth Street was the centre of the old clothes trade; its emporia, however, were generally depressing, filthy rag shops hung about with musty dresses, faded corduroy trousers, canvas waistcoats, worn boots which had a habit of kicking at the unwary head of a customer who might find himself entangled in the billowing, yellowish skirts of some ancient bridal gown, the arms of which leant down to enfold him in a ghostly embrace. The customer, horrified by his spectral bride, would struggle to free himself from the dusty cloud of net – heedless of the threat of breach of promise – only to face the wrath of some uniform jacket of moth-eaten scarlet and tarnished gilding – the enraged groom, perhaps. Could the toothless hag smoking her pipe peaceably in a broken-down basket chair really have once been the bride? Hideously malformed, tea-coloured stays were cast upon deal tables mixed up with suspiciously stained undergarments, and worn-out dancing shoes, the dancers having pirouetted elsewhere to ease their corns – and bunions, judging by the curious bulges near the frayed silken toes. The burial place of fashion, Dickens had called it.

The second-hand clothes shops were usually foul-smelling, greasy, dirty places, the rags for sale often infected with the fever or pox which had, no doubt, carried off the former owners. But Zeb and Effie were a superior sort of dealers. Entering, Dickens found that the floor was clean, the shop carefully dusted and the goods carefully classified. The front and back doors were open so that a breeze came through to ensure that the air was, at least, breathable. Zeb Scruggs, besides selling old clothes, was a 'translator', meaning that he and Effie were skilled at refashioning the better parts of discarded coats, dresses and skirts into something wearable – the skirts of a coat might make a child's cape; a miniature dress might emerge from a larger one; a skirt might make a pair of breeches for a boy or the back of a shirt could be turned into a baby's dress.

Zeb was at the counter turning over a cloak, too shabby for the pawn shop where it had probably spent a good deal of its working life, but possibly offering something salvageable for the translator to use. The seller was a thin, patched and darned woman. She watched Zeb with desperate hope. He gave her two shillings and out she went. Dickens noticed her gaunt face and dark eyes. She looked starved. The two shillings would mean bread today and the rent paid if she had another couple of shillings.

'Not worth sixpence,' said Zeb ruefully to Effie while folding up the cloak.

'Well, she has to eat, poor woman. Sacking will have to do for her instead of the cloak. She has a boy to feed, too.'

Zeb was a large, well-built man with dark, flashing eyes which gave him a gypsyish look, and there was strength in him, Dickens thought, of character as well as physique. Effie was like her brother, thin and wiry, and full of energy, determined to keep a respectable shop, but never a hard-faced businesswoman.

'Occy, brought us a customer, have you?' Effie smiled at Dickens. 'I know who you are, sir. We look forward to your books. Zeb reads 'em to us – Friday night's the night when we all sit down in the back parlour there. Some of the neighbours come in, too.'

'Thank you, Mrs Scruggs, I am pleased that you like them.'

'What brings you here, Mr Dickens? Have you come to tell us what happens next to David Copperfield? What a thing that'd be, eh, Effie?'

'I am not quite sure myself,' said Dickens.

'Mr Dickens is lookin' for a dog – a dog gone missin'. I thought you might be able to help,' Occy put in.

'Not a valuable dog – in money terms at any rate – it belongs to some young friends of mine and I want to get it back for them. There's a boy gone, too, after the dog, I think.'

'Probably taken by a lad – there's boys who take dogs to the big thieves. It happens all the time. There's a house down by

St Giles's, Darling Row, where I know they keep dogs. Might be a chance there, but, you know, Mr Dickens, it could be somewhere else. No ransom asked for?'

'No, we've heard nothing. Occy mentioned dogs and rats at the King's Head in Compton Street –'

'Not likely, I said,' interrupted Occy.

Dickens looked at Zeb. He wanted reassurance. The idea of Poll with a rat at her throat appalled him.

'Occy's right – it'll be a lad, I'm sure, a lad who knows where to get a bob or two. No one seen loiterin' about the house? Experienced thieves work in twos generally – the lurker hangs about waiting for his opportunity and passes the dog on to his mate.'

'I don't think so. I don't know – the boy and the dog went missing at the same time.'

'Not run away?'

'No – definitely not. The boy, Scrap, is devoted to the children and to the dog. That's why I think he's gone to look for her.'

'Let's stick to the idea of a lad who picked her up on the chance then. I can take you to a man I know who knows the dog thieves – he might find out for you – he'll want paying, of course, if you're willing.'

'Mr Dickens, you can't go dressed like that – we can lend you an old coat – best to blend in, if you know what I mean,' said practical Effie.

They found for Dickens an old, long coat and a woollen red scarf to obscure part of his face, a pair of old spectacles to perch on his nose, and a top hat which had seen better days, its being rather worn and having part of its brim missing. He looked at himself in the greenish silver of a tarnished cheval glass and saw an old gentleman with staring eyes looking back at him – no one he knew. He took up the part of a benevolent grandfather who wanted to bring back his grandchild's dog. He shuffled towards the mirror and the old gentleman came nearer and peered at him. He smiled at the old man; the old man smiled back with a mouth that seemed to have no teeth. 'Ssss all right,' he said to his audience of three. His friend Mark Lemon would have recognised him – Dickens had played Justice Shallow to Lemon's Falstaff – and here was Shallow come to life again.

Effie, Occy and Zeb laughed to see him so transformed.

'It's as good as a play,' said Effie. 'Your own wife wouldn't know you!'

Occy went back to his crossing, and Zeb and Dickens made their way to find the man who would, Dickens hoped, be the means of bringing back Poll, and Scrap who, surely, could not be far away from her.

4

RATS' CASTLE

It was becoming dark now, but Zeb Scruggs knew his way through the honeycomb of alleys, blind courts and tunnels that made up the area of St. Giles's with its straggling lines of half tumbledown houses with rags and paper for windows, mysterious shops with their extraordinary jumble of goods: rags, bones, bits of old iron, clothes so ancient that they must have been there for a century or more; with its terrible foetid cellars where resided families living their underground lives like troglodytes. Knots of filthy, half-naked children played mysterious games with stones in the gutters, heedless of the slime or the cold. A helpless drunk lay insensible in a doorway, a woman screamed after a running man who fled into a passageway, vanishing into darkness, and a man with two dead rabbits swinging from one hand shook his fist at an urchin who tried to grab them. A jaunty figure in masculine clothes but with a girl's face winked at Dickens. Man or woman, it was hard to tell. A man with a rudely made coffin on his back stared doubtfully at the hole in the ground where the dead one waited. The smell everywhere was of rotting sewage, decaying food, and filthy humanity. Dickens had been here before, and had written of the sickening smells, the slimily overflowing houses and cellars, and he thought again, with the same astonishment, that only across the road were the great shops of Oxford Street and Regent Street, and the grand houses where men and women, made up of flesh and bone as were the denizens of St Giles's, dined in state, and green parks where the rich strolled away their Sundays – ten minutes' walk to a different planet.

The alleys were narrower now, the buildings almost meeting in the middle so that it was like walking through a tunnel. Occasionally, the light of an oil lamp stared at them through a bleared window, and sometimes there was a feeble light above a doorway where a wretched figure huddled, the face a nightmare in the sickly light. Shadows came and went, real or not, it was hard to tell, so thin and black were they, and so silent as they passed. It was sinister here and Dickens was glad of the company of Zeb Scruggs, large and solid by his side.

They went into a lane where grimy light spilled onto the street and groups of men gathered at the windows and doors. Here was the ancient public house, named Rats' Castle for its customers were chiefly thieves, prigs, cracks, coiners and laggers and their molls. It was built on the site of the leper hospital, founded in the eleventh century by Queen Matilda. And still the home of outcasts, thought Dickens.

The place was packed with men, all ragged, filthy-looking vagabonds, sitting on benches at scarred deal tables. It was lit by tallow candles, giving off a dirty, feverish light and all smoking, and wax dripping down the brown walls. It smelt of unwashed bodies, stale grease and old cooking. No one looked at them – an old man in a long coat and a brawny black-eyed ruffian – why should they? Zeb looked about him and slid through the crowd, helping his old man who tottered feebly, and smiled his toothless smile. They took a table at which sat a young man nursing a pot of ale.

'Zeb, wot brings yer to the Rats' of a cold night. Got sumfink ter sell?' The young man giggled, showing blackened stumps of teeth.

'Tommy Titfer, I wants somthin' and this 'ere gent's willin' to pay fer it.'

Dickens noticed how Zeb's speech had coarsened – no doubt to match that of the aptly named Tommy who wore no hat but whose red hair stood upon his head in a high quiff which owed more to nature than to art. He was altogether an odd-looking young man with a shiny weasel face and sliding eyes which had something oysterish in their glistening opaqueness.

'Wotcher want, then?' The eyes slid away and back again.

Zeb leaned forward to whisper his request. 'The gent – no names, mind – 'as a little girl wot wants 'er dog back. Gone missin' three days or so back – little thing it is – not worth anythin' 'cept to the kiddie o' course. White with brown ears and brown patches. Answers to name of Poll. Any chance of yer findin' out?'

'I could. No names mind.' He winked and leered. 'Don't wanter upset me contacts. Wot's it worth?'

'For yer, Tommy, five shillin's, and fer whoever's got the dog, a sovereign, maybe – mind it's not a pedigree so tell 'em we'll pay wot's fair.'

'Right. Brass up front fer me, if yer will. There's a lot of dishonest folk about these days. Promise yer the money, an' then yer niver sees 'em again – an' all that work fer nuffink. It's an' 'ard world an' that's a fact.' Tommy sighed, regretting the wicked ways of the world in which he found himself.

'Well, old gentleman, are yer willin' to give my friend Tommy 'ere 'is five shillins?' Zeb asked. He was in cahoots with Titfer now. Zeb could act a part when needed.

The old gentleman was ready to part with the money and took out his purse, somewhat injudiciously, considering the company. Tommy's eyes slid and narrowed when he saw the purse. Perhaps he could ask for more later when he brought some information.

'Come back 'ere tomorrer – same time. I'll see wot I can find out.'

It was time to go. It was something, thought Dickens, Tommy Titfer might bring news. He did not know, but what else could he do?

They pushed their way out into the street where all in a moment a fight erupted, flashing out as if someone had thrown a taper on dying coals. They were suddenly in the midst of flying fists, kicking feet, animal grunts and piercing yells, shoved and barged, turned this way and that as if they were caught in a whirlpool. Dickens saw Zeb go down suddenly like a felled tree. Then a meaty fist the size of a hock of ham shot perilously near his nose. He dodged away, snatching at the man's waistcoat to keep his balance. He felt his heel slip in the mud. The owner of the fist roared madly as he and Dickens were whirled in a crazy dance. Then they were down, locked in a stinking embrace, Dickens turning so that he fell on top of his assailant rather than underneath. The man's head hit the stony ground with a thud. Blood spurted. Dickens jumped away, not frightened, more excited by the clamour and his own skill in evading the punch. Then he was plucked by his coat, seemingly tossed back into the melee only to pop out like a cork, his arms flailing. He felt the kick in his back, the sickening dizziness as his feet slid, then he was rolling, covering his head, but the kicks kept coming until the attacker was dragged away by another whose fist broke his nose. Someone trod on Dickens's hand and a last kick rolled him away. Then there was only suffocating darkness.

Somewhere a police rattle sounded, sharp and urgent. There were heavy feet running down the alley. Dickens did not hear any of it, nor did he feel the cunning fingers rifling his pockets for the purse that he had slipped into the pocket of the long coat. Tommy Titfer found it easily and slid away down the narrowest of passages by the Rats' Castle. But, no one saw the great hand suddenly pinning him to the wall; no one heard the hoarse, mad, whispering voice.

'Seen yer, seen yer follerin' me. Wot are yer? Yer shan't foller me.'

Tommy Titfer gasped, terrified. 'I don't fink so, I don't know yer. Gerroff me, yer brute.'

No witness saw Tommy Titfer try to wriggle away, but he was held too fast against the rough black wall. The man's hugeness filled the passage. There was no escape. The vast hand squeezed Tommy's throat, tighter and tighter. When it let go, the limp body slid down the wall into the oozing mud. No one saw the apelike figure, a monstrous shadow of itself, shambling away, dragging its freight behind it.

Who shall say which man's life is worth more? The man lying by the inn wall? Tommy Titfer? He was a villain in a small way, a low, slippery creature whose life began and ended in the greasy slime of the alleys of Seven Dials. Yet later, much later, after the case was over, in a cellar, when Constable Rogers found a starving woman with scanty red hair poking from a dirty cap, and an emaciated child with a curiously high red quiff, he felt only pity for her hacking grief.

Outside Rats' Castle, which had plunged into sudden darkness at the sound of the police rattles, Zeb Scruggs came to, wondering what had happened to Mr Dickens. Blimey! He hoped he wasn't responsible for the death of the most famous man in London. He felt panic, heard the police rattle, and found himself alone, the fighters gone, scrabbling like rats into holes. Someone lay by the wall, the head covered by a long coat, a familiar red scarf trailing like a line of blood in the dust.

When Constable Rogers of Bow Street came into the alley, he saw a big gypsyish-looking man bending over another, a man in a long coat lying by the wall. Injured, obviously. Was the gypsy robbing him? He hurried forward, his bull's-eye lamp held high.

'What's goin on 'ere?'

Borrowed on 01/26/2019 14:33 Till

1) Murder at the Chase : a Langham
   and Dupre mystery
   Due date: 03/09/2019
   No.: 31659041614997
2) Death at Hungerford Stairs
   Due date: 03/09/2019
   No.: 31659045217094
3) Framingham fiend
   Due date: 03/09/2019
   No.: 31659048189969
4) A shot in the dark
   Due date: 03/09/2019
   No.: 31659048333310
5) Bright young dead
   Due date: 03/09/2019
   No.: 31659050600580

Total on loan : 13

The dark-haired man turned, his black eyes anxious in the glare of the lamp.

'He was knocked out, I think – there was a fight. Don't know what about. I was knocked down, too – he's alive though, heard him groan.'

Rogers went forward just as the injured man groaned again and sat up, his white face bewildered.

'What on earth happened, Zeb? I saw you fall.'

Rogers looked astonished, his mouth agape. 'Mr Dickens! What's 'appened to you?'

'An altercation with a pair of boots, I think, hob-nailed ones judging by the pain in my back. I can stand, I think.'

Dickens smiled weakly as Zeb helped him to his feet. Rogers picked up the length of dusty old scarf, remarking as he did so that it surely could not belong to Mr Dickens, and as for the long coat smeared with mud and a tear in its sleeve, well, it was not fit for a rag shop. Zeb was a little offended by this account of one of his saleable goods, but he agreed that it did look a bit mangled now.

'Disguise,' said Dickens. 'We were after information, and when we came out of the pub there, all hell broke loose, and,' he felt in the pockets of the coat, 'my purse is gone – forever, I expect.'

Rogers caught on. 'You was lookin' for Scrap and the dog. You think that there dog's been kidnapped. You wasn't goin' to pay a ransom, was you, sir?'

'That was the idea, and we found a young man who was willing to find out for us – for five shillings.'

Rogers whistled. 'Five bob, sir. Do you think you'll see 'im again? 'E's probably scarpered with it.'

Zeb interrupted. 'I know him – he's a sly one, for sure, but I think he'll come and meet us tomorrow. Otherwise, he knows I'll find him.'

'Are you fit to walk, Mr Dickens? Shall I take you to Bow Street? I don't know what the superintendent'll say when he sees you. We 'ad news, by the way, about that lad found at 'Ungerford Stairs – murder, it was.'

After bidding goodnight to Zeb, Dickens was escorted to Bow Street where the superintendent regarded the old gentleman with astonishment.

'Charles, what in the world have you been about? Why are you dressed in that coat? Where did you get that hat?'

Sam Weller, Mr Pickwick's faithful servant, seemed to come in, as he so often did, when the superintendent and Dickens were together.

'Ta'nt a werry good 'un to look at, but it's an astonishin' one to wear, an' every hole lets in some air – ventilation gossamer, I calls it.'

Sam laughed. 'Very good, Mr Weller, but you ain't answered the question.'

'Ooh,' Dickens winced as he made to sit down. 'If you have the heart of anything milder than a monster, you will pity me and my dented pride.'

'Very well, I do, so sit ye down and tell your tale.'

'I did disguise myself and went into battle – by accident, of course. I was round and about on enquiries, you might say.'

'After Scrap and Poll. You were not alone, I hope, in that den of thieves where Rogers found you.'

'No, I was taken there by Zeb Scruggs, a man of honour, I may say, but we were unfortunately caught up in a riot – and I think I have the bruises to prove it. I don't know what happened – all of a sudden we were in a confusion of arms, legs, staves, wild shouts and everybody hitting everybody else. God knows why – we didn't cause it, by the way, in case you were thinking.'

'No, I was more thinking about who you were seeing and why.'

Dickens looked a little shamefaced. He hardly liked to tell the superintendent that he was prepared to pay a ransom, but there was nothing for it but to confess.

'Zeb brought me to Tommy Titfer who seemingly knew something of the dog thieves and for five shillings would bring us information tomorrow night. I know – one shouldn't be paying thieves and rogues, but, Sam, I am getting desperate, so beset and worried – I cannot even face going to Mr Brim's shop – those children are so upset.'

'I know, so is Elizabeth. However, you have done it now – and no bones broken – I hope. What I suggest is that you go back with Zeb Scruggs tomorrow. If you find out that some-one has Poll then, of course, I won't know anything about it. However, Rogers might be about Rats' Castle. He might, of course, be tempted to follow and when, and if, a big if, mind, you do get Poll back, it might be his duty to make an arrest. My conscience will be clear, at any rate.'

'Thank you, Sam. Of course, this does not necessarily mean that we will find Scrap. I just hope that wherever Poll is, Scrap is nearby.'

'I hope so, too.'

'Occy Grave – my crossing sweeper acquaintance – men-tioned the King's Head in Compton Street –'

'Dogs fighting with rats?'

'Yes, both he and Zeb thought it unlikely, but I wonder, could we – I mean if tomorrow night is no go – should I try there?'

'Mmm – no, but I'll find out when the next meeting is. They advertise: *Ratting for the Million*, it says on the posters, if you please. I'll send Rogers and Stemp in disguise. Rogers knows the dog, and Stemp in disguise with some brute of a bulldog will fit in nicely.'

'Does he have a dog?'

'Not that I know of, but he'll borrow one – very resource-ful, Stemp, and very menacing when he's in the mood. Don't you go – someone might recognise you.'

'I couldn't stand the sight of all those rats – I used to have terrible dreams about them when I was a boy. Comes of listening to my nurse's stories of a talking rat – even now I'm morbidly afraid of finding one in my pocket. I hated masks, too, and talking of which, Rogers told me that Inspector Harker had reported that the dead boy at Hungerford Stairs was murdered. What was the cause?'

'When they examined him at the morgue, the doctor found a slight puncture wound. The boy had been stabbed, but with so thin a blade that it might have been missed. The doctor had very sharp eyes. Stabbed in the heart.'

'Why would someone murder him? He was just a boy scraping a living in the mud.'

'Perhaps he found something valuable – something that was worth killing for. Harker is trying to find out more about the boy – whether he belonged to anyone, whether anyone knew that he had found something.'

'That chalk mark – I wonder now. What did it mean, that masked face?'

The door opened. Constable Feak came in. 'Body been found, sir – a lad – don't know any more. Up by St Giles's in the churchyard. Stemp is there.'

5

ST GILES'S CHURCHYARD

The clock of St Giles's Church was striking seven as they hurried along the High Street past the shops still open for business: the butcher's window which displayed great hunks of bloodied flesh, ghastly in the flaring gaslight; the pie shop with its wares apparently made of cardboard; the general dealers in bird cages, flat irons, old clothes and all sorts of motley goods of no use to anyone; past the baked potato seller, the sausage man, the café with the eels curled up in the window – dead, not just sleeping, one hoped; the oysters like so many dead eyes in their icy tombs, and the pawnbrokers with the three golden balls. They came to the dark churchyard under the shadow of its great steeple, and went through the stone gateway under the resurrection carving with its angels blowing their trumpets and the haloed Christ in the centre. The last church on the route to Tyburn tree, the three-legged gibbet.

A thin rain was falling now. Here were silence and shadows among the ancient graves where victims of the plague had been buried when the old church stood before this eighteenth-century one. It had started here. Somewhere, thought Dickens, deep down, there were the bones of those who had perished, their bodies empurpled with erupting sores, flung into the plague carts and thence into pits. He thought of the skulls piled upon each other, staring into the blackness, the bones heaped and muddled together, waiting to be reassembled on the Day of Judgement when those angel trumpets would sound. Would they, he thought, those poor disfigured bodies, bloom again as they rose, as he had read once?

Stemp called out, and they went to find him by an old door at the side of the church. On top of a tomb, black, solid and cold in the rain, something lay. They walked into the lamplight, and saw the body face down just as the other had been, the arms stretched out above the head. It was a boy, dressed in clothes which were shabby but clean. Someone looked after this boy. He belonged to someone. But he was too small, surely, for Scrap. It was hard to tell in the shifting lamplight. Dickens glanced at the superintendent, and saw, as before, the tightened lips and anxious eyes.

Stemp turned the boy over. It was not Scrap. There was no sign of any injury. He was a singularly handsome child with bright hair and a fine bone structure. What had he been doing in this black place at night? His face was peaceful; there was nothing to suggest violence. It was as if he had fallen asleep there on the tomb and had simply not woken up. He was terribly thin, half starved. Perhaps the cold had killed him, perhaps sickness, perhaps hunger. It happened, but a boy might drown sometimes, and then be found to have been stabbed by a wickedly thin blade, so thin that it had slid so smoothly through the flesh that a boy might not feel it at first. Until there came the wonder, the surprise, the horror of the blood spilling from the heart, filling the space round it, and drowning the lungs, flooding each vital organ, spurting then seeping with each failing heartbeat so that there came unconsciousness, and then the long sleep, fallen heavy on the sightless eyes.

Superintendent Jones murmured his prayer, and then opened the shabby waistcoat to undo the buttons on the darned shirt. Stemp and Rogers raised their lamps so that he could see. The boy's ribs protruded sharply, but he was clean, and the skin showed pale in the light. It was there, tiny, easily overlooked, the little mark where the blade had gone in.

'Same as what Inspector Harker reported,' said Rogers.

'It is – a second murder, by the same hand, I am certain.' Sam's voice was grim.

Stemp moved his lamp, and when they looked down by the side of the tomb, they saw something crumpled beside it, something soft. Rogers picked it up. Gleaming silk rippled in the light like dark water. It was a woman's shawl – not the cheap, scratchy woollen shawl of a poor woman, but something fine and expensive. Stolen, perhaps?

'Odd. Someone might have lost it, I suppose. I wonder – was that someone running away, having seen something? But then, you would think it would be on the path, not by the tomb. How did it come here?'

'The murderer?' asked Dickens. 'A woman?'

'Could be,' said Rogers. 'Look at Mrs Manning. 'Ard as nails, she was.'

'Well,' said Sam, looking at the pattern of red flowers under the light, 'it is quite distinctive. We might be able to trace it. Milliners, dressmakers, that kind of thing. Meanwhile, Stemp, you need to go back to Bow Street to organise the removal of the body – you'll need a stretcher to carry him out of here.'

'Yes, sir.' Stemp vanished into the darkness.

'Let us have a look round,' said Sam, 'see if the murderer left any other convenient clues.'

'A chalk mark – there will be one. There will be a sign,' said Dickens.

And there was, on the old wooden door behind them. The lamplight showed it as they had seen it at Hungerford Stairs. The mask atop the crudely chalked figure of a man.

'What's that all about?' asked Rogers.

'There was one at Hungerford Stairs. We wondered about it then. It didn't look like a child's work, and this confirms it. Suggests disguise, does it not,' the superintendent speculated.

'Perhaps, as if he – or she – is saying "You can't catch me",' said Dickens.

Rogers stayed with the body while Dickens and Jones had a look round the churchyard. They went round the back of the church, deeper into the darkness. When Jones held up his lantern at the sound of something above them, they saw peering down at them the face of a gargoyle, its twisted lips mocking them – another mask, a face laughing at death. They turned away into the rank, wet grasses, picking their way through the black tombstones, walking over the tenanted mounds with no stones, but the cone of light sometimes showed them a worn inscription, barely legible now, and a ruined angel with one hand missing – the blessing for the dead one cut off, leaving only an ugly stump more like a curse. Then they saw something – a shape on the ground – something covered in dark material, a blanket or coat, perhaps. They moved nearer, slowly, quietly, until they stood over two prone figures, asleep or dead, perhaps, so still were they, the arms entwined and the heads close together, black and fair hair mingled on the rough coat that covered them. Two girls.

The superintendent let his light fall on the heads while Dickens bent down to touch one girl gently on the shoulder. They woke suddenly, blinking in the light, pulling at the covering which fell about their ragged dresses. Two blackened faces, gaunt with want, gazed at Dickens and Jones. They might have come from the grave, Dickens thought, so filth-encrusted were their rags. But there was the smell of gin as well as the sharp fish-stink of unwashed clothes and sweat.

'Wotcher want? Leave us alone. We ain't doin' nuffink – jest sleepin'.'

'Can you get no lodgings?' Dickens asked.

'Yers – if we 'ad the money, but we ain't so it's unfurnished lodgins for us, out in the open air, unless yer gotta bob, sir.' The fair girl looked at Dickens. She was desperately dirty, hungry, and probably a drunk, but, as so often, he was amazed at the spark of life, the challenge to poverty and filth which shone in her eyes as she asked him for a bob.

'How long have you been here?' asked Sam.

'Dunno, sir. Come in 'ere, say a couple of hours ago – Katey an' me we 'ad a drink or two, dunno where. Come in 'ere for a rest.'

'See anyone?'

'Dunno – who, like?'

'A boy – with someone older – a man, perhaps.'

'Oh, aye, there was a gent an' a boy sittin' on a grave at the side o' the church. Aksed 'im for a tanner but 'e dint answer.'

'You did not see his face? Either of you?'

'Nah – jest a gent – dark suit – thinnish, though.' The dark girl thought for a moment. 'Young, I think. Dunno – jest an impression. 'Ard ter say. It woz dark.'

'You said "a gent" – what made you think that?'

'A top 'at – 'e woz wearin' one – dunno, just thought he woz a toff, can't say why. Yers, I can – no smell – yer know most folk stink. Only toffs are clean.'

Dickens had smelt it when the girls moved, the stink of unwashed bodies, of filthy clothes, of poverty. Interesting that the girl had noted the lack of smell.

'The boy?'

'Jest a boy, sir.'

'How did they seem together?'

The fair girl frowned. 'Wotcher mean? Do yer mean woz they friendly?'

'Yes – the boy wasn't trying to get away?'

'I get yer – like that yer mean,' said the dark girl, looking at Sam, knowingly. Too knowingly, thought Dickens. She'd seen too much, this girl. 'The man 'ad 'is arm round the boy. 'E woz leanin' against the toff – coulder bin – yer know. Why d'yer wanter know?'

'A boy was found dead just where you said you saw the boy and the man,' answered Sam.

'Blimey – d'yer think 'e did it?'

'We don't know, but I think you two should get away from here, find some lodgings for tonight.'

'If you had two shillings to get some supper and a lodging, should you know where to get it?' Dickens felt in his pocket for the coins and handed them to the girl called Katey.

'Ta very much, sir, we knows a place. 'Opes yer finds the killer. We won't be back 'ere in an 'urry.'

They scrambled away hand in hand through the damp grass, round the bulk of the church to be swallowed up into the labyrinth of lanes – to find lodgings, or more gin, or something worse, unbearable to consider. Katey and me – they were – what? Thirteen? Twelve? The same age as Dickens's Katey and Mamie. The dark girl with Katey's name and colouring, and they were lost, gone in a minute.

'Just children. I tell you, Sam, the sight of them and the legions of others ought to break the heart and hope of any man.'

'I know – and that poor boy over there and the other. We need to find him before he does it again.'

'Well, we have the shawl.'

'A man and a shawl? The two things do not seem to be connected, but I have an instinct that they are. I am not surprised that there was a man with the boy, but I am surprised at that shawl because it's an expensive one.'

Dickens asked, 'Could he have an accomplice, a woman? If he was a toff as the girls said then his accomplice might be a woman who could afford a shawl like that.'

'Could be – but it was damned careless to leave the shawl there – unless they were disturbed, but the girls mentioned only a man.'

'And the drawing – the mask. I don't know, but it seems like someone who is on his own. The mask is some private symbol. You do not think that the boy had stolen the shawl – that it has nothing to do with the murder?'

'Until we find the owner of it – if we do – it is hard to say. We don't even know who this boy is or the other one. But they are connected, and we will need to think of all the connections. In the meantime, tomorrow, I will have enquiries made about this boy – he belongs to someone. There is a mother somewhere – who else would have darned that shirt?'

'And his mother kept him clean. He was loved,' said Dickens.

Dickens and Jones went back to Rogers and saw that Stemp had returned with two more constables who were lifting the boy on to a stretcher to take him to the morgue.

'I will get back to Bow Street,' said Sam. 'You should go home, Charles, after the night you have had. Go and rest those bruises. I will send word tomorrow if there is any news.'

They parted, and Dickens walked away from the church towards the High Street. He would get a cab in Oxford Street to take him home. Now that Sam had mentioned his bruises, he could feel them. Then, he remembered his clothes. He should have gone back to Zeb's to retrieve his own coat and hat. Too late, he had not the energy. He wanted to get home, to seep in a hot bath, to wash away the dirt, and horror that he had seen. That poor boy. Somehow there was the betrayal of innocence in the brief sketch drawn by the dark girl. He could see the little scene as if it were spotlit – a boy trusting a young man who held him, and who, in that embrace, slid the blade into the unresisting heart.

6

POOR ROBIN

Isabella Gordon had gone. Dickens had dismissed her; now Urania Cottage at Shepherd's Bush resounded with sobs, and tearful faces looked at Dickens and Mrs Morson with reproach as if Dickens did not feel bad enough when he had watched Isabella walk away with her half crown, wiping her eyes on the cheap shawl she had been given.

They went into Mrs Morson's own parlour and sat silent for a few moments. Mrs Morson felt that she had let him down; she ought to have been able to cope with Isabella and Anna-Maria Sisini, but their combined mischief and malice, it had to be said, were too much in that they undermined the order of the house, and their relationship, she feared, was too close to be healthy. She felt always a sense of unease about them, and they knew it. They challenged her with their kisses, their caresses, their flirtation which could seem just affection, but which Mrs Morson was sure was not. Not that she condemned them; she had known of a similar relationship between two women in the tiny European community at the mine in Brazil. She had seen how one of them, a young woman abused by a hard-faced husband, had looked at the other woman with such love. Mrs Morson had been so afraid that others would see it too.

But what she feared in Isabella and Sesina was their insolence, and their desire to overturn the order of Urania Cottage. When she and Dickens had gone into her parlour, as they often did when he visited, she had frequently seen Isabella's mocking eyes on her, and she had sensed her exchange of meaningful looks with Sesina. She had felt the beginnings of a blush and had held herself rigid, willing the tell-tale heat to subside. They challenged her authority by being able to discomfort her, and that annoyed her. It made her uncomfortable with Mr Dickens, and she felt that now, though they had always been good friends.

'What about Sesina?' he asked. 'Will she last?'

'I doubt it. She needs Isabella. And I told you before what I suspected about their relationship. I am surprised she didn't go after her just now. I am sorry I failed with Isabella.'

'I do not think anyone could have succeeded. She had to be the centre of attention, and I thought all along that the life we were offering would not suit her. She is so full of spirit, and yet so hardened by what she has been. I suspect we will hear of Isabella and Sesina, together again. We will not succeed with all of them. Alice Drown for example – she told me it was the very thought of a possible marriage in Australia that put her off. She said Australia was bad enough, but marriage was worse – and, you know, I could hardly blame her when she told me about her childhood, and I am not surprised that she got work in the theatre – she said she liked her independence when I saw her that time we were trying to find out who murdered Patience Brooke.'

'Isabella is bright, too, clever enough to manipulate the others, teasing the plain ones whom she thought of no account – remember her spite against poor Lizzie Dagg when Lizzie fell in love with the curate. And clever enough to get the lively, pretty ones on her side by inventing grievances, telling them what a cruel place this is, and challenging our authority – not yours to your face, of course.'

'Alice Drown was clever, too, and Sesina, and Jenny Ding,' said Dickens thoughtfully. 'Sometimes when I watch a group of girls in the street, I think that if these girls were properly educated, they would grow into capable, intelligent women, and yet society offers them nothing except drudgery or prostitution. Ignorance and want are the two great evils. I saw two girls sleeping in a graveyard last night – they could only be twelve or thirteen – same age as my daughters – and they stank of gin already.'

'I know, and it is not much better, in some ways, for girls of the upper class, trained only for marriage, trained to be undemanding, to pretend to be simple and to submit to the authority of first their fathers, and then their husbands. And, still, too many girls have no choice in their marriage partner. I want something better for my girls.'

Dickens looked at her; he was not surprised by the indignation in her voice. He admired her. Here was a woman whose husband had died in Brazil, leaving her pregnant, having to bring home two small girls, and she had done it, had travelled hundreds of miles by mule to find a ship to take her back to England. Even when she was home she found that her husband's brother had embezzled her husband's money. But she had not sat down and wept; she had placed her children with their grandparents, and she had found herself this post – and she was the best matron he had engaged.

Dickens had to return to town. He bade goodbye to Mrs Morson, told her to write if Sesina caused more trouble, and clasped her hand to show that he was not disappointed. They were friends. Once he had felt something more, but it could not be. Outside the house, he looked down the street and thought of Isabella; he pitied her, felt sorry that they had not tamed her, worried what might become of her, and novelist that he was, imagined Isabella, bold and haggard, and flaunting and poor, and translated his image into Martha, the ruined girl in *David Copperfield* who, like Isabella, went weeping on her way to London. Somehow, he thought, Isabella would not weep for long.

His fly took him to Bow Street where he found the super-intendent gazing at the shawl as if in its embroidery he could read the identity of the murderer. Rogers and other consta-bles were out enquiring about the dead boy. Sam hoped that if they could find out who he was then they might discover the owner of the shawl. Inspector Harker had not had any success in finding out the identity of his boy either. But it was early days, Sam said to Dickens; his experience told him that they would have to wait, to follow all sorts of leads, some of which would be dead ends, but something would happen. Two murders, two masks and one beautifully embroidered shawl meant an unusual case, and unusual cases usually had a solution – eventually.

A constable, Semple, came in. 'There's a woman 'ere, sir, says she wants to know about the boy. 'Er son's bin missin' – not a runaway, she says, a good boy – well, they all say that. Still, she's upset all right.'

'Bring her in.' Semple went out. 'I hope for her sake that our boy is not hers,' said the compassionate superintendent, 'even though we desperately need information.'

The woman came in, a woman who had once been pretty but whom poverty had worn out, a woman who was very afraid that the boy who had been found was hers because hers was missing. She looked frozen. A rough piece of sacking was tied at her neck; that was all she had as a cloak or coat. She wore an old brown bonnet – it had once been good but the velvet had been rubbed away and it was tied under her chin with string. Her brown dress was threadbare, and Dickens could see the ancient boots she wore. He thought he had seen her before. She looked not at them, but at the shawl which was hanging off the chair where Sam had left it, its colours seeming to glow in the gloomy office with its utilitarian furniture.

'Where did you find that? It is mine.'

'Yours?' The superintendent was astonished.

'Well, it was, but Zeb Scruggs gave me five shillings for it – weeks ago. But, my boy, have you got my boy?' She forgot the shawl now. Her terror about her boy returned.

'How long has he been missing?'

'Not long – only since yesterday. He wouldn't run away, not my boy, not my Robin.'

The name conjured innocence for Dickens who thought of Ophelia singing of bonny sweet Robin, all her joy. Somehow he felt that this woman had loved her son, that he was all her joy. And he knew, though he did not know how, that the thin boy in the morgue was Robin, and that she would die without him. He felt it all as he looked at the wasted face, with its sheen of hunger shown up in the harsh gaslight, as he looked at the eyes, grey as dark water, in which dread and hope alternated.

'Mrs …' began the superintendent.

'Hart, Mrs Hart. My husband is dead. Robin is all I have. You must tell me. Is it my boy – the boy you found in the churchyard? I must see him.'

'Is there anyone else?' asked the superintendent. He could not bear the thought of showing her the thin boy, and her finding it was Robin. He glanced at Dickens and saw the same thoughts in his mobile face, and how, in the luminous eyes, there was trepidation for this poor woman.

'No, no – only me and Robin. Please, let me see him.'

They had to take her down the ill-lit corridor, down the stone stairs to the mortuary below. Their feet echoed in the cold silence as they descended, going down into what would be a circle of hell for Mrs Hart. Dickens's intuition was correct. It was Robin Hart who lay on the icy marble slab in the white-tiled room where the attendant drew back a sheet to reveal the thin boy with his closed eyes, looking for all the world as if he were sleeping.

'Who has done this?' she asked. 'Who has killed him?' Her voice was strangely calm. Dickens and Jones had dreaded that she might fall, might faint, might cry out with horror. She did none of those things, but Dickens saw as she gazed at the boy how she was diminished, as if she withered away like a dried leaf before his eyes, and he saw how her heart died within her so that there could be no tears, only the arid grief that sounded in the one hacking cough that was like a bark. Then there was silence and stillness. They heard only the drip of water somewhere, and felt a shiver of a draught which seemed to make the blue gas flame flare a moment, illuminating the scene like a painting – the figures frozen in anguish, their faces in shadow except for the white face of the dead child.

Mrs Hart stepped forward before they had chance to stop her. She pulled at the sheet to see her son, and held the naked child to her. Dickens and Jones could not do anything but wait until she was ready to leave him. What then they would do with her they had no idea. She had no one. They turned away, as did the attendant.

It seemed a long time. Not a word was spoken except for the low murmuring of the woman to her dead child. Then she stopped. Dickens half-turned to see her lay the boy down, cover him again with the sheet as if she were putting him to bed, place her hand on his hair and caress the thin face.

'I am ready,' she said. 'I know I must leave him, but it will not be long.'

They took her back upstairs, the superintendent holding her listless arm, and they sat her by the fire in his office, hoping it might bring her to life again. She paid them no attention at all as she stared into the flames.

'I have seen her before. I saw her at Zeb Scruggs's shop,' said Dickens, remembering. 'She was selling an old cloak. Zeb was kind and gave her two shillings – they obviously know her and her circumstances, and she said she sold him the shawl. I wonder if Effie Scruggs would look after her – she cannot be left alone.'

'Yes, a good idea. We can find out if Zeb had sold the shawl and to whom – if he didn't sell it, perhaps it was stolen, and he might recall something about that.'

Between them they helped the woman out of the building and into the clamour of Bow Street; it was always crowded with prison vans bringing in customers or taking them away. A waiting chorus of beggars, brawlers and bagmen cheered or jeered at what they called 'Long Tom's Coffin' which took those who had been sentenced at the police court to the gaols around the city. The prisoners were brought out from the cells in the courtyard behind the station, a procession of starving wretches, sullen or enraged, a band of impudent pickpockets going to prison for the umpteenth time and not a wit cast down, a haggard woman who looked like a governess with her hands over her eyes, and a ragged little dandy who attempted a swagger, but whose eyes were burning, a man whose hooded eyes hid his knowledge that this was his penultimate journey. They were bundled into the van, into the little cells which lined the corridor of this wheeled black prison. A policeman climbed into his watch box on the outside and another took up his position in the inside corridor. Then they were off, the black horses drawing away the great funeral car, for one of them was going to his death. Somewhere a gallows stood waiting.

Scuffles broke out as drunken wretches were manhandled into the station: ragged ruffians abusing their captors in the vilest terms, bedraggled women with children swarming at their skirts, a prostitute in her gaudy red satin, and a scruffy pickpocket who managed to twist out of the constable's grip and was away through the crowd which cheered him on. The constable shrugged – the lad would be back.

Mrs Hart paid no attention; she seemed neither to see nor hear as they walked her away through the crowd. Something in her stopped the noise; curious eyes watched her and the crowd stood back to let them through. Most knew the superintendent and some of the regulars knew the man with him, but no one shouted or jeered. They just watched the woman with the tragic eyes like dark water, and they knew that something dreadful had happened, and what little humanity was left in them was stirred to pity for a few moments.

Dickens and Jones walked with her between them up to Monmouth Street and Zeb's shop where Effie took one look at Mrs Hart's face and took her into the parlour at the back. Dickens followed while Sam stayed to ask Zeb about the shawl. Effie sat Mrs Hart by the fire. She found brandy and a glass, but Mrs Hart waved it away, her eyes fixed on the fire. Effie withdrew with Dickens who explained what had happened.

'Then it's all over with her, Mr Dickens. That boy was everything to her. Her husband died two or so years ago. He had been a clerk, respectable, you know, at Lincoln's Inn and she was educated, and the boy. The husband was ill. They moved to cheaper rooms on Parker Street, but they couldn't pay the rent – you know how it is – people move to a cheaper place, two or three rooms, then one, then a cellar, and then for some, nothing.'

Dickens did know how it was. He remembered only too well his own family's descent from a respectable life in Chatham to dingy Bayham Street in Camden Town. Number sixteen he recalled as a mean, small tenement with a wretched back garden next to a squalid court. It was not long before the creditors pressed in: the butcher and baker were not paid, the books had to be sold, Dickens scurrying to the drunken bookseller; the household shrank as furniture and goods were pawned; then when insolvency proceedings were instituted against his father, Dickens went to the appraiser so that even his own clothes could be valued since a debtor and his dependants must have effects of no more than twenty pounds; finally the Marshalsea where John Dickens was imprisoned for debt, and where Mrs Dickens and the younger children joined him, leaving Dickens an exile in the blacking factory. Oh, it was so easy to fall.

Effie continued, 'Then her husband died and left nothing. Mrs Hart took a room off Moor Street, her and the boy and a dozen other families crowded into the house. Terrible for her.' Effie's eyes filled as she looked at the woman who might have been carved of stone, who gave no sign, nor ever would again.

'How did she live?'

'She sold nearly everything – you saw her sell the cloak yesterday; she had the one dress left, and the boy a few things. She sold things, one by one, a green glass paperweight, a set of spoons, a brooch – her treasures. It was pitiful. Zeb stopped her going to the pawnbroker's – gave her more than she would have got there. We haven't sold any of it. Then she did sewing, and he ran errands – earned a penny or two. Nice boy – honest, you know. People liked him. Who would have killed a boy like that, Mr Dickens? Who would be wicked enough?' Effie's kindly face was troubled. 'Well, I'll look after her, but, I don't know what will become of her.'

Neither did Dickens. She was lost to this world. She would die, he thought. Effie would do her best, but Mrs Hart would not eat or drink; she would simply waste away of longing for her sweet Robin.

Dickens went into the shop to tell Zeb that he would come back later so that they could go to find Tommy Titfer, and maybe Poll and Scrap. He saw on a shelf the green glass paperweight gleaming with the sea inside it. She would never buy it back now.

'Don't forget to bring the coat and hat, and your specs,' said Zeb, smiling at the thought of the old gentleman. Then his face changed. 'And we'll do what we can for that poor woman in there.'

'Thank you, Zeb. Would it be possible for me to contribute?' asked Dickens.

'No need, sir, we have enough. I'll see you later.'

Dickens and Jones went out into the street to make their way back to Bow Street, and the superintendent told him what he had learned about the shawl. Mrs Hart's shawl was still in the shop. Zeb had not sold it; he had thought he would keep it if ever she wanted it back. He knew that she had been given it by her husband. He hoped that she might be able to raise the money though it was unlikely, but, somehow he did not like to sell it and nor did Effie – it did not seem right.

'So, whose shawl is the one we found?'

'Effie said that when Mrs Hart wanted to sell the shawl she told Effie that it had been made by a Frenchwoman, a milliner and dressmaker, and that her husband bought it before he became ill. Effie knew of a Frenchwoman who made clothes and lived in Hanover Street, but she didn't know if the woman was still there. However, we can look for her and see if she made more than one shawl, and to whom she sold it. In the meantime, I suggest we find some supper before you don your motley and go a-playacting. Remember, Rogers will not be far away – and try to avoid getting into a fight.'

7

GEORGIE TAYLOR

By eight o'clock Zeb and his old gentleman were entering Rats' Castle in search of Tommy Titfer. Zeb bought two glasses of brandy and water and they sat at one of the rickety, scuffed tables to wait, but he did not come. Dickens felt a profound disappointment. After all that had happened today, in the back of his mind there had been a pinprick of hope that at least he would find Scrap. Zeb was disappointed, too, and angry. Well, he thought, Tommy Titfer would pay for this when he found him.

St Giles's clock struck nine; it was time to go. Tommy Titfer was not coming. At that moment a weazened little man slipped on to a stool at their table. His face was like a shrivelled walnut, all creases, and jaundiced, too. His nose dripped, and his squint eyes were inflamed with pus in the corners – and he stank. He must have worn those grime-encrusted clothes all his adult life.

'Yer waitin' fer Tommy? 'E ain't comin'. Nobody seen 'im. Vanished 'e 'as. Owed money ter Fikey Chubb – dangerous 'e 'is. Not seen 'im neither. Could 'elp yer. Wanter find a dog, doncher? 'Eard yer talkin' last night.'

They had not seen him. For all they knew he might have been crouching under the table like a dog. Unsavoury as he was, Dickens felt that there was a chance.

Zeb asked, 'Know any fanciers?'

'Could take yer ter Georgie Taylor – 'e's the big man round 'ere. Brother o' Sam Taylor – up at Shoreditch. They 'ates each other, now. Georgie knows all the dog takers round 'ere. They all goes ter 'im – don't matter wot sort o' dog. 'E'll make money – yer'll 'ave ter pay 'im – an' me o' course.'

'We'll pay when we get there. Five bob.'

The weazened man thought. 'Two bob, now. I might lose yer – an' a man's gotter live.'

'All right,' said Zeb, handing him the two shillings.

'Yer bringin' the old 'un? T'ain't really fittin' for 'im – 'oo knows wot might 'appen?'

The weazened man was twice Dickens's age and he almost laughed. However, he nodded his head to Zeb who told Weazen that the old gentleman was stronger than he looked, and that he wanted his grandchild's dog back.

They went out into the narrow passage by Rats' Castle where Tommy Titfer had gone last night with his purse of gold and silver, and where a gigantic hand had squeezed the life out of him. Weazen led them through a maze of alleys which twisted and turned, went off at right angles, seemed to take them backwards, and in circles, so that they were lost in the labyrinth with no skein of thread to lead them out. Sometimes the lanes were so suffocatingly narrow that it was hard to breathe; sometimes Dickens thought he heard steps behind him, shuffling steps as though the feet were shod in rags; sometimes, looking back, he thought he saw a monstrous apelike shadow on a wall, and he hurried, his breath clotted in his throat, to catch up with Zeb who looked back as though he, too, had sensed something.

City of dreadful night. Always, in the solid darkness, pierced by no star, there were sounds: a scream, running footsteps, a child sobbing, a shrill, mocking voice singing a ghastly song, outcries of sorrow, voices high and hoarse quarrelling in a cellar, curses loud and deep, accents of anger, terrible oaths and terrible laughter, a boy shouting, and somewhere, far away, a dog howling. And there were faces, faces marked with weakness, marked with woe; faces that twisted down at them from windows above, like the gargoyles at St Giles's Church, and faces appearing at subterranean gratings, looking up at them as if from hell. And shadowy forms passing and repassing as if condemned to some perpetual traversing of a terrible limbo, forever seeking light and never finding a way out of this blind world, and all the time Dickens and Zeb pressed on, following their ragged and wretched Virgil deeper into the maze.

The creature shuffled behind them, stopping when they stopped, folding into the shadows when Dickens held up his lamp. The creature saw a dead man walking with eyes like small moons. It muttered to itself. It was afraid now.

'No eyes, no eyes. Wot is it? Ghosts all round – hell this is. Dark, always dark. Gotter get away.'

Still muttering its fearful words, the creature took another byway and vanished into the murk. When Dickens looked behind him again, his spectacles shining suddenly in the lamplight, the shadow was gone. He heard a kind of scuttling as though something had darted away in fear then he went on. He did not see the other shadow creeping after them, looking curiously down the alley where a huge man had suddenly turned. He did not see Rogers, but he was there as the superintendent had instructed, and he was armed, his flintlock pistol in his pocket.

Weazen took them out of the alleys, and into a wider road lit by gas. Outside a rough-looking house, a knot of men lounged. Another man knocked at the door. A thin line of light gleamed for a moment and then he went in, carrying a sack in which something squirmed and yelped. Dickens thought of brave Mrs Browning outside the house of Sam Taylor in Shoreditch where she went to rescue Flush. The brother could not be any worse, surely. Weazen looked up at Zeb.

'This is it,' he whispered. 'That's three bob yer owe me. I brought yer like I sed.' His rat's face was eager for the money but his restless stepping from side to side told them that he wanted to be off. Zeb gave him the coins, and he darted away. Zeb gripped his stick tightly.

'I'll go an' ask. Wait here, Mr Dickens.'

'No, I'll come. Two are better than one. Money might talk and I've got my stick. I'm stronger than I look, remember.'

Zeb smiled. Dickens sounded confident, but he could not help thinking that Sam had told him not to get into a fight. And he could feel the twinge of last night's bruises. Perhaps Rogers was somewhere near. If there was trouble, he could rattle up the beat constables. They crossed the road, passed the group of men whose louring faces looked menacing, and went up to the front door. At their knock, a man came out. Georgie was not yet at home, but they could wait inside if they wanted. He leered as he said it, and Zeb glanced briefly at Dickens with a slight shake of the head which said they should wait outside. Zeb said that they would like to know how much to find the old gentleman's dog.

'Wait 'ere,' the leering man ordered. The door shut in their faces. They stepped back, looking round to see where they might escape to if it were necessary. They backed towards the pavement where they stood uncertainly. Perhaps Georgie was really there and talk of money would bring him out.

The door opened again and a woman came out, a mountainous creature with a fat, doughy face and little, cunning black eyes. She looked them over, assessing their worth. Her eyes lingered on the old gentleman. Yes, 'e'd pay, she thought. No need ter say the price – yet. Yer niver knew 'ow much yer could get till yer found out 'ow desperate a cove woz. Shrewd, Mrs Taylor. Dickens would have been most amused to know that a respectable and pious father had called her Charity.

65

'My 'usband won't be long, sir. Should be back in 'alf an hour. 'E'll tell yer 'ow much when 'e comes.' She attempted a smile which was more like a snarl, showing long, yellow teeth.

Husband, thought Dickens, she was his guard dog more likely. Heavens, she was like some great bulldog. He knew a bulldog once who kept a man. Perhaps Mrs Georgie kept Georgie on a tight leash. He hoped she would not come any nearer. He wondered what kind of dog Georgie resembled. Odd, he thought, how people looked like their dogs: Mrs Browning with her long curls exactly like Flush's silky ears and a well-dressed little terrier he knew who looked just like his master, both sporting white gloves and neat black boots, going to the races in a smart painted dogcart.

His idle thoughts were interrupted by Zeb apparently declining another invitation to sample the delights of Dog Villa. At that moment a cab drew up on the opposite side of the road. Dickens said they would wait in the cab. Mrs Georgie looked disappointed. Perhaps she had a good tea service which she wanted to show off, or, more likely, she was brewing up a cauldron of dog meat, and her two visitors might have added a new piquancy to the stew. With that harrowing thought, Dickens stepped smartly off the pavement and crossed the road, Zeb hurrying after him. The cab driver evinced no surprise at being asked to wait. It was all one to him, moving or waiting would mean payment.

Dickens and Zeb stepped inside – safe, they thought – but there was someone there. Rogers.

''Eard it all, sir, I was waitin' in that doorway – followed you in the alleys. Thought you was in danger – some great, hulking feller was following you, but 'e went off. Got the cab, sir, so we can make a quick exit if need be. Slipped away while Mrs there was talkin'.'

'Thank you, Rogers. We did feel a bit uncomfortable out there, but we were not about to go in.'

Rogers settled himself in the corner furthest away from the road, and Dickens and Zeb made sure they could be seen if Mrs Georgie came over. They watched and waited. Mrs Georgie stood on her step, her huge arms folded. From time to time, someone would come with a sack, and go in, but no Georgie came. It seemed a very long half hour.

He came at last, little, cocky Georgie in his fancy jacket and waistcoat, like a little spry terrier whose bite was almost certainly worse than his bark. His nose might be purple but he was cleaner by far than his wife, and with good-natured, twinkling eyes that could turn cold in a moment – if he were crossed. Oh, Georgie would find the grandchild's dog. Little girl, was it? Missin' 'er doggie, was she? Well, Georgie would find the dog if 'e could. Only it'd cost – Georgie 'ad 'is livin' ter make, dint 'e? Way o' the world, weren't it? Couldn't do it fer nothing. The wheedling voice went on until the price was fixed – three sovereigns – cheap as 'e could do it. Finder's fee of two sovereigns and one more when the dog would be brought to – where?

Zeb gave his address. Poll was described. Georgie would do what 'e could, o' course. No guarantees, mind. He twinkled at them again. All heart was Georgie, in this wicked world, an' as for Mrs G, well, yer might not guess it, but she woz a lamb, really, a lamb wiv daughters of 'er own. Dickens glanced over at the scowling lamb – daughters forsooth, he thought – harpies, probably.

The two sovereigns paid, the cab took them back to Bow Street.

'Daylight robbery,' said Rogers, indignantly. 'Well, bloomin' midnight robbery, if you like.'

Dickens and Zeb laughed – from relief, perhaps, rather than Rogers's wit.

Not many streets away, in another twist of alleys, huddled behind the broken door of an abandoned garden, Scrap waited for the house across the narrow alley to fall silent. By day, his eye was fixed to a hole in the door. He could see across the alley a closed door which gave access to the yard of a house. He knew Poll was there. He had heard her bark, and the yelping and snapping of other dogs. Several times, he had scuttled across and peered through a crack in the wood, and he had seen the cages. He had been round to the front of the house and had watched the men, and boys, arrive with their sacks in which live things wriggled and whimpered. He heard the clink of coins as money changed hands. Once, a little man in a fancy jacket and waistcoat came and took away a spaniel which he tucked under his arm. Scrap watched when further down the road the little man put the dog down and walked off as if he were a respectable householder, taking his dog for a walk. Scrap had watched in the back alley when the hulk of a man they called Nat Boney took sacks away; sometimes the sacks moved and writhed, but sometimes, he heaved them over his shoulder where they hung, limp with something bulging at the bottom.

Scrap had seen strange things in the alley. Last night he had seen a giant, a great, stinking bundle of rags which had shuffled along by his door. It grunted and muttered, shaking its huge matted head, and it was dragging something along. Scrap had shrunk back into his doorway, covering himself with the sack he used for his coat, and his bedding, so that he looked just like a heap of discarded refuse. The thing had shambled by and he had heard the sound of something banging on the stones. Before that he had seen a thin stick of a woman struggling with a man who pinned her against the dripping wall, and tore at her, and pummelled her with his fists until she slid down the wall, and the man lay on top of her. Scrap had huddled back through the hole in his door, but he could hear the man grunting, and the woman groaning. Then there was nothing. In the morning, they were gone.

Scrap had no sense of time; he heard, without register-ing the meaning, the distant clocks strike the hours. It was two o'clock in the morning now, and the lane was quiet. He did not know how long he had waited – days, he thought. He was sometimes hungry and always cold, but he had only one fixed idea and that was how to get Poll out. He had talked to a cross-eyed boy who came and went through the blistered door. The boy had no curiosity about Scrap who was just there sometimes and who would give him a penny in return for bread. There were plenty of ragged boys about. This one seemed to live in the ruined garden opposite. He wasn't always there – out on the scavenge, the boy supposed, but he was all right. The cross-eyed boy was glad to get a penny for the bread – there was plenty of food in the house for a boy who knew just when to filch it from the empty kitchen.

Scrap was patient. No sense in hurrying the cross-eyed boy. There would be a moment when he could ask to see inside, ask if there were any jobs, ask if he could earn a bit of bread by helping the cross-eyed boy who sometimes came out of the wooden door with more than one sack which he had to take to a house where a mountainous woman with a face like a bulldog's would pay him. The cross-eyed boy had to take the money back to Nat Boney. Scrap knew it all. He had followed the cross-eyed boy, and he just had to wait for the right time when he could say he had no more pennies, but that he would help with the sacks in which the dogs would twist and writhe. Once, the cross-eyed boy came out with a starved-looking greyhound on a lead which he took to the entrance of a great square lined with white houses where a man in footman's livery took it and gave the cross-eyed boy a purse in exchange. And if, when he helped the boy with a sack, Poll was in it, then he would seize it and run like the wind. Pity the cross-eyed boy when Nat Boney knew he had lost a dog, but Scrap did not care about that.

Tomorrow it would be. Tomorrow, he would get in. If the cross-eyed boy did not come, Scrap would go in, and ask for food, a job, anything. There was a woman. He had seen her throwing bits of food to the dogs. He had seen her come into the alley earlier. He had watched her, a girl, really, thin with fair hair scraped back from a long face where a bruise showed livid against the pale skin. In her slate-coloured gown and drab cloak, she had looked sad, he thought, and crushed somehow, and she had glanced behind her as if she was frightened that someone would follow her. She had carried a basket. He had wondered where she was going and if she would come back. She had come back about an hour later, and she had slipped in through the door. Then he had heard the dogs barking and whining, and he had heard Poll, her high, short yaps, distinguishable to him from the others. Perhaps the girl might go out again, perhaps he might slip in as she closed the door, and perhaps he might see where Poll was. He might be able to hide in the yard somewhere, and release Poll, and take her home.

Home. For the first time in days, he thought of the shop where Eleanor and Tom Brim would be waiting. The memory was sharp as an ache. Did they think he had left them? Not Miss Nell. She would know.

Somewhere a clock struck the half hour. Scrap crept out through the hole in the broken door and waited, crouching like a cat in the darkness. He could see a light upstairs in the house, a candle that flickered. Someone was at the window. Scrap froze, holding his breath. A door banged shut and foot-steps came through the yard. Scrap squeezed back through his hole. The dogs barked and when the figure came through the door in the wall, the noise was stilled. Scrap waited.

The sound of the footsteps in the alley died away, and the silence settled once more. Scrap inched his way out and crouched again, listening. He darted across the alley and flattened himself against the blistered door of the yard.

Through a crack in the door, he whispered, 'Poll, Poll.' A short yap. She had heard him. 'Poll, quiet, now. I'll come fer yer.' He heard footsteps. Voices whispering. A spurt of laughter. Someone was coming down the alley.

Scrap fled. Away from the footsteps. He did not look round. He turned right at the end of the alley, knowing that he could work his way back to the front of the abandoned house. He kept close to the wall, his head down, just a boy – no one, really. He slid into the house, through the empty rooms to the shed in the overgrown garden where he pulled his sack over him, and slept. Cloud covered the bruised moon which dimmed to a hazy glimmer. The rain came, drumming on the roof of the shed, and on the metal roof of the cages, but Scrap slept on. Poll stayed awake, her head on her paws, and her black eyes staring into the night. He would come.

8

THE SEA CAPTAIN

It had rained all night. In the morning, Dickens looked out on his garden where the trees and bushes dripped disconsolately. An air of melancholy pervaded the scene; even the raindrops on the window fell listlessly, pausing and halting as they slid down the window. *How weary, stale, flat and unprofitable*, Dickens thought. November, a dreary month, unforgiving in its gloom when night was always at odds with morning. Even the air looked sodden like a wet rag that needed squeezing. Too early for news.

He turned back to his desk. It was as it always was: the goose quill pens, the blue ink, the bronze image of two toads duelling which always made him laugh, a paper knife, a gilt leaf with a rabbit upon it, the blue slips on which he would write his monthly numbers, and, his eye fell on it, another bronze image, this time of a dog fancier with the puppies and dogs swarming all over him. *How all occasions do inform against me.* He thought of Georgie Taylor, that insinuating little man who might or might not bring back Poll.

He stood pensively, gazing at the desk. With that capacity he had for standing outside himself, he wondered if, when he was gone, the desk would be there waiting for the author to come back to the empty chair and pick up his pen. The deserted seat, the closed book, the unfinished occupation, all images of death; he had written that. Where would his chair be? He loved his house in Devonshire Terrace – he did not know

now that it would be his favourite of all the houses he would live in. He loved his iron staircase leading to the garden – not today, though, when he could hear the drip, drip of the rain on the railings. He loved his garden where on sunny days – if there were ever to be any – he would lie on the grass with a handkerchief over his face, and he loved this room with its bookcases, and the round mahogany table with its secret drawers where he kept his secret keys. But it was only leased, and he had the anxiety of finding another house in a couple of years.

He was worried about Catherine. His wife was never really well, suffering from headaches, nervousness for no accountable reason, faintness and sometimes confusion. He could not reach her somehow; it was as if a space had opened up between them which he could only fill with little kindnesses, talk about the children, plans for a holiday or a stay with friends although Catherine was beginning to become uneasy if she stayed in other people's houses. He thought of Mrs Morson, and Mary Boyle with whom he had acted at his friends, the Watsons. He felt guilty when he remembered what he had written to her. He had said how he seemed always to be looking for something that he had not found in life – he, a man with a wife and eight children, and a reputation second to none. What folly! But it was true.

"'Heigh, ho, Rowley, a frog he went awooing",' he sang to himself – not this frog, though. This will not do – begone, dull care. He sat down at the desk and saw there the masks he had been doodling, remembering the masks at the murder sites. He had always hated masks; as a child he had shrunk from a mask that hid the wearer's face – not a stranger, someone usually kind and laughing, but whose face was translated by the mask into something blank and so fixed that it haunted his childish dreams and woke him in the night, crying, 'O I know it's coming! O the mask!' Perhaps, he thought the mask, so still and expressionless, was, even then, some dimly understood presage of death. He looked again at his sketch. Unconsciously, he had drawn two masks, one smiling, one tragic, comedy and tragedy. Then he remembered. The mask at St Giles's surely had a downturned mouth, or had he made that up? What about the one at the blacking factory? He could not recall. Had it been smiling? Was that why he had felt it to be so sinister? He could not go back there. Perhaps Sam would send Rogers to find out. And what would it mean, anyway, that the murderer had drawn the masks of comedy and tragedy? Disguise? Was the murderer an actor? That might be a lead to share with Inspector Harker. Which theatre, though? Start with those nearest St Giles's. Ignore the inconvenient fact of the murder at Hungerford Stairs. Make a list: Covent Garden, Bow Street; Theatre Royal, Drury Lane; The Queen's, Long Acre, and, he thought despondently, all the penny gaffs that it would be impossible to follow up.

He heard the doorbell ring. A visitor, perhaps, come like a messenger of brightness to clear the shadows of this November day. His friend, Forster, perhaps, though they had no appointment. Zeb? With news of Poll? Or of Scrap? He sprang up in anticipation. No, Zeb would send a message. He waited, listening. He heard John, the manservant, and then an unfamiliar voice. Who?

John came in. There was a visitor, a seafaring man who had offered Dickens's card, saying that Mr Dickens had offered to help him if he could. Captain Ned Pierce, he said his name was. Should John show him in? Indeed he should. The seafaring man from Hungerford Stairs – the man who had lost a boy.

Captain Pierce came in; he was dressed in his pea coat with the red handkerchief at his neck, his cap in his hand, and the rain glistening on his shoulders. Dickens went forward to shake his hand.

'Captain Pierce, I am glad to see you. Come to the fire and warm yourself. I see how wet you are.'

His quick eye saw also the anxiety in the man's eyes, and he thought of the boy who was lost to him. He motioned him to a chair by the fire and they both sat.

Captain Pierce spoke: 'I have heard that another boy has been found. I came to you for you gave me your card. I looked at it only after I had been to see the boy at Hungerford Stairs – he was not my grandson. I don't like to trouble you, Mr Dickens. I know how busy you are – who could not? But you obviously had an interest in finding your boy, and I thought you might be able to tell me – the man you were with – the inspector at the old blacking factory said he was a policeman from Bow Street – I thought he might know about the dead boy. That's why I came.'

'It is no trouble, Captain Pierce – I could see how worried you were. The dead boy has been identified by his mother. He was Robin Hart – does the name mean anything to you?'

'No – I do not know of anyone called Hart. My grandson is my son's boy, Johnny Pierce.'

'How came he to be missing? Before you tell me, perhaps I can get you some tea or coffee?'

'No, no thank you. My son is dead, and the boy was taken, I think, by his mother. I must begin at the beginning. It's a long story – have you time, Mr Dickens? I hate to impose on you.'

'Please, tell me all. If I can help, I will. My companion the other day was Superintendent Jones – he may be able to assist you.'

'I have retired from the sea now, but while I was last at sea, in 1848, my son died. His wife had already left him and the boy to go off with another man. She was an idle, shiftless wife and mother, a spendthrift who loved gaiety and fine clothes. My son was a marine painter, Mr Dickens, a quiet, thoughtful young man, taken in by a pair of shining eyes, and a pretty manner, but he didn't make much money and she tired of him and cared nothing for the boy. However, when my son, John, died, she came for the boy, as I found out from the neighbour who had looked after him. She emptied the house, took all the belongings and vanished. When I returned from my last voyage, I went to my son's house. I had been away eleven months, starting for Valparaiso in January 1848 – I came back in November. You can imagine what I felt when I found the house empty, my son dead, and the boy gone. I had been away for almost a year and in that year all was lost to me, and I have searched ever since. I traced the mother, Rosa – she had died in March 1848, but there was no sign of the child – he'd disappeared completely.'

'There were no neighbours of Rosa Pierce to tell you about the boy?'

'None, Mr Dickens. By then she was living in a slum, earned her money as a prostitute. She died of drink and disease. The neighbours knew nothing of a boy, those who were sober enough to speak to me. I have read your works, Mr Dickens, you know what it is like – it is unspeakable, the dirt, the squalor, people living like brutes, and that poor boy – I could hardly bear it. Perhaps he's dead, perhaps I will never find him.'

Dickens had listened, but, as he always did, he watched the man, too, scrutinising the features, and he had thought all the time that Captain Pierce was speaking, that he was familiar. He had watched his transparent hazel eyes that had still, for all his years, a kind of innocence, and he had watched the mouth, and the way one of the front teeth protruded slightly, and the way, as he spoke, the tooth caught on the bottom lip. How should he proceed? If he were wrong, and told Captain Pierce that he might know where Johnny Pierce was, would the disappointment be crushing? But if he were right, then the risk would be worth it. Dickens was a shrewd reader of character; he believed he knew his man. Captain Pierce who had pursued the lost boy with such dogged persistence would want to know, and he would be strong enough to bear a disappointment.

As he looked at Captain Pierce, Dickens could superimpose the face of a young boy on the older face. He was sure. And so he spoke.

'Captain Pierce, I know of a boy who greatly resembles you, who has your eyes, mouth, and teeth. And, if you will hazard the risk of disappointment, then I will tell you his story and take you to him.'

Captain Pierce did not speak. The hazel eyes were clouded now with doubt and disbelief, but he shook his grey head as if to clear the uncertainty. He looked directly at Dickens as if to read what was in his face, and he saw there in those keen, brilliant eyes something so fixed, almost mesmerising, that he could not resist. Afterwards, he could not remember the colour, only the power of those eyes. Johnny Pierce always said that they were blue.

'Tell me, Mr Dickens. I am willing to take the risk; I have nothing left.'

'At Shepherd's Bush, there is a home for fallen women which I established with Miss Angela Burdett-Coutts. Its aim is to give young women a chance of a better life. It is run by a matron who is a kind, motherly woman with children of her own. I admire her very much, and when I found a boy living on the streets, a boy with eyes exactly like yours, I knew that Mrs Morson would take care of him, that he would be safe.'

'But fallen women, Mr Dickens, how would that be safe for a boy? If it is my boy, surely he's seen too much of that.'

'You will have to trust me, Captain Pierce. I assure you it is a well-run house. Think of it, if you will, as a school. The boy – to whom I gave the name Davey – '

Captain Pierce interrupted, 'But why? Why change his name? I don't understand.'

'He could not tell me his own name – he does not speak.'
'Never?'
'No. He is not deaf so Mrs Morson and I thought that –'
'He had experienced something dreadful.'

'Yes.'

'Then, you must take me to him. I must see if it is Johnny.'

They took a fly to Shepherd's Bush. It was the quickest way which took them along the New Road, into Grand Junction Road and then to Uxbridge Road by Kensington Gardens and the gravel pits.

'You will know him?' asked Dickens, breaking the silence.

'I will know him, Mr Dickens. Now tell me his story.'

Dickens told of the bitter night when he found a boy curled up in a doorway like a lost dog, a boy whose hazel eyes were transparent as the light brown water of a stream, eyes which looked at him with appeal and bewilderment, a boy who could not tell him his name, a boy who wept when an outstretched hand clasped his and took him away to warmth and food. Dickens told the captain of Mrs Morson's care of the boy, and how James Bagster, the gardener at Urania Cottage, had taught him to laugh again, and he told him of Patience Brooke whose gentle care had reminded the boy that he could read and write. He told him about Patience Brooke whose murder had made the boy afraid, but how he had recovered in James Bagster's kindly company. He told him how the boy, Davey, loved the horse, Punch, and the cat, Peg, and he told him how he and Superintendent Jones had thought of what the boy might have seen, what nightmare figures inhabited his memory.

'What secrecy there is in the young, under terror. We could never know. We wondered if he would ever speak or whether his silence is now fixed so that the memories can never be exorcised.'

'I understand you, Mr Dickens, and I fear what he has seen or heard. Is he damaged beyond repair?'

With the question unanswered, they arrived at Urania Cottage. Mrs Morson looked at Captain Pierce and she knew.

'He is so like you,' she said. 'He must belong to you. And I am glad, so glad. Davey is in the garden with James,' she said to Dickens. 'Shall you go out to them?'

They went out through the kitchen door up into the garden where they saw James Bagster at work. He came to them and saw Captain Pierce.

'You have come for him?' He knew, too. They looked across the garden to the open stable door where, in a patch of winter sunlight, the boy sat with Peg the cat, both absorbed, staring at a piece of string snaking along the ground.

'Go to him,' said Mrs Morson.

The three of them watched as the captain crossed the garden. Dickens found himself clasping Mrs Morson's hand too tightly. The cat, which usually walked away from strangers, sat where she was, looking at the man with fixed yellow eyes, and then the boy looked up. The man knelt, and they saw him touch the boy's shoulder. Peg the cat looked at the boy and the man before she disappeared into the stable.

The three watchers turned away. This was not for spectators.

'I shall miss him,' said Mrs Morson.

'So will I,' said James Bagster, 'but I am glad for him and for the captain. You have done such a good thing, Mr Dickens.' He went away, back to his work.

'I must go back to London,' said Dickens. He thought of Scrap and Poll, and it seemed important to get there soon. 'Tell the captain to come to see me soon to tell me about Davey – or Johnny, as we must think of him, now. You will look after them until they are ready to go home?'

'I will. Home – how wonderful for Davey.'

'Home. There's a word as strong as a magician ever spoke.'

'You are a magician, Charles, to have found the captain.'

'He found me, really, though something prompted me to give him my card when I knew he was looking for a boy. Perhaps it was magic. Fate, anyway – we are all connected, I am certain. Now I must go and see if my magic will conjure my missing boy, Scrap. I shall come again soon.'

'Do – I think we might need to settle with Miss Sesina – but not now. Let us not spoil this.'

They looked back over the garden where the boy and the man stood now, their arms about each other.

Dickens went out to walk back to the village. It had been extraordinary, he thought, that his return to the despised blacking factory should be the means of restoring Davey to his grandfather. A rebirth, he thought, but a death, too, and another death. Poor Robin. His pace quickened. Go back. Let us find the murderer before he does it again. Why did he think that? Because of the mask. Did it mean, as he had thought, 'You can't catch me'?

9

HARK, HARK, THE DOGS DO BARK …

The rain that Dickens had watched soaking his garden had poured all night on to Scrap's shelter, and on to the iron roof of Poll's cage where she had lain with her head on her paws, waiting. It had fallen on Georgie Taylor's garden, or rather, on the stunted tree in the sodden earth behind the house. Georgie was not fond of nature in any shape or form. The tree was a leftover from some earlier time when St Giles's was really in the fields, and Violet Lane had bloomed with other things than mud and dog dirt. Not a bank where the nodding violet grows now, unless one counted Georgie's purple nose or the bruises blossoming on the boy's arm where Georgie squeezed it. The boy was Mrs Georgie's son. There were no daughters as Georgie liked to claim – why, he could claim a dozen daughters, twenty nieces if the occasion asked for sentiment. Georgie always understood when a little miss's doggie was missing. No, Georgie was not fond of the boy, the child of nature who perforce must come with Mrs Georgie when she was a slip of a girl, well, not quite a slip, but slimmer than she was today.

Today, Georgie must go to Nat Boney to see if the dog, Poll, was there, and how much out of the three sovereigns it would cost to get the dratted thing back. No, Georgie was not keen on nature; dogs, apart from the profit they made, were a blamed nuisance. He would have liked another trade, he thought, something cleaner, less yappy. Horses, the races, that's what he'd have liked, but Mrs Georgie didn't care for racing – money down the drain. Mrs Georgie liked to keep her money where she could count it – under the frowsty bed where she now lay, an unromantic heap of flesh, gurgling like a drainpipe in her sleep. Lazy cow, he thought, bitterness rising like acid. Lazy bitch. And he was tied to her like a terrier on a leash.

In the kitchen, the boy – not a boy at all, but a thin, simple, shambling creature of nineteen – was eating a piece of bread. Georgie snatched it away and gave a spiteful squeeze to the thin arm before tossing the bread to the black dog with red eyes which snarled in the corner. The boy looked at Georgie and smiled his idiot smile. Georgie's anger flared and died. What was the point? Whatever was done to him, the boy smiled, though Georgie never noticed the hurt in his eyes.

The rain still fell, turning the lane to mud and slush, and the sky was dark and thick as wet wool. Georgie pulled on his oilskin. Bloody rain, bloody dogs, but two sovereigns were not to be sniffed at and, what's more, he might, just might, keep a bit back from Mrs Georgie – a little bit to add to his secret hoard. One day, one day, he thought, the terrier might just wriggle out of the leash. He picked his way fastidiously through the mud and made his way to Nat Boney's.

Scrap watched the cross-eyed boy come out of the door, which he held open with one hand so that he could set down one sack and reach back in for the other. Scrap heard the dogs barking, a clamour of yelps, howls and snarls. Scrap was poised. This was the moment when he could offer to help the cross-eyed boy. He stepped across the alley. Then something amazing happened. The door was smashed to the ground, and a great mastiff stood in the alley. The cross-eyed boy was bowled over, his yelping sack splitting to release a frightened spaniel which stood bewildered. And then a stream of dogs came racing through the hole where the door had been. Cross-eyes had left the cage open. Scrap heard a roar of rage and he saw Nat Boney rush forward into the writhing mass of dogs still in the yard. But the gods were just. Boney slipped on the collop of shit left by the mastiff for just that purpose. Down he went. Scrap heard the sickening thud. And the alley was full of legs, tails, tongues, teeth, barks, yaps. Poll? There she was shooting under the mastiff's bulk, popping out, seeing Scrap, barking her head off, leaping into his arms. Just as he bent to receive her, Scrap saw the astonished face of Georgie Taylor. Bloody hell! Two sovereigns! But Scrap was gone. Exit, pursued by twenty dogs.

He could not take them all. But he could lead them off. Away he ran, like Mr Browning's pied piper, the dogs barking and racing, diving off down alleys, some even running back the way they came, but hearing Boney's curses, leaping away again, mad with freedom, into gardens and passageways, through open doors into hallways where astonished householders tried to shoo them off, over walls, into shops, snatching chops from the butcher's counter, and following the scent of home, Scrap hoped. Home which was where he and Poll were bound. Home to Eleanor and Tom Brim, to Mr Brim and Mrs Jones who were in the stationery shop, about their daily business, but with a space in their hearts where Scrap and Poll should be.

Dickens was wet, too. He had come back from Shepherd's Bush on the knife-board, the narrow seat on top of the omnibus, as uncomfortable a ride as one might get in a coffin, but with the small advantage of being alive and in the open air, wet as it was. There had been room inside, but Dickens could never bear the smell of damp straw nor the smell of even damper clothes. Besides, the fat woman inside had given him such a look with her fishy eye that he had resisted the temptation to risk the smell so had climbed up on top. A man with an umbrella had attempted several times to poke out Dickens's eye, but that was nothing compared to the man who squeezed next to him, sneezing and honking like a sick swan. Leprosy, thought Dickens gloomily, remembering Rats' Castle and noting the sores on the man's face. If I don't catch influenza, then it will be leprosy. Leprous got off on Oxford Street. Too late, thought Dickens, watching a new passenger appear at the top of the stairs like a startled porpoise, dripping with water. Dickens felt the rain trickle down his neck. Home or Bow Street? The thought of a hot bath, a fire, and tea and cake was tempting, but Sam would want to know about Davey, and he wanted to know if there were news of Scrap. It was time he went to Crown Street and the Brims.

The omnibus disposed of him on Broad Street from where he hurried to Bow Street, arriving just at the moment when Mrs Elizabeth Jones, her face glowing despite the rain, was dashing in to find the superintendent. Dickens gazed at her shining face.

'They are back! Scrap and Poll have come home. Charles, I could dance for joy.'

'And, if we were not like to be arrested, I should join you in a polka. Let us get Sam, and be off. A cake – we must have a cake.' Oh, glory, Davey restored, and Scrap and Poll.

'We must, I promised them – on the way.'

The superintendent summoned, good-natured Rogers in his wake, his red face shining, the cake bought, they went to Crown Street, to Mr Brim's stationery shop where they found a party beginning. Lemonade was ready, the plates were waiting for the cake. Tom Brim, aged five-and-a-bit, was sitting on the counter with Poll whose neck sported a red ribbon, and who seemed to be barking in time with the music. A man they had never seen before was playing a violin and Eleanor and Scrap were dancing madly to the tune. Mr Brim leant on his counter, watching it all, his eyes glittering, the tell-tale hectic in his cheeks witness to the disease that would kill him. But not yet, not yet, not until his children were a little older. Elizabeth Jones saw it all, and she, too, thought *not yet*.

Eleanor Brim danced another polka with Mr Dickens who had learned it from his daughters, and who had practised in the middle of one wintry cold night, fearful that the steps were forgotten. He had not forgotten them now. He and Miss Nell flew about the shop to great applause, while Sam Jones sat in the chair where Tom and Poll found room, too, and Elizabeth Jones took Mr Brim by the hand into the dance; though their steps were slower, Scrap saw that Mr Brim was happy, and he was, so he danced in and out of the whirling Eleanor and Mr Dickens, making up the steps. Constable Rogers joined him, and for just a little while, Dickens and Jones forgot about poor Robin and the unknown boy. And so they whirled, danced, and clapped to the wild, sweet music.

Then it was the cake and lemonade. The violinist was introduced to Dickens, Jones and Rogers. He knew of Mr Dickens, of course, had heard much about him from the Brims, how proud they were that Mr Dickens had put a nice dog in *David Copperfield* just for them – it was true. Eleanor and Tom had not much cared for Bill Sikes's dog so Mr Dickens had promised them a spaniel with silky ears, though it had to be admitted that no dog could be as intelligent as Poll. Poll, who had known all along that someone would come for her. And Scrap, the hero of the hour. He had found her and Eleanor declared that she had believed all along that Scrap would come back with Poll.

The cake was just a scatter of crumbs on the counter, the lemonade a sweet memory on the tongue, and the music an echo in the ear. It was time to go and leave the reunited family. Dickens, Superintendent Jones and Elizabeth went out into the darkening November street where the air was suddenly cold after the warmth inside.

'Home, Charles, I think. I am going home, too. Rogers, you go and spend an evening with your shining Mollie Spoon. She'll be glad to see you, I daresay. They know where to find us if they want us. I sent Constable Feak to Hanover Street to see if he could find the French milliner, but there is no sign of her. We will continue our search tomorrow.'

Rogers went off, smiling. A night off. That was something. He certainly would go to see Mollie Spoon. He could not help smiling at the superintendent's pun. Mollie did shine – for him, at any rate. He had met her during the course of the investigation into the murder of Patience Brooke. Now he wondered when the time might be right for him to ask her to marry him.

'I had a thought,' said Dickens, 'about the masks. I found myself sketching them and drew a smiling mask and one with its mouth turned down.'

'Comedy and tragedy?' asked Elizabeth.

'That's what I thought, but I could not recall what the mask was like at the blacking factory. I wondered if it was a smiling mouth and if that was why it seemed so sinister – at least, not a child's work. Have I imagined that the St Giles's one had a downturned mouth?'

'I cannot remember precisely, either. We could go to see on our way home. It is only a step. Elizabeth, would you mind?'

'No – not that I am fond of a churchyard in the dark but with you two to protect me, I shall be safe.'

They walked up from Crown Street to Monmouth Street with its ghostly inhabitants hanging still about the second-hand clothes stalls; the bride was still there though it seemed that her military groom had taken his scarlet coat and gone to war. She was doomed to eternal spinsterhood, her net skirts getting yellower and dustier by the year.

It was early evening and the street was busy – there was the baked potato man with his little tin contraption, and the kidney pie man from whose portable oven sparks flew down the street every time he opened the door to hand a hot pie to a customer. There was all the hurry of coming home and getting out again; who was coming and who was going, it was hard to tell. The still centre of this turning world was the group of idling men gazing indifferently at the drunk in the gutter and the two scrawny women abusing each other like alley cats.

They crossed into Compton Street, passing the King's Head where the poster advertised the prize of a gold repeater watch for the champion rat killer. No need to worry about that now, thankfully, thought Dickens, watching the men going in with their dogs in their arms or on tight leashes. There were plenty of bull terriers, little welsh terriers, and one melancholy, shaggy white dog with a scarred face, very like Sikes's Bulls-eye, gave him a look which seemed to say that he'd had enough of it all and fancied something better. Dickens felt for him, but, seeing Sam and Elizabeth ahead of him, hurried on to the church.

They went in to look for the chalk mark on the old door at the side. Dickens could not help glancing at the cold tomb where they had found Robin Hart. Elizabeth saw the direction of his glance.

'Sam told me. That poor boy – and his mother. What will become of her?'

'She is safe for the present with Effie Scruggs, but they cannot look after her forever. I do not think she will survive the loss of her child.'

Elizabeth understood. She had lost her only daughter. Edith had died in childbirth and the child, too, but Elizabeth had had Sam. At first they had carried their grief with them like a large, unwieldy, heavy parcel that they could never put down, and which had to be handled with care lest it break one or the other. It was lighter, now, and they could sometimes put it down, resting for longer times when they could remember her with some of the joy she had brought them as a child.

Sam held his lamp up to the door. There was the mask with the mouth turned down slightly. The drawn in sightless eyes gave it a sinister look. Dickens wondered if it were more frightening than the other.

'It is horrible,' said Elizabeth. 'I wonder what it means to the murderer.'

'It may mean nothing,' Sam responded. 'It may be his way of leading us on, playing with us.'

'If he is playing, then I might be right – he could be an actor, relishing his ability to disguise himself.'

'The trouble is we do not know the man or the mask. We need to find the owner of that shawl – it is the only clue we have – and for all we know, it could have been dropped there before the murder. It might be no clue at all.'

'And the toff as those girls called him – someone might have seen Robin Hart with a man.'

'Yes, that is a lead. His mother cannot tell us anything about him, but he must have had friends, and he got money by taking messages so someone must have noticed him. I'll get on to that tomorrow.'

They went out of the churchyard and made their way to Oxford Street to take a cab which would take Dickens to Devonshire Terrace and Sam and Elizabeth to Norfolk Street.

'Tomorrow, and tomorrow and tomorrow,' said Dickens by way of farewell. 'At least we have Scrap and Poll back, and Davey has found himself again. It has not been such a bad day.'

'Indeed not – I shall treasure the memory of your polka, Charles.'

'When my biography is written I shall ask that my prowess as a dancer be included – as witnessed by Superintendent Jones of Bow Street. And now, a thousand times goodnight.'

They watched him as he went, his quick step taking him away, replacing his hat he had flourished in farewell,

Odd, thought Sam, how I always think of him walking alone, yet he is the best-known man in London – and the best loved, probably. He has a wife and eight children, but there is something in him, something in his eyes that I cannot fathom. Something missing, perhaps. He looked at Elizabeth who was gazing at the retreating figure, a curious expression of pity mingled with fondness.

10

THE MILLINER

Superintendent Jones was in his office next morning. Rogers had gone back to the blacking factory to check the chalk marks. Sam had no idea what it might really mean if the mask was smiling, but it seemed like something to do. Feak and Stemp were out looking for a French milliner, and he was here, thinking.

Motive. What's his motive? Dickens would say and the superintendent agreed. In crime as in literature, there had to be motive. Greed, jealousy, revenge, power, the need to protect the self from danger. And, of course, there was sometimes no understandable motive – the murderer did it because he could. But then that was power, of course it was. It was the delight in having the power over the victim, and the triumph of getting away with it. Greed? He thought about the novels of Dickens he had read. What was Dombey's motive? Greed. What was the motive of Jonas Chuzzlewit's intention to murder his father? Greed. And Jonas had murdered Montague Tigg because he feared him.

Well, he thought, Dickens was an expert on greed – the ruthless desire to have at all costs, and greed could be avarice, but jealousy was a kind of greed. Carker in *Dombey and Son* – sexual greed, the desire for Edith Dombey was not out of love, and his motive was power, too, power over Dombey. Revenge. A powerful motive – witness Bill Sikes who had believed that Nancy had betrayed him and had clubbed her to death with his pistol.

So, he thought, where does our murderer fit into all this? Avarice was out – these boys were too poor. Why should the murderer fear two boys? Perhaps they knew something that might discredit the murderer. It was possible. And power? Yes, he had power over them. The little vignette of Robin Hart with the murderer's arm round him – that suggested that the young man those girls had seen had power over the boy. A young man and a young boy. Dark-haired Katey in the churchyard had thought of that – her knowing eyes had told him. He, too, had thought of what that might mean, but why kill them? They knew nothing about the first boy. Mrs Hart could tell them nothing about her son, but someone might have known Robin Hart and whether he had a new friend. He wondered if Scrap knew him. Well, it was time to ask.

Rogers came back from Hungerford Stairs. He couldn't really tell if the mask had a smile. 'I dunno, sir, it might 'ave bin a smile, or it might just 'ave bin a scrawl.'

Comedy and tragedy, perhaps, perhaps not. And, if that's what the masks meant, then what? Sam preferred something more concrete. And Rogers was able to supply it. He had met Constable Green who had been at the blacking factory with Inspector Harker. The boy had been seen – with a slight young man.

'Where?'

'Hungerford Market. Jack Green had been making his enquiries in the market 'cos anyone going down the stairs would 'ave to go through the market, and Jim, knowing that our boy had been seen with a young man, asked about a ragged lad, possibly a mudlark, in the company of a young man, a man who was probably a gent.

'There was a lad who knew the dead boy – Jemmy, 'e called 'im. Knew 'im as Jemmy Kidd but 'oo knows, sir? The lad could 'ave 'eard the word kid and thought it was 'is name. The lad said 'e didn't know where Jemmy lived. 'E was a mudlark, as we thought, scraped a livin', as they all do, so the witness was surprised to see 'im with a toff, as 'e put it.'

'Could he describe the young man?'

'Not really – he noticed 'is top hat, 'is dark suit, and that 'e seemed young – probably because 'e was slight – the boy said 'e was thinnish.'

'Where did they go?'

'The boy didn't see. You know 'ow crowded the market is. Anyway, Green is looking for anyone else who might have known Jemmy, whether he belonged anywhere, 'ad a family or what.'

'So, we have a young man. Let us presume it is the same young man in both cases – the descriptions, though vague, fit. We have a possible, faintly possible, link to the theatre, and we have the shawl. And we have our experience which tells us to be suspicious of a young man who makes the acquaintance of young boys and kills them.'

'You think it's sex, sir?'

'I do. What else would he want them for?'

'Crime? Did 'e use them? Was 'e a kidsman – not a real toff, but a flash cove – usin' 'em for stealin'? An' when they wanted to get away, did 'e kill them, or did 'e just replace them when 'e'd finished with 'em?'

'But, remember, Robin Hart belonged to someone. His mother would have known if he had been involved in something criminal.'

'But, 'e might 'ave been new to it. The mother 'ad nothing. 'E might 'ave thought 'e was 'elpin', not realising what it all meant. I dunno, sir, I think it's just that we should – keep an open mind – that's what you always say, sir.'

'How right you are, Rogers. Thank you for reminding me.'

Rogers glowed. He admired his superintendent more than anyone, and he was determined to learn from him, to follow his methods and to get on. That's what his ma said. 'You look an' learn, my lad, an' you'll be an inspector before you know it.' An' 'e would, he said to himself, yes, 'e would.

'Mr Dickens comin', sir?'

'Yes, he's coming from Shepherd's Bush. He sent a message to say he'd come after dealing with Miss Sesina. You remember her?'

'Not 'alf – frightened me to death, she did. Sparks flyin' everywhere. A real temper, she 'as.'

Dickens came in. Rogers was right. Sesina's temper had got the better of her, and as he arrived, summoned by Mrs Morson, Sesina was on her way. Sam Jones and Rogers could not help laughing as Dickens described what Mrs Morson had told him of how she had flounced and stamped her way to her bedroom, how she had flung her nightcap across the room, dressed herself in her own good time, and then declared that the rain was too bad for her to go out. Threatened with Mr Dickens, she had made her exit, threatening to air her many and varied grievances against the Home in a letter to Miss Coutts. Dickens had seen her when he was coming back; she was tripping jauntily up Notting Hill, looking in the shop windows with the air of one who might saunter in and buy something. 'It was quite a performance,' said Dickens.

'She oughter be on the stage,' said Rogers.

'Indeed she should – perhaps she'll find a role as a tragedy queen. I cannot help thinking that she will find her way to Isabella Gordon. What a pair they will make. Still, nothing to be done. We tried to help, but it was not to be. Any news, Sam?'

Sam told him Rogers's information about the boy, Jemmy, seen with a 'gent' at Hungerford Stairs, and the conclusions he and Rogers had come to, explaining that Rogers had suggested they keep an open mind about the relations of the young man with the two boys.

Constable Feak returned with news that he had found the French milliner who had moved her premises to Rose Street, not far from St Giles's. He had spoken to a neighbour who had told him that Mamselle Victorine had lived there for about eighteen months. She was very quiet and reserved and no one knew her very well. She had few visitors, except customers, the woman supposed, and once or twice, she had seen a young man leaving out the back. The woman wondered if Mamselle had a lover, though she was so thin and plain, the neighbour doubted it.

'How did you find her?' asked Dickens, curious.

Feak, who looked about fifteen, and only just tall enough for regulation height at five foot nine, reddened. 'Asked me mam.'

'What?'

'I know it sounds daft, sir, but I thought it'd be quicker. She knows a lot, me mam, an' I thought, 'er bein' a woman an' that …'

Dickens and Jones wondered about the 'an' that', but Feak's embarrassment was so palpable that they forbore to comment. In any case, Mrs Feak was a legend in Bow Street – for Feak, she was an oracle. The superintendent called her the Sybil of Star Lane. And she told fortunes when she was not out nursing. I should have consulted her cards, thought the superintendent, but he merely nodded at Feak to continue.

'Well, 'er bein' a woman made me think that she'd know where the 'at makers are an' she said there was one off Earl Street, an' I knew I'd struck gold when she said she thought there was a French lady in Rose Street. I went straight there.'

'Very sensible, Feak – to ask your mother, I mean. Give her my compliments when you see her.'

Feak's raw, red boy's face lit up. 'Thank you, sir. She will be pleased. She always asks after you.'

'Well, you and Stemp can get out there and ask about Robin Hart. See if you can find out who he took messages for. Try some of the shops, the more prosperous-looking ones, and later, ask some of the street vendors if they saw him about – he might have had a penny for a pie or a potato sometimes.'

'Yes, sir.' Feak went out very pleased with himself. 'E'd felt a fool when 'e blurted out that 'e'd asked his mam, but, well, the superintendent'd thought it a good idea, an' it was – wait till 'e got 'ome – she would be pleased.

'I thought about asking Scrap if he knew Robin Hart, or, if he did not, then he could ask about for us. What do you think, Charles?'

'A good notion. Shall I offer him the usual rates?' Dickens and Jones had made use of Scrap before, and had insisted that he take his wages – sixpence a day.

'Yes, but we should go to Rose Street first and ask Mademoiselle Victorine about the shawl. It is here, ready to take. Rogers, would you go back to Zeb Scruggs's and see how Mrs Hart is? I doubt that she will be fit to answer questions, but you should ask Zeb and Effie if they know who Robin ran his errands for.'

The three of them went out, Rogers for Monmouth Street and Dickens and Jones to walk up Crown Street of which Rose Street was an offshoot. The house was neat and respectable; there was a sign in the window bearing the legend: *Mademoiselle Victorine, Milliner and Sempstress.*

The superintendent knocked. After a few moments, the door was opened by a tall, thin woman in a grey dress with neat white cuffs and lace collar. Dickens observed her as Sam explained that they were trying to find the owner of a shawl which they thought might be evidence in a criminal case. She wore very thick spectacles behind which her rather glassy eyes seemed to be just pinpoints – myopic, he thought. She was plain; her face was unremarkable, pale, almost grey and her hair, of no particular colour, was scraped back in a neat bun. Her lips were pale, too, and there were faint lines from her nose to her mouth and frown lines. Dickens thought how anonymous she was. You would not notice her in the street. In the crepuscular shadow of the doorway she was as faint as a pencil sketch, easily erased. But she seemed entirely unmoved by the superintendent's announcement that they had come from Bow Street, merely murmuring to them to enter.

They went into a front room which was obviously her workshop. There were a few hats perched on stands like exotic birds, their bright plumage rustling faintly from the draught as she opened the door. There was a deal work table with tapes and scissors and a garment that she had been cutting out when they knocked, and there was a shawl, very like the one the superintendent took from his pocket.

'Is this your work?'

She looked at it, and said, 'Yes, monsieur, I made it.'

'Did you sell it to someone? Can you remember to whom?'

'Yes, monsieur, I remember the shawls I have made. They take a lot of work. I do not make them now – my eyes. The work is very fine – the birds and flowers – you see.'

'It is very beautiful,' said Dickens, hoping for a reaction, but she merely looked at him and nodded.

'This is quite an old one. See, some of the fringe is missing and there is a little wear here where the stitching is loose. A pity. Perhaps she did not look after it.'

'Who?' asked Sam, 'who bought it?'

'An old lady – she lives in George Street at number twenty-seven. She was my client when I lived in Hanover Street. I used to make hats for her, but I do not see her now. You see, I had to move here. It is cheaper. I do not know how it is, but sometimes people stop coming. They find, perhaps, someone they like better. Rich ladies like change. They follow their friends, perhaps. Now I do not make shawls. I must make these gaudy hats for the gay young ladies.'

'What was the name of your rich lady?'

'Madame Outfin – curious is it not – the English have strange names, do they not?'

'I suppose French names sound odd to us – I have a friend, Monsieur Le Beau – I find his name amusing.' Dickens tried to draw her out, borrowing Le Beau from Shakespeare. Perhaps she might answer the questions he knew that Sam wished to ask this odd, self-contained creature. She is like a snail, he thought. She draws in her horns.

She looked at him, her little eyes indifferent behind the thick lenses. She did not answer, and the silence was thick suddenly. She had nothing further to say. Sam, however, was not to be put off. He thought about the young man, leaving by the back entrance.

'You live alone here?'

Her eyes flickered slightly behind the spectacles, just a movement – alarm, perhaps? But the impression was so fleeting that Dickens wondered if it were just a trick of the light on the lenses rather than the eyes.

'Yes, I live alone, monsieur. I prefer it. I am a foreigner here. It is not easy. The English do not like foreigners.' She shrugged. Such a French gesture, Dickens thought. He felt he ought to pity her, but there was a coldness in her which repelled him. He could not imagine her with a lover, but then, who knew? Though she was sexless, he thought, neutral. What would move her?

Sam asked, 'Have you no family here in England?'

'No, monsieur, I had a brother, but he must go back to France. My mother wished him to take over the shop. Now, they are dead, and there is nothing there for me to go back to. So, here must I stay to earn my living.' There was finality in her tone. Not sadness, not regret, just a cold acceptance of facts that could not be changed.

There was nothing else to say. Sam thought he could hardly ask her who the young man was who had been seen at the back of the house. It might have been her brother. It might have been no one at all; someone the neighbour had seen, and had assumed was coming from Mademoiselle Victorine's house. It might have been an idle piece of gossip. Victorine waited in the silence. It was clear that she wanted them to go. She glanced at her work table.

'If there is nothing more, monsieur …'

'No, thank you. We will see if we can trace the shawl to Mrs Outfin.'

She went with them to the front door which she locked as they went out.

'An odd young woman,' said Dickens. 'A sad story, but why did it fail to move me?'

'Something cold about her. I could hardly believe the story about the lover. I wonder if it was just gossip.'

'I had the same thought about the lover. There was so little to her, not physically though she was thin enough, more that she had so little personality. But there was a sense of secrecy about her.'

'At least we have the name of the shawl's owner. We'll go to George Street to see if Mrs Outfin is in – or out. A fishy sort of name – though I doubt that she is our murderer.'

'Perhaps she has a son, or grandson who might turn out to be an actor who wears a beautifully embroidered shawl as a disguise, or, even better, a son who is really a lunatic, kept locked in the cellar, but who has escaped on nights when the moon is full, and wearing his mother's shawl, stalks the streets intent on murder …'

'It was raining two nights ago – no moon.' Sam grinned. 'Sorry.'

'Ah, my theory dashed to pieces.'

'Well, it is as good as any other at the moment. Shall we take lunch first? Frustration is making me hungry. A chop and a glass of ale might well restore my good humour.'

They walked to the George to order their chops, potatoes and ale and sat by the fire. They ate first so that the superintendent's usual equanimity might be restored. When he had finished, he looked at Dickens.

'Motive. That's what I want to know. I want to know what the relationship was between the boys and their killer. Rogers, bless his open mind, thinks crime – that the murderer was using them to thieve for him, but I'm not sure how Robin Hart fits in to that theory. Could be, I suppose, but –'

'You think that it is an unnatural desire that is his motive? That when he has finished with them he kills them.'

'It happens – we find boys abused, dead, as well as girls. That poor girl we found in that wretched garden when we were looking for our murderer back in February – no one claimed her. Boys and girls so young that they should still be playing with their toys. It's sickening, and what is worse, there are men, wealthy men who will pay for this – that's why it is so hard to uncover – there are closed ranks, Charles, which I can never part.' Sam sounded angry.

He and Dickens knew well that children could be bought and sold, and often there was nothing to be done. Money changed hands. Silence was bought. Victims vanished into the cellars and holes of the alleys where they might die of neglect, starvation or of the disease with which perverted sex infected them. Some were murdered to stop their mouths. Sam was right. It was vile.

Sam continued, 'You have shown the suffering of neglected and abused children, but you can't write about that – you would be accused of every kind of perversion.'

'I know. There were comments on the lowness of my subject when I wrote *Oliver Twist*. Some did not want to read about thieves' kitchens and boys trained into criminality, but I could not write about such abuse anyway. It is too horrible. How could one describe what is done, what the effects are? Surely the post-mortem will tell us if they have been abused.'

'It might – it depends on how long the abuse went on.'

'Then I think Rogers is right. We should also consider other possibilities.'

'Such as?'

Dickens grinned. 'I have no idea at the moment, but I'll think of something, I daresay. Shall we go on to Mrs Outfin and hope to find a gibbering maniac in the cellar?'

'Now, that would be something.'

Number twenty-seven was a handsome house with white pillars, smart black railings and a shiny black door. It spoke of wealth and privilege. No wonder Mademoiselle Victorine had resented Mrs Outfin. Dickens imagined the contrast between that ghost of a woman and perhaps a well-fed, stout, ungracious client who dropped her milliner when her fashionable friends recommended another. For a moment, he felt something like pity. The shawl showed that Victorine was an artist, in her way, but her poor eyesight had robbed her of her skill in creating those beautiful things. He forgot her coldness then, and thought he had been too hasty in his judgement. Perhaps all the blows she had suffered had simply left her numb, not indifferent.

A solid, box-like woman, probably the housekeeper, answered the bell. The superintendent asked if they might see Mrs Outfin on a confidential matter. He introduced himself as Superintendent Jones from Bow Street.

'I am sorry,' said the woman, looking puzzled. 'The Outfins do not live here now. Mrs Outfin is dead. She died about a year ago.'

'I see. The family – where are they now?'

'Mrs Outfin had a son. He is married with two children. They live in Montague Place, just behind the museum, number forty.' She closed the door.

'A son – I said she had a son, and children. I wonder how old she was. Victorine said that she was old, but we do not know what she meant. He might be in his forties. Perhaps he has a son,' Dickens said eagerly.

'It is possible, but we might be on a wild goose chase. Still, they ought to recognise the shawl. It is distinctive.'

Montague Place was lined with the same white Regency houses as George Street, though in this case the houses were embellished by an elegant wrought-iron frieze running along under the windows of the first floor. The door was opened by a flustered maid. Dickens handed in his card and asked if he might speak with Mr Outfin. They were admitted into a cool hall with a black and white tiled floor. Other smartly clad maids and a uniformed footman were carrying hatboxes and other parcels up the stairs. The maid vanished with the card. When she returned, she led them to a library where Mr Outfin waited. He was about fifty years old, stocky with the same box-like build of the housekeeper at George Street. Dickens's imagination conjured him briefly as a love child. He reproved himself silently as Mr Outfin came forward to meet them. He was evidently not the slight man.

'Good afternoon, Mr Dickens. I am very glad to meet you. I know of you of course – your books.' He gestured to his shelves. 'How may I help you?' He was courteous, and smiling, but his eyes were wary. What had brought the famous novelist to his house with this commanding stranger? He looked uneasily at the superintendent.

Dickens introduced Sam who explained that they wished to find the owner of the shawl as they had been told it belonged to Mr Outfin's mother. It might be a significant clue in relation to a crime. Mr Outfin could hardly understand. He looked puzzled, but Dickens observed an uneasiness about him as he acknowledged the superintendent. Perhaps it was natural – a policeman coming to the house. Mr Outfin explained that his mother was dead. He did not know if the shawl had been hers. He looked at it but it meant nothing to him. His wife had dealt with his mother's clothes. Perhaps they would like to see her – he would fetch her. She was upstairs – busy – their daughter was to be married – everything was topsy-turvy – but he would see. He went out.

Dickens could not resist going over to the bookshelves. Yes, they were there – attractive editions of *Pickwick*, *Oliver Twist*, *Nicholas Nickleby*, *The Old Curiosity Shop*. He touched them for luck. Sam watched him, amused.

Mrs Outfin came in, a slender, pretty woman who smiled agreeably, though her thick fair hair was escaping from its bun and tendrils were loosened attractively round her face. She looked good-humoured and sensible, but there was anxiety in her eyes.

'Mr Dickens, how very nice it is to meet you. We have all read your books. My favourite is *Dombey and Son* – how I cried at the death of little Paul, and of Little Nell, too. But, I beg your pardon, my husband says you are here about a shawl. May I see it?'

She examined the shawl. 'I think it might have belonged to my mother-in-law, but I cannot be sure. She had so many, shawls, gloves, bonnets – she was like a magpie, always collecting – and then discarding. A difficult woman – not that I should say so.' She paused as if conscious that she had betrayed something. She went on quickly. 'But she was very fond of my daughter, Sophia. Sophia might remember. She went often to see her. Shall I ask her to come? She is here. We are preparing for her wedding – to Mr Wilde, Oliver.'

'But I know him,' said Dickens. Oliver Wilde had helped them in their pursuit of the murderer of Patience Brooke.

'A nice young man. I am very fond of him,' said Mrs Outfin.

'He is, indeed.' Dickens was curious. When last they had met, Oliver Wilde was in love with someone else though Dickens had thought she would not return his love. So, sensible lad, he had found someone else.

Mrs Outfin went out, leaving them to ponder on the coincidence of their knowing Oliver Wilde, and to hope that Sophia Outfin might remember the shawl, and to think about the faint but discernible tension in both Mr and Mrs Outfin. It might be the bustle of the wedding, but Dickens could not help wondering. Families had secrets.

Sophia came in with her mother. They were alike: slender, fair and good-humoured. There was an innocence about the girl, however. Whatever might be wrong here, Sophia was not party to it. She looked at the shawl.

'Yes, it was grandmother's. I remember it. It was made by Mademoiselle Victorine who had her workshop in Hanover Street. She made some hats for grandmother, but then grandmother took a dislike to her and found another milliner.'

'Do you know why your grandmother disliked her?' This was interesting. Mademoiselle Victorine had not told them this.

'She said she was surly, cold, and that she never smiled. Grandmama thought she was ungrateful. She always expected people to be grateful for her custom. I suppose she was difficult in that way. Poor Mademoiselle Victorine – she was rather odd, though.'

'You met her?' asked Sam.

'Yes, only once. She was hard to like, I think, but I felt sorry for her. A lonely woman, I thought. You could not get behind those thick lenses.'

'Do you remember what happened to the shawl?'

'No, I am sorry. It is a little worn in places. Grandmother would not have worn it like that.'

Sam asked, 'Mrs Outfin, what happened to your mother-in-law's clothes after she died?'

'Some of the newer dresses were remodelled for Sophy and me. My mother-in-law had good taste and an expensive one. Most of the things were given to the house-keeper, Mrs Mapes, to dispose of as she pleased. She would have sold most of them, I expect. Some she would have kept for herself. Perhaps she sold the shawl?'

Dead end. If the housekeeper had kept it, how had it come to be in the graveyard? If she had sold the shawl, it would probably be impossible to trace, though she might remember to whom she had sold the clothes. Even so, over a year ago, it might have been sold, stolen, lost, found, lost again. The shawl was rapidly becoming a useless piece of evidence. But they ought to know where the housekeeper was so Sam asked.

'She went to live with her daughter, out at Cricklewood. Mary Mapes married a blacksmith there.'

Dickens and Jones thanked Mrs Outfin and Sophia who came into the hall with them. Sophia made her way up the stairs. The door opened to admit a young man, slender and fair. The son, they presumed. Not gibbering but certainly tense. Dickens observed his thin face, almost girlish. He might have been the twin of his sister were it not for a slight beard at his chin. Mrs Outfin could not avoid introducing Dickens and Jones.

'My son, Theo. This is Mr Dickens, and Superintendent Jones from Bow Street. They are making enquiries about a shawl which belonged to grandmother.'

Sam spoke quickly. He wanted to gauge the young man's reaction, and Dickens knew that it was his role to observe.

'The shawl may be an important clue in a crime I am investigating.'

Dickens watched as Theo's eyes flickered towards him. Green eyes like his mother's and sister's, but veiled, not inno-cent. Theo did not look at Sam. He seemed to force himself to address Dickens.

'I am glad to meet you, sir. Of course, I know your books.' He glanced up the stairs. They knew he wanted to go.

'Do you remember the shawl, Mr Outfin?' Sam insisted.

Theo glanced at it. 'No, it means nothing to me.' He did not look at them.

'Your father wishes to see you, Theo. He will be in the library now.' Mrs Outfin spoke gently, filling in the awkward pause. But Dickens noticed the faint red that flushed at her neck and jaw.

'Not now, Mother. I must go upstairs to change. I have an appointment to keep.' He went, taking the stairs swiftly, passing a maid as he ascended. But he did not look at her. Mrs Outfin watched him, and Dickens saw how anxious she was, and how, when she turned back to them, she switched on her smile.

'I am sorry we could not have been more helpful.'

'Thank you, Mrs Outfin. You have given us valuable information. We may be able to trace the shawl, now.' Sam was polite. Neither Dickens nor he betrayed any trace of the curiosity they felt about her son.

They went out into the quiet street, walking in silence until they were well away from the house. They stood looking through the iron railings into the private garden which was empty of nursemaids and their charges on this gloomy November day. A solitary man stood coatless with his top hat pushed back on his head, staring at the darkening sky. What was he reading in the louring heavens? For what sign was he looking? Dickens and Jones gazed up, too. But there was nothing – only a faint pinprick that might have been a star, but no answer to their fears.

'I hope not,' said Dickens, still looking at the motionless figure.

'You hope Theo Outfin is not our man?'

Dickens turned to look at Sam. His face was grave. 'For the sake of that innocent girl and for Oliver Wilde. And for Mrs Outfin. The scandal would destroy them all.'

'Yet, you observed his manner and you felt Outfin's uneasiness, and Mrs Outfin seemed anxious. There was tension in that house, something unspoken. They are afraid of something. The boy, perhaps, a source of that fear?'

'Yes, I think so. But his glance at the shawl, his dismissal of it might have been simply indifference. He might have something else on his mind, but if he is our murderer –'

The word seemed to freeze in the air. It was almost as if they could read it there before them, and all its implications for the Outfins.

'Let us not get ahead of ourselves, Charles,' said Sam. 'He'd have to have amazing self-possession if he had left that shawl at the scene of the crime and was able to reveal nothing but indifference when he saw it in the hands of a policeman from Bow Street. Nevertheless, we will remain interested in him. As we have said before, the shawl may have nothing to do with the murder.'

'I could meet Oliver Wilde to offer my congratulations about his marriage. I might ask about the family. He might know what is troubling the boy. I sense tension between him and his father. Theo didn't want to see him, and Mrs Outfin is obviously the one in the middle.'

'A good idea. I would like to exclude him.'

'What about the shawl? Ought we to follow up the housekeeper at Cricklewood?'

'We must – there's a chance that she will remember how she disposed of it, but I am not hopeful. Still, she might be able to tell us something about the family. Now, it's too cold to be standing about here, let us go to see Scrap, and set him to work on the history of Robin Hart.'

Scrap was out on an errand when Dickens and Jones arrived at the Crown Street shop. Mr Brim was behind his counter; he looked well enough though he was gaunt. He greeted his visitors with a smile though Dickens thought he discerned strain there as if Mr Brim was worried about something.

'Scrap should be back soon. He is out delivering – I have a good many orders thanks to you, Mr Dickens. And your wife is here, Superintendent, giving Eleanor a lesson with Tom listening in. Poll is with them – she is not too keen on going out just now.' He smiled, more easily this time. 'We are not letting her out of our sight, either.'

The bell rang as the door opened to bring in Scrap. 'Wotcher, Mr Dickens,' he said cheerfully. 'An' you, Mr Jones.'

'I have a job for you,' said the superintendent.

Scrap grinned. 'If Mr Brim can spare me.' Scrap was proud of his responsibilities and of his being needed.

'You can do it between deliveries, Scrap, if that is all right, Mr Brim.' Mr Brim nodded. 'We are trying to find out about a boy, Robin Hart.'

'Murdered weren't 'e? I 'eard yer found 'im in St Giles's. Want me to find out 'oo knew 'im? 'Oo 'e went about with?'

'Yes, but be careful, Scrap – talk to the street boys. And, there is another boy we need to know about. A boy called Jemmy, possibly Jemmy Kidd. We don't know if he was from here at all, but if you hear anything about a boy of that name, it could be useful.'

'Right, Mr Jones – I'll be careful. I knows 'oo to ask, don't yer fret none.'

Elizabeth came out with Eleanor, Tom and Poll who threw herself at Scrap – the hero who had rescued her.

'How are you enjoying your lessons, Eleanor?' asked Dickens.

The usually grave little girl gave him the smile that transformed her face. 'I love them – and Tom enjoys his, too, don't you, Tom.'

Tom frowned. 'I think so – I do like the letters, but I like the pictures better.'

They all laughed. Dickens said, 'Have you seen the archer – what did he do?'

'A is for archer, and shot at a frog. And apple pie too,' cried Tom. 'Apple pie is my favourite.'

Sam and Elizabeth watched Dickens sit Tom on the counter. He was very good with children, able to enter into their world, understanding their childish fears. Here they saw him drawing out the little boy, making learning a game. He took him through the verse for B about the bee in his hive, the one for C, and then, improvising to Tom's delight, Dickens taught him a new one for D.

> *D was a dog,*
> *And Poll was her name.*
> *So bold and so clever,*
> *That wide was her fame.*

Poll was delighted too and barked at Dickens approvingly. Of course, it had to be said again and again until everyone but Tom and Poll wished they could move on to E, F and G. Then it was time to return to Bow Street to review the evidence, and as Dickens put it, to discipline their thoughts like a regiment, putting each soldier into his rightful place.

'On, on, we noble English,' he declaimed as they walked back. 'I will send a note to Wilde this evening.'

11

CAT'S HOLE

Secrets. Behind every murder there were secrets. Secrets concealed like stolen goods buried deep, but still on the conscience. Secrets, thought Dickens, as he walked home after he and Sam had reviewed the evidence. Murder was composed of secrets just as any three-volume novel. Secrets were the staple of the novelist; they provided the mystery, suspense and tension. In murder, the identity of the protagonist was secret, the characters in the story – for murder was itself a terrible story – possessed secrets, sometimes harmless ones, sometimes ones that were the key to the mystery, and it was the investigators who must uncover those secrets, and, this was dreadful, too; they must lay bare the lives of all enmeshed in the net of the murderer's making. Horrible, thought Dickens, who had secrets of his own, a hidden life about which he had spoken only to John Forster, his closest friend, and that hidden life was connected to the blacking factory where the boy Jemmy had been found in his mud coffin.

Theo Outfin had a secret, Dickens was sure; a secret, perhaps, which tainted the air of that respectable house, the secret that caused so much unease in his parents. And the shawl? Who had dropped it there in the churchyard? Who was the secret visitor seen at Mademoiselle Victorine's? What secrets were hidden in those dull eyes behind the thick lenses? Who was the toff seen with the victims? And, this was a thought, what secrets did the victims have that brought about their deaths? Sam had said that often the key to the murder lay in the victims' own lives – it had been true of Patience Brooke. But these boys scarcely had any lives to speak of. Yet, did they know the young gentleman who had lured them to the blacking factory and the churchyard of St Giles? And had their knowledge of him killed them? Did the killer feel his secret murders sticking on his hands? And, most dreadful of all the questions – would he strike again? Only he knew that secret, a chilling thought that set Dickens quickening his pace along Regent Street which took him away from the blind courts and alleys where Scrap was even now pursuing his enquiries.

Scrap was not having much success. He hung about the alleys near St Giles's, lounging at corners, tossing an apple in the air – bait for any passing lad; he had several more in his pockets for the same purpose. He heard the sound of a police rattle somewhere across the alleys and the sound of rushing feet, and shouts. After a thief, he thought, hoping it was not someone he knew.

Running feet towards him. Kip Moon leaning breathless against the wall, a little girl following.

'Wotcher, Scrap. 'Ow's tricks? Not seen yer for ages. Where yer bin?'

'Out an' about, Kip – takin' messages – earnin' a bob or two. Apple?'

'Don't mind if I do.'

'Tilly, yer want one?' Scrap saw her hungry eyes, and offered the apple.

'Ta, Scrap.'

Scrap, who in his way was as perceptive a reader of human nature as the great novelist, knew how to wait. The three lounged against the wall, munching on the apples. Give 'em time, thought Scrap, and I'll find out if they know anythin' about Robin Hart. He watched as they ate.

Tilly Moon's bonnet had slipped off, and Scrap watched her unusual violet eyes. Tilly fascinated Scrap. She was an albino child, her white, almost silver hair like a halo under the blue gas light. She always wore her bonnet but running had dislodged it. Mrs Moon worried about her strange white child and wrapped her up against the curious, sometimes hostile stares of others, and against the appraising stares of men who sometimes caught a glimpse of silver hair. But Mrs Moon could not keep her in. She hoped Kip would look after her. Mostly he did. Mr Moon was crippled, his legs crushed by barrels falling from a wagon. Still, there would be no more children, now, thank God – she would have to bear no more the deaths of children. Little Lucy Moon had died at three years old and there had been a stillborn baby, a boy whom in her heart she had named Joey after her father. But she had enough to do looking after these two and the bitter, crippled man whose curses cut through the air like cruel knives, and whose hatred of the slight, white child broke her heart.

Bad luck she brought, Mr Moon said, like 'avin' a friggin' ghost in the 'ouse. Look at me, he would snarl like a tethered dog, useless, cos that white freak 'as put a curse on me. The voice like a saw would go on and on until Mrs Moon pacified him with gin, and then he would weep because he was ashamed, and because of the agony of his pain. Then Mrs Moon would stand in the dungeon of a back yard, clenching and unclenching her hands, wishing that he were dead. And Kip and Tilly would roam the streets until they judged it safe to go home. Home, Mrs Moon would say to herself, a prison more like, and then she would go in to put a blanket over the sick man because he could not be got to bed.

Tilly Moon had brains. Scrap could tell. They were there, bulging out behind the bony forehead. And he was right. Tilly was smart, but when she looked in the green, tarnished mirror she saw a ghost and it worried her. She did not know that she was an occulocutaneous albino, and that the blurring of the image in the mirror was the result of her myopia, caused by albinism. She saw the world as shadows, except Kip who kept close to her and whom she could see was her best friend. Tilly did not know that, in her way, she was beautiful, and that Scrap wondered if she were a fairy, if there were magic in those nearly purple eyes. Nor did she know that such ghostly strangeness is dangerous.

The apples were finished. Tilly put her bonnet back, remembering that her mother told her to keep her hair covered.

'Wot woz yer runnin' from?' asked Scrap.

'Perlice found a dead man in one o' the alleys. Murdered. 'Eard a man say 'e'd bin strangled. The giant, it woz – someone seen a giant. Lots o' people seen 'im.'

'I seen 'im,' said Tilly.

'Niver told me,' said Kip. 'When? Where?'

'Cat's 'Ole.'

'Wot woz yer doin' there? Tilly, no one goes in Cat's 'Ole – yer know that.'

'Rosie Jinks dared me. Said she'd give me a farthin' if I'd run down Cat's 'Ole to the corner – if I stepped round the corner, she'd give me two. An' I did – we spent the farthin's – yer remember – on them toffees.'

'Yer niver said.'

'Yer niver asked. Anyway, when we got 'ome, Pa woz shoutin' so I forgot to tell yer.' The violet eyes darkened to deeper purple at some memory.

'Wot about the giant?' asked Scrap. Was it, he wondered, the man he had seen in the alley behind Ned Boney's? And what then was the thing that had bumped so horribly on the stones?

'Stepped round the corner, an' 'e woz there. 'Uge, he was, about ten feet high – an ogre.' Tilly produced the last word triumphantly. Before the catastrophe struck, Tilly and Kip had possessed books. Tilly could still read, but the story of Jack the Giant Killer had long gone. She remembered the picture on the front, though, of the giant with his great club over his shoulder, his long hair and bushy beard. Oh, yes, she had seen that very giant in the alley.

'Yer not romancin', are yer, Tilly?' Kip was cautious.

'Saw 'im – big as an 'ouse – filled the whole passage, 'e did. I ran fer me life – but I got that ha'penny didn't I? Bet that's where 'e lives – that's 'is lair.' Another word came back to her. The long-remembered story coming to life. 'We could go an' find 'im an' tell the perlice – get a reward. An', an', with the money, we'd get medicine for Pa, an' e'd be better an' 'e wouldn't …'

Kip's heart twisted. He knew what Pa said. He had seen it often enough, the black mouth spitting its vile words, and he had seen the pale child with her hands over her ears, the silver tears mingling with the silver hair, and had known that if Pa could have walked he would have killed her. He had seen him struggling to rise and the wasted arm half raised as if to strike. Mebbe, just mebbe, he thought.

Scrap wondered, too. He did not know about the thin blade that had entered Robin's heart. He did not know about the toff. Perhaps the thing dragging on the stones was Robin Hart. And what about the boy called Jemmy? Had the giant got him? They could go and see. Then they could tell the superintendent, and he would go and get the giant. And there might be a reward for Tilly.

'We'll go then, Tilly, but we gotter be careful. I seen 'im, too. The other night. Seen 'im draggin' somethin' along – a body, mebbe – a victim.'

'Aw right,' said Kip. Kip was a link boy. They could find another boy with a torch so that Kip could light his. They did not want to go down Cat's Hole in the pitch dark. They only needed a glimpse of the giant and then they would run for it.

Cat's Hole was the narrowest, dankest, slimiest alley. It slid like some night worm just by Rats' Castle, the alley into which Tommy Titfer had gone with Dickens's purse. He had not come out again. Kip's torch created shadows on the walls; there were giants with them, monstrous shapes walking beside them, bending with them, pointing with them, their grotesque heads turning when theirs turned. When Kip dipped the torch so that they could see where they were walking, the shadows seemed to crowd in on them as if pressing them down. Then they reared up, elongated in the sudden flare of the torch in a draught coming up from some underground cellar. Sometimes the light showed water running down the greasy walls. The air was damp and thick with the smell of rot and filth and human excrement. It was so narrow that they had to walk single file with Tilly in the middle, and Kip in front with the torch. They dared not speak and it was so quiet that they could hear themselves breathing. Occasionally, they could see red eyes peering at them. Rats. Rats which scuttled away at their approach. Nothing human here. Once in the flickering light, Scrap saw something that might have been blood – something dark red, encrusted. He saw it again a bit further on, and he thought about the thing trailing behind the giant, and a head, perhaps banging on the cobbles so that it bled into a trail just like this.

Cat's Hole widened out a little as they neared the corner where Tilly said she had turned to see the giant. When Scrap looked back at the narrowness of the tunnel-like passage through which they had come he could not help hoping that the giant would not be there. There was little room to escape. He began to think that he had been a fool. The superintendent had told him to be careful, and here he was, perhaps walking into a trap, and bringing two others with him. Gawd, he thought, wot an idiot, carried away by the idea of reward – oughter know better. An' Tilly – bringin' a girl into this.

They stopped. The light seemed to go dim and the shadows moved in, closer, seeming to surround them. Tilly saw only shapes moving. She stepped forward, suddenly terrified, her bonnet slipping off her head. The lamp flared, illuminating her whiteness. Then something horrible came at them, something huge and shapeless, something which stank and roared, and grew, monstrous in the shifting shadow and flame, and reached out for her.

The giant saw the ghost. He had seen it before. It had come round the corner. He had seen its white halo of a head, and then it had vanished, this thing which haunted him now. It had come again. The giant roared its terror and reached out to crush the life out of it. It had not seen that there were other figures.

Tilly screamed. Kip stepped back, slipping in the slime, the torch falling from his hand. Scrap heard the hiss of the flame as it touched the wet ground. He saw the shapeless thing reach out for Tilly. He seized the torch and flung it at the terrible figure, simultaneously grabbing Tilly. The thing was on fire. Flames suddenly licked at the rags it wore. They saw its great hands beating at the fire, heard its bellowing fury. Then they ran, Scrap dragging Tilly, Kip behind, all three stumbling and gasping in the thick darkness. Kip fell once but was up and away after them, not caring that his hands were bleeding, scraped by the rough stones. They did not look back.

They were out. But they did not stop. They ran on through the crowded street until they were in the alley behind the Moons' house. Only then did they stop running. Kip opened the back door which led into the yard where Mrs Moon stood clenching and unclenching her hands.

12

TILLY MOON

Dickens was in his library in the morning looking out at the winter garden; everything was still. The scene before him looked like a grey and white picture on which black lines had been etched. The blue slips were on his desk, ready for the scratch of the goose quill. *David Copperfield*, Chapter twenty-two, *Some Old Scenes and Some New People*. Steerforth and David were in Suffolk. Dickens was contemplating the ruin of Little Em'ly by Steerforth, Little Em'ly who must fall, he thought, there was no hope for her. He was preparing for it with the introduction of Martha Endell, the fallen girl. He was thinking, too, about Isabella Gordon, and that last sight of her going slowly and miserably away, wiping her face with her shawl.

He looked down at the blue slip on the desk and began to write:

Then Martha arose, and gathering her shawl, covering her face with it, and weeping aloud, went slowly to the door. She stopped a moment before going out, as if she would have uttered something or turned back; but no word passed her lips. Making the same low, dreary, wretched moaning in her shawl, she went away.

Dickens knew what Martha's fate would be in London; he did not know what would be the fate of Isabella nor of Sesina, but he feared for them, and felt again the sadness of Isabella's departure; it was a failure, he thought, not necessarily his, but of society in general which offered nothing to girls as lively and intelligent as Isabella, and which corrupted them so deeply that some could not be saved.

He took up his pen again and wrote about Little Em'ly's distress and fear which would be explained later when her elopement with Steerforth was to be discovered. He heard a knock at the door. It was John with a note from Superintendent Jones, asking him if he would come down to Bow Street earlier than they had arranged for they were to go to Cricklewood in the afternoon.

Scrap was there. Dickens thought, perhaps, that he had news of Robin Hart. Both he and the superintendent looked grave.

'Robin Hart?' asked Dickens. Scrap looked very miserable. 'You have found out something?'

'Scrap has been tilting at a giant,' said Sam. 'Last night, a man was found murdered – strangled – in a lane near St Giles's. Scrap's friend, Tilly, said she had seen a giant, and off they went to find him – what did I say, Scrap, about being careful?'

'I knows, sir, an' I'm sorry – I knows it woz stupid, but I woz thinkin' that we could find 'im and then tell yer, an' yer would catch 'im – an' there might be a reward fer Tilly an' Kip. Tilly thought they could get medicine fer their pa – 'e bein' sick. She thought 'e wouldn't be cruel to 'er no more if 'e could get better – leastways that woz what I thought she meant. Their pa 'as no legs.' Scrap's eyes were wet.

He is just a child, thought Dickens. We forget. He is so smart and streetwise. He has a child's imagination, believing in the giant, wanting Tilly, whoever she was, to get her reward, wanting to cure a man with no legs, setting off, in the dark to slay an ogre. He had rescued Poll. He must have thought a giant could be defeated.

The story was told of the dark, frightening walk down Cat's Hole, the giant suddenly materialising out of the shadows, the danger to Tilly who had run from the giant before, Scrap's hurling the torch at the beast, the flames, the howls and the terrified dash to safety.

'I have sent Rogers, Feak and Stemp to search. The dead man is in the mortuary – it is clear he was strangled. He was just an ordinary labouring man – no money to steal. A fight got out of hand, perhaps. We don't know. But now we have two murderers to catch.'

'I thought 'e might 'ave murdered Robin,' said Scrap.

'No, that was different – Robin Hart was seen with a gentleman in the churchyard. In any case, he was stabbed as was the other boy, Jemmy, I mentioned to you.'

'I seen 'im, yer see – that's why I thought – I seen 'im near Nat Boney's when I woz waitin' ter get Poll, an' 'e was draggin' somethink be'ind 'im – I think it could 'ave bin a body.'

'When?' Sam's question was sharp.

'I dunno – two, mebbe three nights ago. 'E woz 'uge, sir, 'e woz, honest ter gawd. 'E stank, too – smelt it last night.'

'So, he could have killed twice. What did he do with the first body, I wonder?'

Dickens was remembering the night the weazened man had taken them to Georgie Taylor's, and the sense he had that they were being followed. He saw again the monstrous shadow on the wall. And he remembered how the shadow had vanished. Rogers had followed them. Perhaps he had seen.

'What is it, Charles?' Sam had seen the expression on his face – his shudder.

'When Zeb and I were taken to Georgie Taylor's, I felt something behind us – heard a shuffling, you know, and I saw a great shadow on the wall – it made me nervous, I can tell you. Frankenstein's monster, I thought. Madness, Scrap, to go after him.'

'I knows, Mr Dickens.'

'And, Sam, Rogers might have seen him – Rogers was following us in the alleys.'

'Then, he is real enough – and dangerous. Scrap, you have to tell your friends to keep away.'

'They will, sir, we woz all terrified. Will they get a reward, though – wot am I ter tell 'em?'

'You didn't mention a sum?'

'Nah – dint know wot yer give fer information.'

'Well, the rate is usually ten shillings. Would that be acceptable?'

'Oh, I reckon – could they git medicine with it?'

'I think so,' said Dickens. 'I could make it up to a pound.'

'Cor, they'll be thrilled. Can I take it now?'

'You can.' The superintendent went over to his cash box for the money which he gave to Dickens who fished a sovereign from his pocket.

'It will have to be a sovereign, then. All right?'

Scrap beamed. He thought of Tilly's violet eyes.

'Perhaps, Charles, you would go with Scrap. You could speak to the mother.'

'Don't tell 'er wot we done, will yer? Saw 'er last night – got a lot on 'er plate, she 'as. We jest said we'd seen the body. Kip, 'e dint want 'er scared. Worries about Tilly, she does.'

'Very well, Scrap. We will say the sovereign is a reward for the information you have given about the body – that they saw a man running away and described him to you.'

'I am waiting for Rogers to come back. Will you return here, Charles, for our journey to Cricklewood?'

'Yes, I will go back to the shop with Scrap and come here afterwards. Oh, there's something else I've remembered. When we met the man who took us to Georgie Taylor's, we had been waiting for Tommy Titfer whom we met the night of the fight. The old man mentioned a Fikey Chubb – dangerous man, he said. Tommy Titfer owed him money. I do not know the old man's name. Weazen, I called him, because he was.'

Sam smiled. 'Oh, we know Fikey – a scoundrel. Has a shop in Dudley Street – a collector, he calls himself. It's a pawn shop, too – not official. He has many interests, you might say: money-lending, theft, drugs, prostitution, though I have not heard that he is interested in children. However, some of the prostitutes are what we would call children. Still, if he and Tommy Titfer were seen together at Rats' Castle, he may know something about our gigantic man. Rogers can bring him in.'

'Someone must know him – a man of that size could hardly be missed.'

'Mr Jones, I remember – Tilly said people woz talkin' abou' 'im – the giant. She said lots of people seen 'im.'

'Then Rogers may find out where he has been seen. We need to get him off the streets before he kills again. Scrap, I still need you to ask about Robin Hart and the boy, Jemmy. I should have told you that they had been seen with a gentleman. But, please, don't go chasing after anyone. Just report back.'

'I will, sir. I won't do nothink stupid.'

'By the way, Sam, I dine with Oliver Wilde tonight – I may find out more about Theo Outfin.'

'Good.'

Scrap took Dickens to the lane off Dulcimer Street where the Moons lived. On the way, Dickens asked about Tilly and Kip and the sick man.

'I'll 'ave ter find Kip first,' said Scrap. 'We can't go in – Mr Moon, 'e's queer. Allus shoutin' or cryin' an' Mrs Moon, she don't want nobody ter see – that's wot Kip says.'

'What about Tilly? Why does Mrs Moon worry about her?'

'Yer'll see.' Dickens had to be content with that gnomic response.

In the alley, they saw Kip coming towards them. He looked at the stranger curiously.

'Brought yer reward,' said Scrap.

'Nah, yer kiddin' me.'

'Sed yer'd get one. Mr Dickens 'ere 'as come from the per-lice. This is Kip, sir, wot woz with me last night.'

'Scrap tells me that you do not wish your mother to know about the giant.'

Kip blushed. 'Don't like lyin', sir, but Ma, she's got enough ter worry about – an', sir, we won't do it again. Scrap an' me, we woz daft goin' after 'im – dint think o' the danger. Tilly could 'ave bin killed – '

Kip looked horrified at the thought. Dickens felt sorry for him. He did not want to lie to the mother either, but he could see how frightened they had all been, and he felt he could trust Kip – and Scrap – not to go anywhere near the man again.

'No, Kip, you must not think of doing anything so foolish again. I thought I saw him the other night and he terrified me. This is a matter for the police now.'

Dickens held out the sovereign which gleamed golden in the dingy passage. Kip looked at it. He had never seen one before.

'Is it real, sir?'

'It is – but before I give it to you, I must have your solemn promise not to go giant hunting again.'

'Cross me 'eart, sir. We won't, honest, sir. But, I'll 'ave ter tell me ma about the reward.'

'If you fetch her I will tell her that you gave a description of the wanted man which Scrap passed on to us.'

Kip went into the yard. A few moments later, he came back with Mrs Moon, her harassed face all angles where poverty and worry had worn away the flesh. As the yard door opened, Dickens heard a man shouting incoherently and the sound of banging as if someone were hitting something hard with a pan or something. It was a demented, nerve-jangling sound.

The metallic noise seemed to reach a crescendo then there was the sound of something hurled at a door. Then he heard weeping, a horrible wrenching sound as if the sobs were being torn from the throat. Mrs Moon looked back. She looked at Dickens; her eyes were large with fear. She could hardly understand what a well-dressed man was doing in the alley. She closed the yard door and from behind her came Tilly, and Dickens saw what Scrap had meant.

She was the strangest child he had ever seen with her silver hair, white skin and large, myopic violet eyes. It was like seeing a sprite which had wandered from some enchanted wood. Dickens smiled at Mrs Moon.

'Your boy gave a description of a man we want to question in relation to a murder which took place last night.' He let her assume that the 'we' meant the police. 'Superintendent Jones of Bow Street has sent a reward for the information.'

As he said the words, he felt that they sounded unconvincing, but Mrs Moon simply gazed at the sovereign in his hand.

'I have told Kip that he must not do anything else – he must not try to find the man. It is a matter for the police.' He offered her the coin.

'Thank you, sir. I thought somethin' 'ad 'appened. They looked frightened when they came back, said they'd seen a murderer. They shouldn't be out, but Kip earns a bit of money, and it's better sometimes for Tilly to – my 'usband's not always ...' She looked back at the closed door. 'I ought to go in. 'E's bad today – it's the pain. He imagines ... Kip, Tilly, you'll stay in the yard until I tell you to come in.'

The pale child stared at Dickens. She saw a pair of luminous eyes looking at her as if he understood something about her. She wanted to tell him. Perhaps, he would know, he looked wise. She forgot the others.

'Pa says it's my fault 'e's sick. 'E says I'm wicked cos I'm a freak. I sees a ghost when I looks in the mirror. Is it true?'

Dickens glanced at Mrs Moon's despairing eyes, and then back at the child's eyes which gazed at him with such yearning in them. Strange, almost purple eyes which knew too much of cruelty. What to say?

He squatted down to meet those eyes. He looked silently at first, willing her to believe him. The others looked on, still as death. The very air was still. Magic in it.

'No, Tilly. It is not true. You are as real as I am, as Kip is, as your mother is. Your pa is sick – you know that. One day, he will see you as I do, but for now, remember that your mother loves you, and Kip, and I will always think of you so that you will be protected. Scrap here will tell me about you, and you will know that I remember you.'

Tilly nodded. It was enough. The gentleman knew. He had told the truth, she was sure.

Dickens stood up to meet Mrs Moon's eyes. Her face seemed to collapse, almost to dissolve before his eyes as the tears spilled out. He thought that here was a woman who was on the point of being overwhelmed by hopelessness. Kip watched her and Dickens saw the terror in his eyes. What if she were to give up?

'Ma, don't forget the sovereign – it's gold, real gold.'

Mrs Moon looked at the money in her hand then at her son's strained face. 'Thank you, sir,' she said to Dickens.

'Keep her safe,' he said.

'I will try,' she said. 'I will keep her from him when I can.'

She went in followed by Kip. When Dickens looked back as he and Scrap made their way out of the alley, he saw Tilly watching him, the silver hair suddenly alight in the gloom. Not for this world, he thought.

Dickens and Scrap walked away. 'Will yer come again, Mr Dickens? Mebbe, it'll help – somethin' wrong there, I knows it. Tilly, she wants lookin' after. 'Er pa, 'e may be sick but that don't mean 'e should –'

'No, you are right, it does not excuse him, but we must hope that the money helps, and that Mrs Moon can keep Tilly away from him.'

That was all he could say. He knew there was little to be done, and he wondered if it would do any good to go back. Perhaps that moment in the alley was all that he could do. To go again might displace the magic of it. Daylight, he thought metaphorically, might simply reduce him to ordinariness. It was better for the child to remember just his words, to hold on to them as a talisman, words she could repeat to ward off the devil.

Scrap went back to Mr Brim's stationery shop and Dickens made his way to Bow Street where Rogers was explaining that people had seen the enormous man running away from the body, but no one had actually seen the murder. No one knew where he was or who he was. He had simply vanished down some alleyway. No one had dared follow. They said he was mad – he had been seen before. It was assumed that he lived rough somewhere in a cellar or a broken-down house, or in a yard somewhere.

'I wonder if your man Weazen saw him – if he was following you that night, then your man might have seen him around Rats' Castle. Rogers, did you get a glimpse of Weazen, as we must call him?'

'Not really, sir. Saw 'im scuttle away – very small, 'e was. P'raps Mr Dickens could describe him.'

'I promise you, Rogers, you will know him. He looks like some ancient gnome, stinks to high heaven, yellow face like a shrivelled walnut, looks sick, and you will observe the pus in his eyes.'

'Should be enough to go on.' Rogers grinned at the description. 'Stemp and me can go and have a look.'

'And, I want you to find Fikey Chubb and bring him here. Keep him in a cell until I come back.'

'What shall I charge him with?'

'Just tell him we are making enquiries about the murder of two children, a man, a missing person – anything at all. Tell him his name has been mentioned. Mr Dickens's Weazen mentioned him in connection with Tommy Titfer – I wonder where he is. If you find him, bring him in, too.'

'I'll take Stemp and Semple – might need three of us for Fikey Chubb – you know what 'e's like.'

'Good. Make sure all the beat constables know who we are looking for. He has to be somewhere. Now, Mr Dickens and I are going to Cricklewood. I'll speak to Inspector Grove, let him know where I am, and you can report anything to him, if you will.'

The superintendent and Rogers went out. Dickens went to the desk to pick up the shawl. He unfolded it and thought again about the woman who had made it, and the contrast between her plainness and the beauty of the shawl. He looked at the flowers and birds and more closely at the stitching which formed little paths between the images. It was like a maze, he thought. You tried to follow the paths to the centre, but your eyes would not stay focused so you found yourself straying from the path, bumping into roses or exotic birds, but you could never get to the centre where Mademoiselle Victorine had embroidered a bigger flower. Dickens stared at it until his eyes were blurred and he could see only red like a huge blot of blood. He folded up the shawl. Murder, he thought, was like a maze. You followed one path and found yourself on another which wound its way back to a dead end so that you had to turn back to where you started. And, in the centre of the labyrinth, there was blood, the stain left by the murderer.

13

MRS MAPES

Cricklewood was a small village, a mile or so in length, situated in a valley between five hills. The road there was often deep in mud, and highway robberies used to be frequent, but in the afternoon when Dickens and Jones arrived, it was quiet: a few cottages, a windmill, a village green where the Crown inn stood, and a blacksmith's. The sun had come out and, although it was still cold, the village lay peaceful in the pale sunlight. It could have been fifty miles from London not five. They had come by hired fly and had asked the driver to wait for them at the Crown.

The forge was not hard to find; they could hear the beating of the hammer on metal. In the yard, a large, shaggy horse stood patiently, waiting for his new shoes. He looked peaceable enough, though Dickens gave him a fairly wide berth – he had been bitten once by a deceptively tranquil beast which had attacked him for no good reason. It had torn off his sleeve and he had felt the terror of the moment for days afterwards – in fact, he had not been able to write.

They looked in through the door to see the smith working on a horseshoe at the anvil. There was a stone chimney with its raised hearth on which coke gleamed deep red. A boy stood by with his bellows which wheezed and clanked as he worked them and the fire gave out a glittering shower of sparks. The smith, in his leather apron, was a young, well-built man whose face shone in the firelight. He frowned in concentration, not looking up. They watched and waited for him to finish the shoe.

They watched him beating the shoe which burnt white as the iron shot out another fountain of sparks under the blows. The smith hammered it on the anvil and turned it on the beak so that they could see it taking shape. When the white turned to a yellow glow, he put the shoe back in the fire with the tongs. They heard the angry hiss of the metal. He hammered again, the gold changing to a dull red. They watched him hammer in the holes where the nails would go and saw how the red changed to blue grey, and then it was finished. The smith looked up.

'We are looking for Mrs Mapes. I wish to ask her about her former employer, Mrs Outfin.'

The smith came forward, the hot shoe steaming on the tongs. They stood back as he passed them; the boy followed and held the horse by its bridle as it moved restively, hearing the smith come out.

'And you are?' the smith asked as he lifted the great feathered hoof and stood astride the horse's leg, ready to assess if the shoe was a fit.

'I am Superintendent Jones from Bow Street. I wish to know if Mrs Mapes can identify a shawl which we have in connection with a crime. This is my colleague, Mr Dickens.'

The shoe fitted and the smith picked up his hammer and nails. They waited. The boy murmured reassuring words to the horse. Dickens noted that its eye rolled, and then it stood still.

'You'll find her in the house. Just by the barn over there.'

They left him and walked to the neat cottage with its white door, the upper half of which was open. A young woman came at their knock, the smith's wife, they thought. She carried a rosy-faced child on her hip who looked at them with saucer eyes. So did the young woman. She looked puzzled, and slightly anxious.

'We are looking for Mrs Mapes. I am Superintendent Jones from Bow Street. I wish to ask her about her former employer, Mrs Outfin.'

The young woman's expression changed; she was curious now. 'Ma's inside – come in.'

They stepped into a neat room, warm from the cooking range on which a pot of something which smelt delicious bubbled. The room was clean and there was the scent of freshly washed laundry in the air. Mrs Mapes, a strong, cheerful-looking woman with bright blue eyes like her daughter's, was folding linen at a well-scrubbed pine table. Near the range, there was a cradle in which a baby lay asleep.

'I heard what you said. You want to know something about Mrs Outfin – I take it you know that she is dead?'

'We went to her son's to ask about this shawl. Do you recognise it? Can you tell us what happened to it after Mrs Outfin's death?' Sam produced the shawl, loosening the silken folds so that she could see it clearly.

Mrs Mapes came forward. She took a pair of spectacles from her apron pocket to look at it closely and she fingered the worn places.

'Yes, I recognise it. It belonged to Mrs Outfin – the pattern is very distinctive. After her death, I gave some things to the maids – the younger Mrs Outfin gave me permission to dispose of the clothes and other things which were not wanted. It was generous of her – she knew we would all lose our places – and she promised characters to the servants who needed them. Well, there were hats and gloves, and dresses, shoes, too, and I made sure all the maids got something. The rest I sold.'

'Do you remember to whom you gave this shawl?'

'I do. Mattie Webb – she had admired it, and she was thrilled with it. Loved the birds and flowers, she said. Never had anything like it. How did you get it, Superintendent? Has something happened to Mattie? She wouldn't have sold it,

I'm sure.' She sounded concerned suddenly. It was clear that Mattie Webb had treasured her gift.

'It was found – it may be a clue in a crime we are investigating. Where is Mattie Webb now?'

'She found a new position – at a house in Charles Street, off St James's Square. Family named Du Cane. Mrs Outfin – the younger, that is – got her the position. The Du Canes are friends of Mr and Mrs Outfin. Mattie is a very capable girl, and a very good maid. I thought she would do well there. She would have no need to sell the shawl. Unless she lost it – found, you say?'

'Yes – she may have lost it, as you say. We shall have to ask her.'

'Oh, I hope it won't bring her any trouble – employers don't like the police calling. Oh, dear, she's such a good girl. She wouldn't have anything to do with anything wrong, I'm sure.' Mrs Mapes's pleasant, open face was crumpled now in her anxiety.

'Don't worry, Mrs Mapes. I'm sure that you're right. We will be very discreet, but I do need to know how the shawl came to be where it was found.' Sam tried to be reassuring. He did not want to say that the shawl had been found at the scene of a murder.

'Do you remember anything about the woman who made the shawl?' Dickens asked by way of diversion.

Mrs Outfin looked at him curiously – this younger man who had not spoken before did seem familiar. She wondered who he was.

'Mamselle Victorine?'

'Yes,' said Sam. 'Can you tell us about her?'

Mrs Outfin looked at her daughter. 'We knew her only because she came to the house. Mary, my daughter, worked as a maid sometimes at Mrs Outfin's – when we needed an extra hand. The milliner – she was a strange young woman. Very quiet, reserved, I suppose.'

'Yes,' said Mary. 'She was odd. Once I was in the drawing room when she was waiting for Mrs Outfin. I tried to talk to her, but she wasn't having it. Probably thought she was too good to speak to a servant. Cold, I thought, you know, never smiled.' She thought a moment. 'Lonely, though, now I think of it. Perhaps she didn't know how to talk to people.'

Mrs Mapes went on, 'Mrs Outfin didn't care for her much. She changed to another milliner, said Mamselle Victorine was too sullen. Mrs Outfin liked her servants good-humoured, and so we were, whether we felt like it or not, but Mamselle didn't see any need to be friendly – suppose she thought her work was enough and she wasn't a servant, after all. I felt a bit sorry for her when I had to tell her that she was no longer required. It had to be me, of course. Mrs Outfin would not condescend to dismiss her.'

Sam thought. Could they risk a few questions about the rest of the family? He had noted the address of the Du Canes and that they were friends of the Outfins. Not that far from Hungerford Stairs. He thought of Theo Outfin.

Dickens had the same idea. He smiled at Mrs Mapes and Mary – the smile that would persuade them to answer, that would prevent them from wondering at the questions.

'A difficult woman, Mrs Outfin?' His tone was light, inviting her confidence.

'Sometimes.' She smiled back at Dickens.

'A regular tartar.' Mary was charmed into the truth. 'Bad tempered old cat. Wanted gratitude all the time. She wanted slaves not servants.' Her blue eyes were indignant.

'Mary, don't exaggerate. Yes, she was a bit cantankerous, but she could be generous, especially to her grandchildren.'

Gold. Here it was. Thank you, Charles, Sam said to himself.

'Yes, we met them. Sophia Outfin is to be married – a lovely girl. I know her fiancé, Mr Wilde.'

'Yes, we heard. Miss Sophy could always put Mrs Outfin into a good mood – she had that way with her, you know, soft and patient. Now, Mr Theo, he could be moody – didn't get on with his father – mind, he was only a boy then. Probably grown up a bit since. But his grandmother spoilt him a bit. Left him a lot of money in her will. Gets it when he's twenty-one. He'll be rich then, I daresay.'

Dickens took another risk in that confiding gossipy atmosphere. 'We met him. We thought he might not get on with his father. I wonder why.'

'A bit girlish, I think. They look so alike – Sophy and Theo – when they were young, Miss Sophy used to play at being a boy, and, you know, she looked exactly like him. She was a bit of a tomboy, but Mr Theo, he was quiet, didn't like boyish things. Always reading. His father used to get impatient with him then sent him to school, Eton it was. Thought it would make a man of him, I suppose.'

'Perhaps it did. Families are not always easy,' said Dickens. He could not help feeling sympathy for Theo Outfin. Dickens had been a solitary boy. A terrible boy to read, his nurse, Mary Weller had said, and he remembered being too sickly to play cricket with the other boys, the spasms in his side so painful that he could only watch the others running about. Perhaps Theo Outfin had been sickly. But what was he now? And was there a connection to the dead boys? Charles Street where the Du Canes lived was not far from Hungerford Stairs.

Sam thought it was time to go. 'We must be on our way, Mrs Mapes. Thank you for giving us Mattie's address – I assure you we shall be discreet.'

They left the warm cottage. They could hear the hammer on the anvil. The smith was still at work though the large horse had gone. They walked across to the Crown where their driver waited, passing a cottage gate where a flock of white geese hissed at them. There was a bench outside the inn and they sat where there was a patch of sunshine which gave a little warmth. Sam looked across at the smithy where a farmer was bringing a horse to be shod.

'My father was a blacksmith,' he said, musingly. 'I might have been one myself – a good life, it was – regular. My father was a contemplative sort of man – not given to many words – like our smith over there.'

'Could you shoe a horse? Among your many other gifts?' asked Dickens. He had not known of this before. He was intrigued by this new dimension to his friend. 'I thought you came from policing stock.'

'I could once – not very well, but I was learning the trade. My father died when I was ten and his brother took over the forge. He had a son so there was no room for me. In any case, my mother wanted to go back to London – couldn't stick the country without my father. She took her share of the business and we went to live with her sister whose husband was a police-man. However, my mother did not want that for me – at fifteen, I was sent to be a clerk in a lawyer's office at Lincoln's Inn.'

'Just as I was myself – though at Gray's Inn.'

'Dull, wasn't it?' Sam laughed. 'When I thought of the future, I felt I was looking down a tunnel to the cramped years ahead, the drudgery, the pointlessness of it all – my large self chafed at it and when my mother died, I was free to go for a police-man – river police at Wapping, then in 1829 I joined the Peelers, proud in my blue coat and top hat – and here I am.'

'Regret it?'

'No, though sometimes the flood of human misery we encounter depresses me – still, we sometimes do some good – as you do yourself.'

They sat quiet for a while listening to the strike of the hammer on the anvil; it was soothing somehow, timeless, and Sam thought of those long-ago days at the forge. Life had been simple then, but if he had stayed there would have been no Elizabeth, and, he thought, he would not have met

Charles Dickens, and they would not be sitting here in peaceful companionship.

'Well,' he said, at last, grinning at Dickens, 'we certainly got more than we bargained for – thanks to your charm with the ladies. I was thinking that I hardly dared ask about Mrs Outfin's family when you came to the rescue. What are your fees for inveigling innocent witnesses to talk?'

'Modest, Sam, very modest – a brandy would be welcome. This sun is a deceiver – my feet are freezing.'

They went inside the old inn with its low beams and oak settles, and seated themselves by a blazing fire waiting for the landlord to bring them their brandy. The driver sat at the bar and was glad to be treated to another drink.

'I will send Feak to discover Mattie Webb – he can do a bit of detecting – or, perhaps I should send the Sybil of Star Street. I will tell him to be discreet – go round to the servants' entrance. He can use the usual tale – thieves about, that sort of thing. I want to know what happened to that shawl. Of course, she may have lost it but –'

'It is all very suggestive – the shawl at the Du Canes, the Du Canes are friends of the Outfins, Charles Street is not far from Hungerford Stairs – Theo Outfin could have visited the Du Canes. Jemmy and Robin were found in two different places. Theo Outfin might now be connected to Hungerford Stairs and St Giles's is not too far from Montague Place.'

'And, we know a bit more about Theo – solitary, girlish, a disappointment to his father. Was he interested in small boys? That is the question. I need the results of the postmortem – if Robin and Jemmy were sexually abused then we must consider that Theo might be our man.'

'And, if not, where does that leave us? What is the motive for the killings, then?'

'Well, Rogers thought crime might be a factor – the man using the boys, and killing them to stop them talking.'

'But the mask? That does not fit at all to the idea of a thief turned murderer. It means something, I am sure. The murderer has something to say to us.'

'Such as?' asked Sam.

'"You cannot know me." Is he telling us that he is too clever for us? That we cannot catch him?'

'But, we must, and we will know him. We will peel off that mask, and we will see his face stripped of its cleverness, and he will see us and know that he is caught.'

They went out of the inn with the driver and made their way back to the roaring, clamorous city. Dickens would go home, and afterwards dine with Oliver Wilde. The superintendent could not help looking forward to rattling the bones of Fikey Chubb. It would relieve his feelings, he thought, to see Fikey Chubb sweating.

14

FIKEY CHUBB SWEATS

Fikey Chubb did sweat – far more than the superintendent remembered. His office was filled with the man's rancid stench. Not fear, yet. Fikey blustered: 'e was a respectable shopkeeper and business man; 'e knew nothin' about no friggin' Tommy Titfer. Wot did they mean about 'im bein' dangerous? 'Oo, said it, 'e'd like ter know? Known for 'is generosity was Fikey. Blimey, the things people said. It made yer lose yer faith, it did.

Sam was patient, listening to the indignant recital of Fikey's virtues. 'Tommy Titfer has not been seen. We just wanted to ask if you had seen him. It was said he owed you money. A man doesn't generally lend money to a man he doesn't know.'

'Dint say I dint know the bleeder – thort you woz askin' if I knows where 'e is. Entrapment, that's wot it is – I'll be makin' a complaint. Gotta lawyer, I 'ave. Respectable citizen I am – yer –'

'I'll make a note of your concerns, Mr Chubb – the money, if you'll oblige me.'

'Well, if yer puts it like that, I don't mind tellin' yer.' Fikey was gracious. Give the rozzer somethin' an' they'd git off 'is back. 'Titfer owed me money. Bit of a sly one is Tommy, bleedin' all over the carpet abaht 'is ma an' 'is brother – dire straits, 'e said. Well, wot woz I ter do? I lent 'im a few quid – an' I ain't seen 'im since. Bleedin' disgrace, it is – a man acts in good faith an' then wot? Let down, that's wot.'

'But you are a frequenter of the Rats' Castle?'

'Fre – wot? Wot d'yer mean?' Fikey was suspicious. Wot woz bein' pinned on 'im?

'You drink at Rats' Castle – often.'

'So what? Niver 'eard it woz a crime ter take a glass now an' then.' Fikey grinned at his own wit. They 'ad nothin' on 'im, he thought. Jest fishin'.

'No, indeed. Though I am surprised that a respectable businessman such as yourself should find it congenial.' A draw, so far, thought Sam. Time to press him a bit. 'Know anything about the dead man in the alley off the High Street?'

''Eard abaht it. Nothin' ter do wiv me.'

'Story is there's a giant on the loose. Seen him? About Rats' Castle?'

'Nah. Madman, I 'eard.'

'Mad? How?'

Fikey was relaxed now. None of this was to do with him. He wiped his sweating brow with a grimy rag. 'Dunno. Jest said 'e woz rambling, talks to 'imself, that kind o' thing. There's talk, yer know, 'ow 'e's a monster, some kind o' beast. Stranger, though. No one seems to know 'oo 'e is. Sorry I can't 'elp yer, Mr Jones, but I'm a busy man. Can't stay 'ere all day chattin'. Yer've wasted enough of me time, as it is. Been 'ere long enough, ta very much.' He smiled condescendingly. 'E'd bin right. Jest fishin'. He rose to go.

'One more thing, Mr Chubb. Two dead boys. Murdered.'

Fikey sat down. He was sweating again. The stink of fear suddenly sharp in the room where the stench of sweat had faded. This was closer to home, Sam thought. Fikey might know something.

'Wot boys? Don't know nothin' abaht 'em.'

'You must have heard about the boy found stabbed in St Giles's churchyard. Seen with a toff, apparently. I wonder if you know about men who might be interested in young boys.'

Fikey looked worried, as well he might since his business involved young girls and the kind of toffs who might be looking for a girl. Boys might not be his business, but he would know whose business they were. And he would not want to tell.

'I don't know nothin', I'm tellin' yer, Mr Jones. Yes, I 'eard about the poor little sod, but boys ain't my line o' business.' He corrected himself, aware of the implication that perhaps girls were his business. 'I deal in fings, Mr Jones, not people, not kids, niver.'

'No one told you who might be involved.' Sam pressed him. 'A name?'

'Nah, I swear ter yer. I 'eard the lad 'ad bin seen wiv a toff, but no one knows 'oo – independent, 'e must be, actin' on 'is own – not through the usual channels – yer get me?'

Sam got it, indeed. Fikey would know the identities of the 'usual channels', but they had no evidence on which to press him, and they had no evidence to connect Fikey with the dead boys. It was interesting that there was speculation about the toff whom no one knew.

'Most helpful, Mr Chubb. Of course, I may wish to speak to you again – you might remember something about those boys or you might hear something. You know where to come. My constable here will keep in touch, of course. We know where your shop is.'

It wasn't much of a threat, Sam knew, but it might make Fikey keep his head down for a bit if he thought the police were keeping an eye on him, and he might hear something which he would be willing to offer if he thought it would get the police off his back.

Fikey went and Sam opened a window, out of which he and Rogers leant, breathing in the cold air. They pulled in their heads, but stood there till until the reek of Fikey's presence had evaporated.

'I'll throw a bucket of water over him next time – cold,' Rogers said.

'He'll complain to his lawyer.'

Rogers laughed. ''E'll be a crook like Fikey. But it was interestin', sir, what 'e said about the toff – no one knows 'im.'

'Yes, I thought that, too. Still we cannot discount the idea that the killer is known to someone who deals in boys procured for sexual purposes until we get the results from the post-mortem. We need it – go down to the mortuary, will you, and hurry them up.'

'Yes, sir.' Rogers went out.

Sam looked down at the busy street below. He was out there somewhere, perhaps wearing his mask of respectability. That young man there, he thought, the one in the black suit and top hat – it could be him. Or that slender young man in blue with gilt buttons or that one with the extravagant bow and the silver-topped cane. He looked like an artist – perhaps he had drawn the mask? Or Theo Outfin. Or Mademoiselle Victorine's mysterious visitor – they ought to follow that up. True, he might not exist at all.

But he would put a watch at the house – just in case. And where was Feak? He had sent him to the Du Cane house. He ought to be back. Perhaps Mattie Webb could tell them something about the shawl.

Sam went to his desk. The mask troubled him because he did not know its meaning. He drew it on the paper before him. He looked into its sightless eyes, but they told him nothing. He thought of Theo Outfin's averted eyes and of Mademoiselle Victorine's colourless eyes behind the thick spectacles – they had told him nothing.

And what about the giant? Stemp was investigating him. A madman – that was interesting, too. Where had he come from, and more importantly, where was he?

In a cellar underneath the abandoned house next to the one where the Moon family lived, a heap of stinking rags whimpered and moaned. It dipped its poor burnt hands into a tank of dirty, cold water that had dripped in through a rusted grating. It muttered to itself. It did not understand this world of shadows and spectres – it wondered if it were dead. It did not know what it had done, only that things followed it, and that it was terrified and crazed with pain. Perhaps, here, in the quiet and dark it might be safe.

Of course, he wasn't a beast or monster, but he was huge with the great, protruding frontal boss and preternaturally large, jutting jaw that signifies gigantism. This hideous cliff-face of a forehead hung over his black eyes where the bristling hairs grew shaggy and straggling. The matted mane of black hair hung on his great misshapen shoulders. The gnarled nose was too big and his skin was thick and coarse in texture, and so begrimed with dirt that his face appeared black, especially in the darkness of the alleys in which he had wandered, pursued as he thought by phantoms. He could not see clearly, plagued as he was by double vision, so he struck out blindly, baffled in rage by the followers. When he spoke his voice was deep and hoarse and his words scarcely intelligible such was the thickness of his over-large tongue.

And he was mad. Mad with fear. Mad with loneliness. He had always been an outcast, though at first he had travelled with his mother who had trudged the roads, dragging with her this deformed thing which she had borne and could never be rid of, and which had grown and grown like some malignant tumour. They were hounded and stoned from village to village; they passed on year by year, more ragged and desperate, begging and stealing what they could to keep alive, sleeping under hayricks, in ditches and graveyards where death touched them with his icy fingers, always following them until, at last, death found them sleeping in the dark shadow of tombs and took the woman where she lay. The giant could not wake her, and so he shambled on until he came to the city. But the crowds terrified him. This was hell, perhaps, and the phantoms pursued him, taunted him, jeered at him, stoned him so that he could only strike back, not knowing his own strength, desiring only that they leave him alone. And then there was fire. He beat at it and the agony was searing. At last he slept and in his sleep the flames roared and licked at him, and he saw through the wavering blaze of yellow and red, the shining spectre from the lanes, the ghost with the silver hair which had run when he had reached out for it. And with it was a face with moons for eyes – another ghost come to torment him.

15

FIRE

Dickens had left Sam at the junction of Edgeware Road and Winchester Road. From there he walked along the New Road to Devonshire Terrace. He thought about the giant and the danger which had brushed at Scrap, Kip and Tilly. He wondered if Tilly Moon were safe. And he thought of Robin Hart – he must enquire after Mrs Hart and wondered if it would be possible to question her yet, and to find out for whom her son had run errands. Somehow, he doubted it. And what about Jemmy – who was he? And had Theo Outfin known him? Was the connection with the Du Canes the link between Jemmy and Theo Outfin? Well, at least dinner with Oliver Wilde at Dickens's club the Parthenon might produce some useful information about Theo.

Dickens had met Oliver Wilde during the investigation into the death of Patience Brooke; Oliver had been in love with Laetitia Topham whom the suspect had pursued in the hope of enriching himself. However, since he was now to marry Sophia Outfin, his suit of Miss Topham could not have been successful. Dickens was not surprised. Miss Topham, he thought, was not the girl for Oliver. She was too serious, too intelligent, too scholarly and Dickens had wondered at the time if she would marry at all. His brief meeting with Sophia Outfin suggested that her good nature and what Mrs Mapes had called her softness would fit Oliver's amiable, open temperament. Dickens had liked the young man, had thought him uncomplicated and honest which was why he felt a little uncomfortable about quizzing him on the subject of Theo Outfin. He certainly did not want to alarm Oliver with talk of murder. He would have to be cautious and hope that the information would come out naturally.

Oliver Wilde greeted Dickens with his natural friendliness, complimenting him on what he had read of *David Copperfield* so far.

'I love your new book,' he said. 'Oh, the pathos of young David's early life! Miss Murdstone is a veritable dragon. Reminded me of a housekeeper we had when I was young – all steel, hard as nails she was. My mother was frightened to death of her. Then, we found out that she drank, and off she went, thank goodness.'

They went into the dining room, Oliver still enthusing about what he had read, commenting on David's schooldays – made him shudder, he said, arriving at Steerforth, guessing that he would be fatal to Little Em'ly, pausing only to order their dinner of baked oyster, cream soup and loin of mutton with roast potatoes.

In the pause after the baked oysters and the soup when they enjoyed a glass of chilled hock, Oliver thanked Dickens for his invitation and his congratulations on the forthcoming marriage which Dickens had written in his letter.

'And, you met her, my Sophy. Lovely, is she not?'

'She is, indeed. You are most fortunate – and Mrs Outfin – you shall have a charming mother-in-law. She obviously approves of you.'

'Yes, it is marvellous – I am a fortunate man to have found Sophy – she is just the girl for me, so happy, so gentle yet so lively. We talk on everything – we have read the instalments of *David Copperfield* together – and are so much in agreement. Sophy said that you must have meant us to take particular note of "the black shadow" following Little Em'ly – symbolic, she said. Is she not a perceptive reader, Mr Dickens? She is so clever as well as beautiful.'

'I think she must be. Naturally, I hoped that the best readers would take note of the shadow – my compliments to Miss Sophy.'

'I have such hopes, Mr Dickens, such hopes of our perfect felicity.'

Dickens lifted his glass in which the cool wine gleamed. 'I believe you will be happy – you are made for each other.' They addressed themselves to the loin of mutton. Oliver Wilde had the hearty appetite of a healthy young man who loved life.

Dickens could not help but be charmed by Oliver's infectious enthusiasm and his love for clever, lively Sophy – love that was returned, he was sure. He envied the boy's innocence, his trust in the future that was unfolding in his imagination. He remembered his intense and painful love for Maria Beadnall when he was but eighteen. Love is a boy's fancy, his friend, Bulwer-Lytton had written. But when he remembered how Maria had toyed with him for three years, and how he had felt the pain of rejection so deeply, he could not call it fancy. Even now he believed that her failure to return his passionate feelings had created a caution in him so that he was wary of expressing his deepest feelings. And in his marriage, he thought, there was something wanting. Even with eight children! The Responsibilities, he called them, joking, of course, but sometimes all his responsibilities overwhelmed him, and he knew he could be a blight on the household. Oliver would do better, he knew it. Oliver did not have secrets to hide so deep that they were like a wound over which the scar had never quite healed.

They ate their mutton and an apple pudding, all the while discussing Dickens's books, Sophy's virtues, their hopes for the future and Oliver's career prospects until he returned, as Dickens hoped he would, to the marvellous coincidence of Dickens's visit to the Outfin home.

'Sophy said that you were with Superintendent Jones and were asking about a shawl belonging to Sophy's grandmother. Are you investigating another crime?'

'The shawl was found near where a boy was murdered. Of course,' he added quickly, 'it may have nothing to do with the murder. We spoke to the housekeeper who worked for Sophy's grandmother. She told us that it was given to a maid, Mattie Webb. I suspect she lost it, but the superintendent simply wishes to clear up a loose thread, you might say. Your Sophy recognised it,' Dickens took a chance, 'though her brother did not.'

'You met Theo, too?'

'Yes, he came in just as we were leaving so it was an opportunity – just to check, but it did not matter. Sophy was quite clear about the shawl. I was much struck by the resemblance between sister and brother – they might be twins.'

'Yes, though they are not. Theo is a year older than Sophy. He is twenty. But they are not alike in character. Theo is …' Oliver's open face clouded momentarily, 'more reserved. Difficult to know, I suppose – I wonder sometimes –'

Dickens trod carefully. This was an opening, but he must not be clumsy nor, he felt, must he take advantage of Oliver's openness. Yet, if there were something, then better for it to be discovered before – before what? The damage, the ruin might already be in motion.

'You are not sure about him?'

'That is just it, Mr Dickens. He is so shut off from them all – Sophy is hurt by his distance. They were so close once. She worries, too, and so does Mrs Outfin. You are very perceptive, sir – if I tell you about him, perhaps you can give me advice – I would do anything to protect Sophy. I cannot bear her to be hurt.'

'What is it that you fear, Oliver?' Dickens was gentle.

The young man hesitated. Dickens understood. His loyalty was to his new family. He saw the conflict shadow the clean-cut face as Oliver tried to put his fears into words. Oliver looked at Dickens, whose eyes seemed so bright – mesmerising even – telling him that he could confide his anxieties.

'I fear that he is in debt. I fear that he gambles. He is to inherit money at twenty-one, but his father will still have power over it. Still, I think that Theo has gambled on the strength of his inheritance. I fancy his creditors do not know about his father's hold on the money, that Theo has given the impression that he will have money to pay his debts and more. There are hangers-on – you know that, Mr Dickens. Theo is young, and – I do not like to say so – but I think he is weak. He is girlish, in some ways. His father has not been easy with him, and I think Theo may have tried to impress his so-called friends with his generosity –'

'What is the basis of your fears?'

'Gossip at the clubs – Boodles and worse, the Polyanthus – you remember we went there when you were looking for Edmund Crewe. Theo is a member and the chief recreation is gambling.'

Dickens remembered going to the club to find the man who was a suspect in the earlier murder case he had investigated with Sam. 'Has he borrowed money elsewhere?'

'You mean moneylenders?'

'Yes.'

'I do not know. His father would be horrified.'

'Gambling, borrowing, moneylenders – they all lead men into strange byways. Do these fellows visit more insalubrious places, about Seven Dials, St Giles's – you know of the places I mean?'

'Illegal gambling dens?'

'Yes.'

'I know they do but whether Theo has – I do not know – but he is very secretive, and he looks – ill, sometimes, as if there were something weighing on him. What can I do, Mr Dickens?' If there were a scandal, it would –'

Oliver looked increasingly worried. It was obvious to Dickens that he knew more than he said he thought or feared. The word 'scandal' showed that. But was it only gambling debts that weighed on Theo Outfin's conscience? Dickens needed to know more.

'You do not think he is involved with a woman? Perhaps his peregrinations into the underworld have led him into low company. That might make him terribly afraid.'

Oliver looked more troubled than ever. The conflict was there again in his darkened brow.

'I do not know. He is girlish, sensitive – perhaps he might be led by some designing woman. I did not think – I mean I thought him too young – not in years, obviously – but there is something feminine about him as yet. He has not shown interest in the young women who are Sophy's friends. This is dreadful. I must do something – but what? I cannot bring suspicions or gossip to his father and what would Sophy think if I were to accuse her brother of dreadful things? What do you advise, Mr Dickens? Perhaps, if you met him –'

'It is very awkward. I understand your difficulty. You need to know for sure before it goes too far and threatens the family's reputation – and happiness. Theo Outfin needs to be got away from his hangers-on. Perhaps, you could introduce me. I could judge how deeply he is in trouble. It would be done casually, of course – a chance encounter, you with your friend, Mr Dickens.'

Oliver took the bait. 'We might go to the Polyanthus this evening – it is only nine o'clock. Theo might be there. I could introduce you – he would be delighted to meet you – like Sophy, he is a great reader, and then you might find out – you are so good at drawing people out, Mr Dickens.'

Dickens felt a momentary twinge of guilt – yes, he had drawn out the information about Theo Outfin from Oliver Wilde and the boy was unaware of the meaning of the information to Dickens, and, of course, to the superintendent. Still, even if Theo Outfin were only a foolish young man too deeply in the wrong company, it would be good for Oliver and Sophy if Dickens could help to free him. And if Theo Outfin were something worse then he had to be caught. But Theo had seen him with the superintendent − that might make him wary. He would hardly trust the man he had seen in the company of a policeman. To see him now might warn him off, but Theo could not just disappear. Damn, it was too late now. He could hardly tell Oliver that he had changed his mind.

The Polyanthus club was in a little lane off Dover Street, and it was at the corner of Dover Street and Jermyn Street that they saw Theo Outfin, a solitary figure coming towards them. Oliver looked uncertain. Were they to speak to him? The matter was resolved as they saw the slight young man get into a cab. As it passed, Dickens caught a glimpse of the face as it looked briefly at him. The face of a murderer? Of course, it was impossible to tell, but Dickens had an impression of inexpressible weariness and misery. What did it mean? And what were they to do? He looked at Oliver. If Oliver suggested they follow, Dickens would concur, but he was not going to suggest it. Oliver looked anxious and unsure.

'Ought we to follow him? I wonder where he is going.'

'I think we might, Oliver. I caught a glimpse of his face. He looked exhausted and infinitely miserable. Perhaps we may be able to help.' Dickens was not being hypocritical. He had felt a twinge of pity for that face, so young and yet so full of misery. Whatever he had or had not done, he needed to be helped. And, it would be useful to know where the boy was going.

An empty cab came by. They asked the driver to follow the one they could see waiting to turn left into Regent Circus. Their cab caught up with the first as it turned. It went round the Circus into Coventry Street, left again into Princes Street and right into Old Compton Street.

Dickens was anxious. He had hoped Theo Outfin would go anywhere but towards St Giles's. However, his cab stopped at the bottom of Crown Street where they saw him alight. Dickens paid their driver and they got out of their cab just in time to see Theo Outfin walking listlessly into Crown Street. He looked like a man who did not know where he was going. They followed him. They were not far from Rose Street where Mademoiselle Victorine, that enigmatic milliner, lived. Theo turned into a narrow alley off Denmark Street; it was in these narrow lanes and twisting passages that the Moon family lived their desperate, uneasy lives. Dickens remembered the noise of banging, the dreadful wrenching sobs and Mrs Moon's starved and worn countenance.

In the mean little lane off Dulcimer Street, Mr Moon was asleep, befuddled by the gin that Mrs Moon had fed him to shut out the noise – if it was gin. How should she know? That's what the woman two doors away called it. It was cheap, though – tuppence a jug. God knows she could hardly afford that, but she would have given him anything, methylated spirit, white spirit, laudanum, anything to shut out that noise. She might have poisoned him and he knew it. She could tell. When she came to him with the cup, he would look at her through the tears, and she would see in the little, knowing eyes that she thought must be like a snake's, his fear of her and his hatred. And she wanted him dead – God forgive her – of course she did. He was a weight on their lives, so heavy that of late, Mrs Moon wondered if she could carry on at all.

It was night and Kip and Tilly were in bed. She stood in the dank yard looking up at the veiled moon and the clouds through which she could just about see the faint, far-off pinprick of a star. What was the meaning of that distance? she wondered. Mrs Moon was not an ignorant woman. She could remember her childhood, ordinary, respectable – her father a modest farm worker who had sent her to the village school, her mother, loving, and Mrs Moon, a cherished child. How had she come to this? The sky gave no answer; it stretched away, on and on, the clouds deepening to black in the furthest distance, so far that as she looked, she felt her own smallness. What was she to those remote stars and planets and what were they to her, this sublunary woman with her feet planted in the mud and grime of the alley off Dulcimer Street?

There was a noise at the yard door, a scratching – a dog, perhaps? Mrs Moon opened the door. She was not afraid; she was past fear except for Tilly, and Kip, of course. There was no one in the alley. Mrs Moon's house was the end of the terrace. Next to her yard there was a bit of waste ground where someone had kept a donkey once. The children had fed it grass, sometimes going as far as the river to find it, and it would gulp carrot or turnip pieces from their hands. Once Kip had put little Lucy Moon on its back and they had persuaded the beast to walk around the brick-strewn ground. She remembered their joy – they loved that donkey and had cried when it was led away. Joyless, now, she reflected. Little Lucy gone, Mr Moon crippled, and Tilly – oh, Tilly – what would happen to her?

Beyond the waste ground there was a workshop, a dilapidated affair of planks and bits of old doors where Harry Sutch, the carpenter who owned it, kept his wood and tools. On the other side of the Moons' there was an empty house, practically falling down. Mrs Moon had forbidden Kip and Tilly to go in there. It was dangerous. Sometimes she heard noises from there but she had not seen anyone. What business was it of hers if some poor, homeless creature had found refuge there?

She stepped into the yard and looked down past the empty ground, past the workshop to where the alley turned the corner into Dulcimer Street, then into the High Street across which were the grand squares with their quiet gardens where one could sit in a green-shaded peace, and the museum where they exhibited creatures from a past as distant as the stars above. She could walk that way; she would come eventually to the fields and gardens beyond the houses and squares, to the open country, to Kingsbury where she was born, and she would walk on like one of those tramping women she remembered passing through the village when she was a child. And she would never come back, ever.

Mrs Moon began to walk, not knowing that she did so. Harry Sutch locked up his workshop and looked at her curiously as she passed him. Where could she be going? She simply stared ahead, he thought, as if she were seeing something far away, somewhere only she could see. Poor creature – she 'ad a lot to put up with. Harry had heard the man shouting; he had seen the children running away, given them a penny or two, once or twice. You 'ad ter feel sorry for that child with the white 'air – odd little thing, like a fairy or wot yer thought a fairy might look like, there not bein' so many round St Giles's. Harry walked away. Mrs Moon reached the end of the alley and stood looking towards Dulcimer Street. A boy came towards her. She recognised him – the boy, Scrap, who had come with the strange gentleman. Tilly had not stopped talking about him. A kind man. Strange eyes – hypnotic, almost, she thought. And he had brought the golden sovereign which she had in her hand though why she did not know.

Scrap knew her, wondered where she was going, wondered where were Kip and Tilly. Seeing her far-away eyes, he knew that all was not well. 'Mrs Moon, where yer goin'? It's late. Where's Kip and Tilly?' He saw the glint of gold in her hand.

Mrs Moon saw him clearly. 'Kip, Tilly, I must get back. Tilly should not be alone with –'

She turned back and started to run clumsily with Scrap following. They went back into the alley, stumbling towards the back door. Then the world exploded.

Inside the house, Tilly had not been asleep. She had been watching her pa as he rolled and writhed in his restless sleep. She had heard him moaning and had felt sorry for him. She had heard the back door. Then she had crept down. How could she stop those sounds which tore at her childish heart? She stood motionless at the bottom of the stairs willing him to see her and love her. He woke up and saw the white child standing, staring at him with those strange eyes which looked black and malevolent in the gloom. He hated her and was afraid. Her eyes could kill him.

He seized the lamp from the table by his chair and flung it at her. It caught the grimy curtain which burst into flames, and it fell with a crash on to the laundry basket in the middle of the floor, and more flames flared up. Through the orange blaze, father and child saw each other, the man's eyes wide with horror. Tilly took a step forward, but the fire leapt at her as it licked at bits of paper and straw. She could still see him, trapped there in his chair. There was a clattering on the stairs. Kip ran down, grabbed her, and hauled her back up the staircase as the blaze took hold. Looking back, she could see nothing but red, gold, copper as the room was engulfed. The fire sprang after them. The crippled man's screams filled the roaring air.

Outside Mrs Moon and Scrap stood watching as the house filled with flame. Somewhere voices screamed 'Fire!'

Near the front of the house, Dickens and Oliver were swept up by the crowd which surged towards the house. Theo Outfin had vanished. Dickens realised which house was on fire. He ran with Oliver at his heels into the lane beside the carpenter's wood store. At the back yard door of the house he saw Mrs Moon and Scrap. Banners of vermilion and gold flame flew in the air and showers of sparks blazed in fountains and cascaded down the darkness. It was terrible and beautiful. Mrs Moon and Scrap stared, transfixed, until Dickens and Oliver came to them.

'Tilly? Kip?' Dickens's voice was urgent.

The flames burnt in Mrs Moon's eyes; she could not speak.

'In the 'ouse, trapped. Oh, gawd, wot can we do?' Scrap came to himself.

'Up there!' Oliver shouted.

They looked up to the roof where Kip and Tilly crouched, working their way along the tiles to the wrecked house next door, the fire rearing at them like some wild tiger which might leap upon them in a minute. Dickens, Oliver and Scrap darted along the alley, hoping to find their way in to the yard of the old house. Perhaps Kip and Tilly could jump. Mrs Moon stood gazing up.

They pushed into the yard of the house. Kip and Tilly were on the roof. There was a lean-to shed to which they might jump down. They saw that Kip had seen it. He stood upright, pulling Tilly with him. A flame reached out to snatch her. Then there was a roar, a terrible cracking as of timbers falling, and the roof fell in. Kip seemed to fall backwards and Tilly simply vanished into the furnace. A huge spume of flame spouted upwards with a great whoosh.

Dickens ran back to the alley. Mrs Moon was not there. A sense of horror possessed him. Heedless of the danger, he pushed his way into the yard, feeling the searing heat, smelling the acrid stench of burning wood, and through the smoke and wavering flames, he saw her walking into the burning house. He saw a great flaming light spring up then she was gone in a whirl of fire blazing all about her.

As at a distance, he heard the shouts of the firemen at the front of the house. There would be the burnished engine, the men with their leathern helmets and hatchets, the jets of water pumped out to still the fiery cauldron; there would be a cordon round the burning houses; there would be the police; there would be the volunteers manning the pumps; there would be the onlookers gasping and cheering; there would be the men, women and children swarming from their tenements, and the dogs, cats and rats leaping from the cellars, drains and hideous hovels, and at last the fire would die down, the beast tamed. But the firemen and their water could do nothing for Mrs Moon.

And Tilly? In his lair, the giant woke and saw fire descending, and in that fire, he saw flying down towards him, ablaze in gold with silver about its head, the ghost of his nightmares turned now to a fiery angel come for him. Vapour filled the cellar, flames rushed at him, and that enlarged heart, damaged by terror and starvation, stopped.

16

THE MORGUE

Dickens woke later than usual, exhausted from the events of the previous night. He had arrived home at nearly midnight, blackened with smoke. He could smell it still even though he had bathed and was wearing fresh clothes. His throat was sore too; it felt raw from the smoke he had inhaled. He thought about the terrible moment when he had seen Mrs Moon devoured by the flames before his helpless eyes. It had contained all the unbearable reality of a dream. And he thought of Tilly consumed in the fire, and Kip fallen from the roof. He had taken Scrap back to Mr Brim's shop. He was worried about him. Scrap's eyes had been so wide with horror when they had seen Tilly vanish. Thank God he had not seen Mrs Moon go to her blazing death. It was bad enough for him – he thought the sight would haunt him for the rest of his days. And, yet, he knew why she had done it. He remembered Kip's terror as he had looked at her despairing face and his own thought that she might go under. And she had. And not just the Moon family. What about all those others whose houses had collapsed and who had been left homeless? The workhouse? Perhaps. Some other dismal cellar into which they would crawl and try to resume their maimed lives?

Oliver had gone home afterwards. They had forgotten about Theo Outfin, but Dickens remembered him now. He hardly had the strength to think about it. Yet he had to go to Bow Street. Sam would want to know what he had found out – which was not very much. The misery of that young face – not exactly evidence, he thought. He did not know why but somehow, he doubted that Theo Outfin was a murderer. A deeply unhappy young man, yes, a man weary of his life, a man with something on his conscience, but surely not a killer. However, it was no use telling Sam that he had seen a face with despair written on it and did not believe it was the face of a murderer. Sam would be interested in his impressions, true, but it was not evidence. After breakfast, he would go down to see Sam.

Sam was in his office. He had heard about the fire from Inspector Lang, who had been there. He knew about the dead girl, Tilly. And he knew that when the police had searched the abandoned house, they had found the child and the giant, both dead. And they had found a purse of sovereigns – Sam believed it must be the one that Dickens had taken out at Rats' Castle and which had been stolen in the fight. Perhaps Tommy Titfer had taken it. He had certainly seen it. And since he was missing, perhaps his was the body that Scrap had seen being dragged by the giant – he would send a couple of constables to have a look round the alleys where Scrap had waited for Poll. And more strange and sinister, he knew of something else which he must tell Dickens.

Dickens came in. Sam looked with concern at his white face and strained eyes. 'A dreadful night – I heard from Inspector Lang about the death of Tilly.'

'Have they found her?'

'Yes, and the giant, too.'

'What?'

'They found him with the child in the cellar of that old house – the house had collapsed around them. She must have fallen into the cellar from the roof. He must have been hiding there.'

'How strange, how terrible – he had lunged at her before. What did he think she was, I wonder, when he saw her first in the lane and then again? What does it mean that they were brought together in this death by fire? Both outcasts in their way – poor little girl – she was strange and beautiful in her odd way – not quite of this world, I thought when I saw her. And Mrs Moon, if you had seen – she walked into that flaming house after she saw them fall. I saw her like a column of fire and I could do nothing. Oh, the pity of it, Sam, the pity of it.'

They fell silent then, thinking of that tragic family, gone in a moment. The clock ticked. Time moved on, leaving Tilly, Mrs Moon, the angry crippled man and the poor, bedevilled giant, all consumed by the flames, their bones fired by the heat to rest at last, cold in the grave.

'Did they find Kip?' asked Dickens after a while, thinking of the boy falling backwards on the burning roof.

'He is alive and, mercifully, hardly hurt at all. When he fell –'

'Yes, we saw him topple backwards.'

'The neighbours who had gathered at the first cry of "fire" had held a sheet out, thinking that someone might escape from the upstairs window. Kip fell into that. He is being looked after by neighbours.'

'That is something – though, poor lad, he loved little Tilly and his mother. I must try to do something for him. I think, perhaps, that he could replace Davey at the Home. Mrs Morson would be pleased to have a useful boy about the place. I liked Kip – he did not want to lie to his mother about the giant. A good lad, I thought. I will take him to Mrs Morson. Scrap will be glad – he was very distressed last night. I took him back to the shop. Mr Brim is very compassionate.'

'I will ask Elizabeth to look after him. And there is something else. Another body was found in the ruins of the house. A boy.'

'Who? I did not see anyone else although I suppose some-one could have been in there.'

'He was brought to the morgue – blackened with smoke, but not burnt, and when he was cleaned up I saw that he had been stabbed – a small puncture wound, exactly like those in Jemmy and Robin Hart.'

'He has done it again. Oh, God, Theo Outfin was there. Oliver Wilde and I followed him and then we lost him in the crowd when the fire broke out. I had thought this morning – I must be wrong – I had hoped –'

'What did you think?'

'I saw his face – such despair. I thought he could not be a murderer. There was something so young, so hopeless about him, but now –'

'And I have had the results of the post-mortem on Robin Hart. There is no evidence of sexual abuse. Neither was there for Jemmy. I had word from Inspector Harker. So, why were they killed?'

'What about the shawl – did Feak find Mattie Webb?'

'No, the Du Canes are in Paris and Mattie Webb is with them – she is Mrs Du Cane's personal maid, now. But they are back tomorrow. I will go myself. I know we promised Mrs Mapes that we would exercise discretion, but there is not time for that now. We need to know if she lost it or if it came into Theo Outfin's hands somehow though for the life of me I cannot see how.'

'No, it seems impossible – why should he steal it? What would he want it for?'

'Then we are left with the mysterious man at Mademoiselle Victorine's. I have a constable watching her house. Rose Street is also not far from the scene of the fire.'

'What do we do about Theo Outfin?'

'Watch him. That is all we can do. Is it possible for you to meet him through Oliver Wilde? Perhaps you might discover what it is that troubles him. You may be right, you know, it could be something else. Did Oliver tell you much about him?'

'He thinks he is heavily in debt – that he is involved in illegal gambling. He thinks that Theo has become involved with a bad set. He does not appear to be a ladies' man, however – Oliver told me that he pays no attention to Sophy's friends, but that does not mean he has not had contact with other kinds of women through his friends. And since neither Jemmy nor Robin Hart was sexually assaulted, it does not seem that Theo Outfin used boys.'

'He might have wanted to,' said Sam sombrely, 'and if they were not willing then he might have killed them – we cannot dismiss him altogether, but I trust your instinct – you saw his face and you felt pity for his young hopelessness. Now I want you to come with me to the morgue to see the third boy, if you will. I want you to tell me what you see.'

They descended the stairs into an air which was suddenly colder as they approached the morgue where they had watched as Mrs Hart held her dead boy. I must go and find out about her, thought Dickens. I cannot just leave her to Zeb and Effie, though I do not know what can be done about her or for her. He felt again that she would never recover, that she would simply waste away, willing her own death just as Mrs Moon had chosen her death when she had seen Kip and Tilly fall into the flames. Oh, would that she had waited to know that Kip was alive.

Dickens paused in astonishment when they went into the white-tiled room where the water dripped still. It smelt of carbolic – razor sharp in the throat but not wholly erasing the sweet, sickly smell of death. On the marble slab, he could see two fair heads, the bodies being covered in sheets. The boys were laid out on their fronts so that he had the impression that twin brothers were sleeping there. The hair was the same colour and there was uncanny similarity in the shape of the heads and the delicate, vulnerable necks and sharply protruding shoulder blades. He thought of his own boys whom he had so often seen sleeping thus – Charley at twelve was much the same age as these two, bright, sensitive Charley, his first son who would go to Eton next year, perhaps. What a difference, he thought. What might these two have become? These ragged boys who were his other self, the boy who had laboured in the blacking factory, but whose own son had all the world before him, and who would not be a victim of ignorance and want.

'*An apple cleft in twain is not more like*,' he quoted, 'but they cannot be brothers. Robin Hart was her only child.'

'They are not brothers, but I wanted you to see. This one was killed in the same way – a small puncture wound. And now, I must show you something else.' Sam went over to the marble slab and gently turned over the boy on the left who was not Robin Hart. He could not have been for Dickens saw something that made his heart contract with pity and horror.

Instead of Robin Hart's sensitive, delicate face, Dickens saw that this boy was terribly disfigured. His mouth was deformed by a hair lip and his nose was partly eaten away, a black, hideous hole where the nostrils should have been.

'What does it mean?'

'I do not know – they are alike and not alike. If the murderer is a man who uses boys then I can see that Robin Hart would be attractive, but this other?'

'I know. It is hard to believe that he would be desired – Robin killed for his beauty; this one killed for his ugliness? But what ties them together? What about Jemmy? We did not see him very clearly. We were only concerned that he was not Scrap.'

'I know and I think we must go to see him. We have seen these two and it is our impression of Jemmy that will count. It is no use my sending someone else. Are you able to come with me now?'

'Yes, but I would like to go to Mr Brim's to see how Scrap is. Is Elizabeth there?'

'Yes. We will call at the shop before we go to the morgue at Scotland Yard. I will send a note to Inspector Harker telling him that we want to see Jemmy.'

The note written and despatched to Scotland Yard by a constable, Dickens and Jones made their way to the stationery shop. Scrap was out on a delivery, but Mr Brim would tell him the news about Kip. Elizabeth was in the back parlour giving Eleanor and Tom their lessons. Mr Brim's face bore the mark of strain which Dickens had noted before. What troubled him?

'I am grateful to your wife,' said Mr Brim, abruptly, 'but I think it is time for Eleanor to go to school. I cannot impose upon your wife any longer, Superintendent. She has done enough. I shall engage someone to look after Tom while I am in the shop.' Mr Brim looked embarrassed at his own brusqueness. There was an awkward silence.

Sam thought what it would mean to Elizabeth to be deprived of the children's company. Dickens saw how Mr Brim was uncomfortable about the charity he felt he was receiving and that he could not pay back. 'I am sorry,' Mr Brim continued, 'if I seem ungrateful, but I feel that your wife, Elizabeth, is giving up all her time and I cannot –' He began to cough, unable to continue and they saw how the hectic in his cheeks burnt more deeply. He looked wretched, angry that his illness betrayed him, that they would know he could not take care of his own children.

When the coughing subsided, Sam spoke. 'You think it is all on one side, Mr Brim, that you are receiving all the benefits, but I beg you to see it from my Elizabeth's side, too. We had but one child, a daughter. She is dead and your Eleanor is filling that terrible blank in Elizabeth's heart where my Edith should be. If you have any compassion, Mr Brim, let her continue.' Sam was silent and Dickens saw how he looked at the sick man, begging him to reconsider.

'I beg your pardon, Superintendent. I thought only of myself and I curse my wretched pride which I will not excuse. My children love your Elizabeth. I do not know how I could, in truth, deprive them of her company. Forgive me.'

'No need,' said Sam. 'I understand your feelings and am glad that you spoke for it is good that we know that we can help each other, and I thank you for allowing Elizabeth the company of your two children, and to help you when you need it. Come, we are friends, are we not?' Sam held out his hand for the other man to take. 'I hope I can be Sam henceforth and not Superintendent.'

'Indeed and I shall be Robert to you both.'

They left him then and went on quietly to Scotland Yard where they saw that Jemmy, lying on the cold marble, was exactly the same sort of boy as Robin. He had been washed and his bright head shone. Dickens remembered what he had thought that day when they had found him encased in mud – that he had been alive, had wondered at the great river and its ships, and had played, perhaps with that unknown dog. But no one had been to enquire for him, no one had missed him, no one had mourned him. They might never know for his quiet face, so like Robin's, and his closed eyes could tell them nothing now.

On their way back to Bow Street, they stopped for lunch at the Lamb and Flag, a favourite of Dickens who enjoyed its poky rooms with their bare pine floors, low beams and wooden panelling. He liked its history, its associations with the poet Dryden, and there was a story of a murder, a young man killed after winning at cards. Naturally, he was said to haunt the building. A thick, steaming wedge of steak and kidney pie having restored them, they lingered over a glass of brandy and water in front of the fire. Time to discuss what they had seen.

'Three boys not unalike if you saw them all from behind. No evidence of sexual abuse. So what is the reason, Charles? Why is it done?'

'As you suggested before, it might be that he did make advances to them, at least to Robin and Jemmy – they reject him, are horrified by what he proposes, and he, in his rage, kills them.'

'And our third boy?'

'The murderer follows him, thinking that he is like the other two. When he accosts the boy, he sees the disfigured face and kills him for not being what he wanted. He sweeps out of the way a detested object. I think he hates them, Sam – perhaps for what they make him feel – perhaps he hates himself, too. And this corroding, growing hate gives birth to monstrous and mis-shapen murder.'

'It makes sense. And what frightens me is that he could do it again if, as you say, he is filled with such hatred. He does not care about the consequences – he does not think he might hang.'

'No, his is a terrible isolation, he is shut off from all consideration of others, estranged from his life, his family – like –'

'Theo Outfin?'

'I do not want to think so. I do not know, but I cannot believe it of him. I remember his face – so young, so despairing. And, the mask – it seems so calculated, mocking us, if you like. I do not read Theo Outfin as the author of that drawing. Oliver Wilde says he is sensitive as Mrs Mapes did – not a hater, surely. Not the man you describe as having the arrogance to believe we cannot catch him.'

'I take your point about Theo and the mask, but we still have to consider him. He is hiding something, and we can connect him with at least two places where murder has been done. And, he could have been in possession of the shawl – he knew Mattie Webb.'

'I know, I know. The unimaginable secrets of the human heart.'

They fell silent then, Dickens pondering the idea that in Theo Outfin there was some darkness that he had read wrongly as a secret sorrow. Perhaps it was fear and guilt. It was true, he had often thought, that every human creature is a profound mystery to every other. But Sam was a policeman. He had to regard Theo as still a suspect. He had to be practical, do his duty and find Theo Outfin, and if he were the murderer, and there was not the shadow of a shade of doubt, then he must hang and Mrs Outfin and Sophie and Oliver Wilde would have to bear it though their lives would be blighted.

Sam watched him. He did not want it to be Theo Outfin either. That was the trouble with murder. You didn't want it to be a man you knew or knew about. Years ago, he had been present when his old chief, Inspector Stone – hard as – had arrested a man with whom Sam had been to school. He had strangled his wife. Sam had not been able to believe it: the boy at school so tender with his pet white mice. Dickens was right about the human heart – it was unfathomable at times.

'Did you find a mask anywhere in that yard?' Dickens asked, breaking the silence. That mask, it haunted him.

'No, we didn't, but then everything was burnt – the fire might have destroyed it.'

'So it might. What next then?'

'Back to Bow Street. I need to see Mattie Webb as soon as she returns from Paris – we need to know how the shawl came to be in St Giles's churchyard – did she lose it? Or sell it? Or was it stolen? Or, and here's a thought, has she some relationship with Theo Outfin?'

Dickens looked at him. 'I hadn't thought of that, but it is possible, I suppose. An affair with a servant girl – that would be a reason for estrangement from his family – but, then he wouldn't be murdering boys, and from the way Mrs Mapes spoke of her, I can't see her as an accomplice.' He sighed, 'Wot a mystery it all is.'

'Shakespeare?' asked Sam, grinning at Dickens's change of voice.

'Topping.' Topping, the coachman, was given, at rare times, to philosophical musings of a peculiarly gnomic kind, much to Dickens's delight.

'Oh, let's get back. All this mystery and speculation simply makes me want to do something.'

'Speculation is the thief of time as much as procrastination so let's collar them both.'

Sam grinned again. 'Good. Drink up and let's be away.'

From Garrick Street they walked back to Bow Street where Constable Rogers was waiting with news. The constable watching the milliner's house had seen no one enter or leave, but Oliver Wilde was waiting for them in the superintendent's office.

'He came about half and hour or so, sir. Mr Theo Outfin is missing.'

They went into the office where they saw Oliver Wilde whose usually amiable face was lined with anxiety.

'Theo did not go home last night. I went to call on Sophy this morning – by midday, there was no sign of him so I came here, Mr Dickens. I thought you should know – after what we discussed last night. He may be in danger – where we last saw him, it's not a particularly salubrious area and I am afraid – he might have been attacked. Can you help, Superintendent?'

Dickens exchanged a glance with Sam. How much to tell Oliver? Sam shook his head slightly. Nothing, yet.

'I will instigate a search, Mr Wilde. Do you know of any places he might have visited regularly?' Sam made no sign that Dickens had told him anything about Theo's difficulties.

Oliver looked embarrassed. Was it his place to tell the policeman what he feared about Theo Outfin? Yet, if they were to find him, he needed help – he could hardly go searching on his own. Sam understood as he watched the fleeting shadows of doubt flicker on Oliver's face.

'You are afraid that he might be a frequenter of some dubious places? Many young men are. Not many come to harm. Still, if you are worried, perhaps you ought to tell me about him. It will go no further.'

'I told Mr Dickens last night. Theo has been deeply troubled, almost estranged from his family – yet he and Sophy were once so close – they are very alike to look at. If Sophy were a boy, she would be practically his double, and he, well, he is girlish in a way – sensitive, you know, and he has found friends in a disreputable group of young bloods – I do not know how, but I think he gambles. Mr Dickens asked me about illegal gambling dens – I think it must be so. Why else would he be in St Giles's?'

'Then we will know where to look. What I suggest, Mr Wilde, is that you go back to reassure Mr and Mrs Outfin and Miss Sophy that the matter is in my hands, and that we will do everything we can to find him. Of course, he may come home and then you must let me know. I will send to you as soon as we have news. You will stay at the Outfin house?'

'Yes, I will. Are you sure I cannot help in the search?'

'No, Mr Wilde. We know where to look.'

Oliver Wilde departed somewhat reluctantly. Sam was glad. He did not want the complication of Oliver's presence. He did not know if he were looking for a murderer or for a victim.

'Well,' said Dickens, 'what are we to make of this?'

'It is quite possible that Theo Outfin is sleeping off a long night of illegal gaming. On the other hand, he might be in danger, and of course, we must consider the idea that he is in hiding. Whichever, he must be found. And, we need to do the finding discreetly. If he is not our murderer then we will be glad to have been discreet.'

'Rogers?'

'Yes.'

'What about Zeb – and Occy? Scrap, too, would be useful. I need to see him anyway.'

'I agree, and I will recruit Feak – he is not a blabberer, young as he is.'

Rogers and Feak were detailed to meet Dickens and Jones near the burnt-out house of the Moons where Dickens had seen Theo last. They would go first to the stationery shop to collect Scrap and then to Zeb Scruggs's shop where Dickens thought he would check on Mrs Hart, too.

The dreary November afternoon light was fading as they came out of the police station. The sky was darkening; dense tiers of clouds, edged with a feverish yellow, suggested rain and, thought Dickens, feeling a thickness about his brow, thunder – a storm brewing?

17

DENS OF VICE

Dickens and Jones hurried to Crown Street under that ominous sky where the clouds boiled. Fat drops of rain fell; there was a splitting crack of thunder followed by the sudden, sharp flash of lightning. Passers-by unfurled their umbrellas and scurried homeward, their faces white in the lurid light. Dickens turned up his coat collar and jammed his hat tightly on his head. *It was a dark and stormy night*, he thought ruefully, remembering the opening line of *Paul Clifford*, his friend Bulwer-Lytton's novel of 1830. It was indeed, and truly, the rain was falling now in torrents, except at occasional intervals, when it was checked by a violent gust of wind which seemed to bustle them along the crowded streets, snatching at their coats with a malicious impudence. By the time they entered the door of Mr Brim's shop they were drenched.

Scrap was there. He looked downcast – poor lad, thought Dickens. No doubt he was thinking of Tilly and Kip. His eyes brightened when he saw Dickens and the superintendent.

'Kip's alive, Mr Dickens – that's good, ain't it. But poor Tilly and Mrs Moon. 'Ow could it 'appen? T'ain't fair, Mr Dickens, Tilly dint do no 'arm an' Mrs Moon, she woz allus worried. I went ter see Kip. 'E don't know wot ter do.'

'I have a plan for Kip,' said Dickens. 'I shall find him a job with my friend Mrs Morson at Shepherd's Bush. He shall be a gardener's boy, and there will be a horse and a stable for him to look after. He will be safe there, Scrap, and one day you will be able to go to see him. I will take you. What do you think? A good plan?'

Scrap beamed. 'A good plan, Mr Dickens. Kip'll like that – 'e sed 'e 'ad a donkey wonce – does Mrs Morson 'ave a donkey?'

'I do not think so – but, if Kip wanted one, I daresay it could be arranged. Company for the horse, I suppose.' I shall have to buy a donkey, then, thought Dickens, grinning as he caught sight of Sam's face. Sam had the same thought and grinned back at him.

'We need you tonight,' said Sam. Scrap smiled. This was better. To be needed by Mr Dickens and Mr Jones – well, yer couldn't say nah, could yer?

'Wot's up? Yer want me ter find someone?'

'Yes, we want you with us, keeping your eyes and ears open – a young gentleman's gone missing from near where the fire was. Not been home all night. You might hear something in the alleys. Mr Dickens and I will be looking, and constables Rogers and Feak, but you know how it is, Scrap, the kids might have heard something. Listen in, will you?'

'Do you have a coat, Scrap? Is there an oilskin in the back somewhere?'

Scrap vanished into the back of the shop as Elizabeth came out to see her husband.

'We are borrowing Scrap,' said Sam.

'Out in this rain?' asked Elizabeth.

'I am afraid so – though we cannot get much wetter.'

'Take care of him – and yourselves. I will see you at home later, I hope.'

'You will. Take a cab home.'

Elizabeth smiled at her husband as Scrap came back.

When they went out, the rain had died down to a lighter drizzle though there was still a rumble of thunder in the distance as though some giant hand were rolling a cannonball to demolish a set of giant skittles. They walked to Zeb Scruggs's shop to ask if he would help with the search, and to find out if he knew anything about the errands Robin Hart had carried out. While the superintendent talked to Zeb, Dickens went in the back to ask about Mrs Hart.

'She's in bed, Mr Dickens,' Effie told him. 'Though, she doesn't sleep – just lies there with her eyes closed or some-times just staring into the dark. Won't eat, neither. Mrs Feak's been to see her – the nurse.'

Sam's Sybil of Star Street, Dickens thought, Feak's redoubt-able mother. 'What did she say?'

'She's dying, Mr Dickens. That's what she said. Nothing to be done. Mrs Feak said she'd seen it before – when a body wants to die, then they does – dying of heartbreak, she says, and it's true. We'll just keep her here until …' Effie's eyes filled. 'She'll not wake up one o' these days – that's what'll happen.'

She took Dickens upstairs to the small room where a dim oil lamp burnt. Shadow time, thought Dickens, seeing the dark coming in from the corners of the room to gather round the little bed with its white counterpane. The feeble light showed Mrs Hart with her eyes closed, the pale face unmoving and her thin, almost transparent hands, still on the whiteness – like a marble effigy of herself. They went out of the quiet room, leaving her to Time. Time would take her when he was ready. It would be too late for Mrs Hart when, and if, they found the murderer, but there would be justice of a kind for Robin and for Jemmy, and for the as yet unknown boy whose poor, disfigured face had, perhaps, brought about his death just as the beauty of the other two had brought about theirs.

Murder, thought Dickens, how the single act, the knife gleaming in the dark, the poison drop in the glass, the thick hand at the slender throat, created ripples which rolled out-wards to touch so many others. Did the murderer consider the harm to all those connected with his victim? No, because murder was a supremely selfish act. The murderer thought only of himself, of his own desires, his own anger, his own loss, his own hurt or rejection – never of his victims' hurts, never of those who might also die for loss of what they had so loved. Every death, he had once written, carries to some small circle of survivors thoughts of so much omitted and so little done. What did Mrs Hart regret now? Did she think that she could have saved him, that she had not paid enough attention when he was away, out in the streets? Well, they would never know from her whom Robin had seen, who had taken him to that shaded graveyard. He followed Effie down the stairs. They trod as quietly as they could but she would not hear them even if they were to clatter their way down.

In the shop, Sam exchanged a brief glance with Dickens who shook his head slightly. They walked to the door while Zeb put on an oilskin which made him look as if he ought to be standing on the deck of a fishing boat. He looked not unlike Mr Peggotty of Yarmouth.

'She is dying,' said Dickens sombrely. 'Mrs Feak, your Sybil of Star Street, has been to see her and says so. It is only a matter of time.'

'Then, it must be true,' said Sam. 'A wise woman, Mrs Feak.' His face darkened as he thought of Mrs Hart and her poor Robin. 'We need to find Theo and we need to know about that shawl, but if it is not Theo then I do not know – unless Mademoiselle Victorine's so-called visitor is the answer. Zeb tells me that Robin did errands for a stationer up the street. A respectable man, he says, not likely to be our murderer. Still, I will send a man to question him. He might know something about Robin's other acquaintances. Let's get going.' He looked out at the street, slushy with mud where the rain, heavier again, added to the misery of the scene.

Zeb offered Dickens an oilskin cape. 'Keep the worst off, Mr Dickens.'

Dickens tied it round his shoulders, conscious suddenly of the smell of fish, and a faint whiff of the sea which reminded him of Captain Pierce and Davey – and Kip. He must get on to that tomorrow. Tomorrow – what would it bring for Theo Outfin, Oliver Wilde and Sophy?

They went to meet Rogers and Feak who were waiting wrapped in oilskin cloaks and with a collection of bull's-eye lanterns. Rogers, that considerate fellow, had brought one for his superintendent. Scrap was to follow them, to keep open his eyes and ears round and about the places where the policemen and Dickens would make their enquiries.

First, a notorious gambling den down a set of precipitous stairs. It was a dank, close cellar with a deal table where cards were laid out and benches where were sitting the company of men with sallow cheeks and matted hair – men who did not seem ever to have seen the clear light of day. There were no girls or women present. There was immediate tension in the room. They knew Superintendent Jones and they recognised Rogers. Someone sniggered, a coarse, ugly sound, as Feak slipped clumsily down the last two steps. Dickens remained above, but he could see into the room; he could see Sam's profile and he knew that his face would be set like stone and that his eyes would be flashing steel in the grimy darkness.

'Playing cards, eh? Who wins? Got lucky, have you, Mr Click?'

Eyes were lowered but Click, a thin, greasy-looking, snuffling, yellow-faced individual, essayed politeness.

'Can we 'elp yer, Mr Jones, sir? No 'arm doin' 'ere, sir, jest a light supper an' a game o' cards for the boys.' The voice wheedled. 'No 'arm, sir, to be sure.'

'A light supper.' Dickens wanted to laugh at the incongruity of such a genteel phrase. Perhaps the speaker was once a superior sort of servant who had lost his place. His sycophantic air suggested that.

'I daresay not, Josiah Click. I am looking for a young man, a toff, as you might say – any toffs been here at all?'

'No, sir, Mr Jones – we don't get no toffs 'ere 'part from the Earl of Warwick, an' yer know 'im, sir. An' Mr Rogers – allus nice to see yer, sir.'

The so-called Earl of Warwick stepped forward nervously, a little foolish, a little sickly, now he was the centre of attention. How he came by his appellation is uncertain, but it was what he was called – an impersonator, perhaps. He had the air of a down-and-out actor with his soiled velvet jacket and dirty shirt.

Rogers, who knew him from old, teased the unfortunate man. 'Take your hat off, my lord. Why, I should be ashamed if I was you – and an earl, too – to show myself to a gentleman with my hat on!' The company roared with laughter, at ease now. What a jolly game it is, when Superintendent Jones comes down – and don't want nobody!

Of course, there was method in his madness. Rogers knew that while he was joking with the company, Feak was in the room beyond, searching, and the superintendent had moved, stealthy as a cat, into all the corners where his lamp would show if there were someone who did not want to be found. Feak came back – nothing, he signalled to his chief. The superintendent had seen only shadows. Rogers was still entertaining the company with his chaffing of the poor earl whose sense of humour appeared to have been filched from him or his discomfort may have arisen from the knowledge of the stolen watch in his pocket. Rogers knew, of course he did. The hand that stole in and out of the pocket gave the earl away as did the sickly grimace that he hoped would serve for a smile. But that was not what they were here for. The earl would keep. They bade goodnight and mounted the stairs, leaving the roars of laughter behind – relief?

St Giles's clock struck six. Scrap was outside. 'Nuffink,' he said, and on they went, deeper into the alleys, now mud-filled trenches where beetle-browed tenements skulked in the dark; where houses like so many rough-hewn packing cases huddled together as if shrinking from the rain. A jaundiced light showed down a foetid alley. There they went. The door was fast against them but Rogers hammered loudly until it was opened by a poor wretch of a girl. They pushed their way in to find a party on the go. Plenty of gin and ale, judging by the reeling of the singers and dancers. The music, from a wheezy piano accordion stopped as if the instrument had died suddenly of old age.

'Don't mind us,' said the superintendent cheerfully as they made their way to the makeshift bar presided over by a sour-looking landlady whose coal-black hair appeared as a coating of lacquer on her narrow head. Feak and Rogers separated to look in the nooks and crannies of this tumbledown wreck while Sam addressed the hard-faced woman.

'Looking for a gent, Mrs Brine,' said Sam. A vinegary name, thought Dickens. Suited her. 'Slight, fair hair, very young face,' Sam was saying. 'Gone missing – family want him back. Could be a reward. Name of Theo. Know anything?'

Mrs Brine obviously did; her shrewd eyes gleamed for a moment at the mention of a reward. She weighed up the risk – to tell or not to tell. She looked appraisingly at the policeman's companion, a younger man with a serious, almost severe expression. Religious, pr'aps, she thought – do-gooder, most like. Dickens read her thoughts and arranged his face into a suitable expression of piety. Sam had to turn away.

'We gets the toffs sometimes – lookin' for a good time when the girls are willin' – can't get no such at 'ome.' She winked, grotesquely and laughed, opening a mouth revealing blackened teeth and he smelt the gin – and decay – on her breath, but Sam steeled himself not to recoil. He waited. Don't push. She'll tell. 'Your young man – girlish, ain't 'e – dint come 'ere for Miss Laycock, yer know what I means.'

Sam nodded. He knew who – or what – Miss Laycock was; the phrase was aptly descriptive, but he kept a straight face. Dickens managed not to laugh, contorting his face into an expression of what he hoped was incomprehension. It was a new one on him – the collector of street slang.

Mrs Brine went on. 'Likes boys, I 'spect, but we don't 'ave none o' that sort 'ere. Tell yer wot, though –' She poured a glass of gin. 'Want a glass? Good stuff – not dilute for me best customers.'

Dickens declined. 'Temperance, ma'am.' He arranged his lips into a line of disapproval.

Sam almost choked. Dear God, it was strong whatever it was – vitriol added perhaps? It was not uncommon and, by the look of them, Mrs Brine's customers liked their drink strong. Still, needs must – if Maggie Brine were to talk. He drank, feeling the blood rush to his face. With heroic strength of character, he suppressed his urge to cough, confining himself to a wheezy splutter.

'Good, ain't it?' Maggie drank another. 'Well, I'll tell yer – that boy, 'e came wiv some bloods – yer know the type, flashin' their money, noisy, drunk as eels writhin' on a slab, but 'e, yer lad, if it is 'im – I 'eard the name, I think. Teasin' him they woz – 'e was wiv 'em and not, if yer gets me, on the edge of it all.'

'What about?'

'Dunno – abaht the girls, I think, cos 'e dint wanter go wiv Dolly over there.'

I don't blame him, thought Dickens as they looked at the girl Mrs Brine had pointed out. She had the build – and complexion – of a coal-heaver and looked as though she might have consumed Theo with the same relish with which she was drinking her gin. She winked at Dickens and licked her lips. He lowered his eyes modestly and turned away to see Mrs Brine looking at him mockingly.

'Too big fer yer, Mister Parson – good girl is Dolly – do yer good – yer look a bit bloodless ter me an' –'

To Dickens's relief the piano accordian started again and the singing resumed. Mrs Brine's words were lost.

Sam continued. 'Were they here last night?'

'Nah, sorry, Mr Jones, wish I could 'elp yer.'

Sam leaned towards her, knowing that she would not want his words overheard. 'So do I, Mrs Brine, but if you do hear anything, remember, there's a reward – you could slip down to Bow Street – discreetly – on your way to market.'

She understood. He knew she would not want to advertise her going to Bow Street, but the reward might tempt her.

'Temperance, forsooth,' he said to Dickens as they went out. 'Lucky for you – I nearly choked to death.'

'I know – I saw. You are a man of heroic proportions, Sam. Saved me from Doll Tearsheet there. I might have been eaten alive.'

Out in the alley, Scrap was waiting. He had news. He had heard talk about a boy called Nose – cos he hadn't got one – so the urchins said. The boy was missing, taken by the giant, some said, but there was no talk of his being seen with a toff – nothing at all. One night he was there and then he wasn't. Though, they all knew about the fire. One lad thought he'd seen Nose there, but then he was gone. Interesting, thought Sam, that there was no suggestion of his being befriended by a toff. Perhaps the death of Nose was, as they had thought, an angry reaction to his appearance. He was not what the murderer wanted – though, as yet, they did not really know what he wanted.

Zeb Scruggs and Occy Grave came to meet them at St Giles's. They had been at Rats' Castle where no one had anything to tell them though Zeb had met their old friend Weazen, looking, if anything, filthier than before. He had been ill, he had told them, sick with fever. Nevertheless, he had promised to keep a look-out and good-hearted Zeb had given him sixpence on account.

'Poor devil,' said Zeb. 'I have to feel sorry for him, though more than a minute or two in his company turns my stomach.'

They carried on, splitting into pairs, searching the alleys, the lanes, the little tomb-like courts, the whistling shops – illegal drinking dens, the common lodging houses, empty houses, and yards where men, women and children crouched like wild beasts under broken-down sheds and outhouses with rats for company. Scrap disappeared down cellar steps, found urchins to ask who were playing football with a ball of rags in a ginnel, talked to women sitting on front steps, asked the pieman whose stand was near the church, questioned the baked potato seller while warming himself by the little four-legged tin stove, resisted the temptation to buy one even though the smell sent his taste buds reeling, and caught up with Rogers and Feak in Dulcimer Street near the alley from where Rogers was coming, having looked again at the burnt-out house and squeezed his way out of Harry Sutch's shed.

Meanwhile, Dickens and Jones were making their way up a set of broken stairs in a tumbledown building situated in a miserable rain-flooded court. The sound of shouting and a woman's scream had caused them to turn into the alley that led to the court. They heard the sound of running feet. Whoever had screamed had gone. They were about to walk away when the sound of breaking glass stopped them. Something was hurled through a window and landed with a smash on the stones. A bottle. Sam raised his bull's-eye lantern. In the yellow light thrown up on the window they could see the figure of a man. He seemed to be pushing at the broken glass. A slight figure – young, perhaps. Then he was shouting.

'No, no, let me go. He's there, I see him. Let me go to him.' The voice of a gentleman. Theo Outfin?

Someone pulled him back. Someone smaller – possibly a woman. Dickens and Jones made for the door. But they had to go gingerly up the worm-eaten stairs, Dickens holding on to the rickety bannister, Sam shining his light downwards where they could see the holes in the treads. They could hear voices, muted now, the shouting over. A door crashed open. A sudden glimpse of light, but flickering and shadowy. A clattering of feet and then someone shot down the stairs, stumbling, almost falling. Sam seized Dickens by the arm and thrust him against the wall. In the light of his lamp, they saw briefly a white face, two black holes for eyes and a snarling, dog-like mouth. And the glint of a knife. They felt the figure's passing. The figure fell down the last few stairs, picked itself up, and vanished through the open door.

'Sorry,' whispered Sam. 'You all right?'

Dickens nodded, shaken by what he had seen and how close he had been to collision with whatever had passed them.

They stood still, listening to the darkness above. Someone had closed the door. There were voices again. Someone shouted. A man. The sound of madness, Dickens thought. Then a lower voice, trying to soothe.

Sam signalled to Dickens that they should go on. He shone his lamp upwards, so that they could see where they were going. A few more steps would take them up to the landing. They stood outside the door. It was quieter now, the voices barely heard. Sam turned the handle.

They found themselves in an opium den, filled with a kind of brown fog, where they looked upon two somnolent forms lying on their filthy cots, murmuring and chattering in whatever nightmares the drug had induced. They could feel the cold air coming through the broken window, but those on the beds seemed not to notice.

Under the window, on a bed, lay a young man. Sitting on the bed with his head in her lap was a young woman in a ragged shift which hung off her thin shoulders, exposing her breasts. Sam lowered the lamp, but she didn't seem to care, only looked at him with dull eyes.

The young man began to shout again. 'No, no, not yet, not yet!' The girl looked down at him, her black, matted hair covering her face, but she stroked his face with surprising tenderness as if he were a child in a bad dream.

What fear possessed him? Dickens wondered, gazing at the tortured face. The face was young, fine-featured and his clothes, though terribly rumpled, were those of a young man of means. What had brought him to this pass? But, and he felt a relief that made his knees weak, it was not Theo Outfin. Sam heard him breathe out and saw him shake his head. Not the man they wanted.

In the corner by a curious-looking screen, a Chinese man was blowing at a kind of pipe. They could see a pinpoint of red light which swelled as he blew then died down again. The slanting eyes looked at them and the pale, thin-lipped mouth grinned as he offered the pipe. Sam shook his head. No point in saying anything. They just looked at the occupants of the cots – only four, two Chinese, the Englishman and the girl. This was a small concern, not like the packed, sweating dens near the docks. And, thought Sam, he would have it closed down. The Chinaman could go back to Wapping with his customers, and one of his constables could escort the young man home – if he had not gone already. And the girl? They'd have to bring her to the station. She'd have no home, that was certain.

They went out, back down the stairs and heard the nine strokes of St Giles's clock telling them that the case was hopeless. They returned to the churchyard where Rogers and the others would meet them. Nothing – not a word, not a sign. Theo Outfin had vanished. Or not – they could not look everywhere. Their search had concentrated on the small area around the scene of the fire but he could easily have gone further afield. Why not? He might be asleep in a bed in a grand house belonging to one of his set. He might be asleep in some foul lodging in a hidden yard. They might have passed it. He might be dead.

It was time to call a halt. Sam would have some men look about tomorrow if Theo were still missing. Rogers and Feak went back to Bow Street, Zeb and Occy back to the shop, promising that if they heard anything they would let Sam know. Dickens and Jones would take Scrap back to Crown Street and then walk home. Dickens noticed Scrap gazing hungrily at the pieman. He nudged Sam.

'A pie apiece, I think,' said Sam, handing threepence to Scrap who darted to the pie stand.

'One thing,' said Dickens, 'Mrs Brine – she described Theo as on the edge of the group of toffs. Not belonging – it fits my impression of his loneliness. I wonder, you know, if he has reached the end of something. Could he have –?'

'Killed himself? God forbid. I hope not – I hope it would not mean that he is our killer.'

'Tomorrow, I will take Kip to Mrs Morson. At least we'll have done some good for one lost boy.'

'And I'll go to the Du Cane house to question Mattie Webb about that shawl and Theo Outfin.'

Scrap came back with the pies on which they blew to cool them down. Impatient, Scrap almost burnt his lip. Dickens lost his appetite suddenly. Scrap obliged him by eating a second.

'Waste not, want not, me ma used ter say.'

'Me ma,' thought Dickens. It was the only time Scrap had ever mentioned her. There was a pa somewhere but Scrap rarely went home. It was easy to think that Scrap had just materialised in the world, fully formed as the boy he was with all his smartness and good humour. Who was she, this woman whose precept Scrap remembered? The few words conjured for Dickens a sensible, thrifty woman, strict with her offspring, but something in Scrap's voice suggested that he remembered her fondly. Dead, he supposed. Pity – her son was a credit to her.

They left him at Mr Brim's shop and walked back up Crown Street, across Oxford Street, then up to Norfolk Street where Sam lived. Dickens walked on to Devonshire Terrace. The rain had stopped but the sky was still heavy with cloud. No stars tonight. No moon. How right Thomas Hood was about November: *no warmth, no cheerfulness, no healthful ease.* Just the dripping of rain on the bushes in the garden, and a pain in his side, the old disorder that had begun in childhood and flared up at times of exhaustion and overwork. But the lights were on upstairs in the drawing room and there would be a fire, dappling the room, and Catherine and her sister Georgy sewing in the golden lamplight. Home.

18

BRIDIE O'MALLEY'S TALE

'Mrs O'Malley, sir, says she wants to see you – got information – for your ears only.' Rogers grinned at the superintendent's raised eyebrows. 'Won't take no for an answer an' I didn't fancy tryin' to get rid of 'er – not in front of the lads, anyways. She's a bit too big fer me to 'andle.'

Bridie O'Malley was an old friend of Sam's. They had grown up together, as it were, having met when the superintendent was just a lad like Feak, and Bridie was a pretty, slender Irish girl whose mother had kept a respectable house where Sam had lodged. They had both risen in the world and Bridie now kept the lodging house – girls only, though men did visit – and Sam became a superintendent of the police. Bridie had more than a soft spot for the superintendent which was why he grinned back at Rogers. She would stay outside all day, immoveable as a mountain, until she got into Sam's office. And it was only nine o'clock. He had too much to do to be distracted by the knowledge of Bridie anchored in the corridor like a battleship. Battleaxe Bridie. He smiled. He would have to see what she wanted.

Bridie, when sober, was as good-hearted a woman as you could meet. When drunk, she could land a punch which would fell a man. Last time he had seen her at the station she had been brought in after she had almost done for a customer who had beaten up one of her girls. He had not pressed charges, preferring that his wife and family were left in the dark about his nocturnal visits to the purlieus of St Giles's.

In she came, enormous yet handsome, hair still improbably black, eyes sparkling green and dressed to kill with peacock feathers in her hat and a red dress – a bit garish for Sam's taste, but you had to admire her. She would go down fighting.

He stood, made her a bow – she loved his manners and it was not often you met a man as tall as he was, who could look down on you – well just.

'Bridie, as always, a pleasure to see you. Lovely hat, if I may say so.'

'You're looking grand yourself, Sam.'

Rogers sneaked a grin behind the broad back where the red satin strained. He did not need to make himself scarce. She only had eyes for the superintendent.

'Take a seat, Bridie, and tell me about this information you have.'

'Heard you lost a young man – they say you were searchin' last night round St Giles's near the burnt-out house. Sure, it was terrible it was – Mrs Moon an' that kiddie – funny little thing – not for this world, I thought, like a fairy –'

Just what Dickens had said. Bridie had poetry in her soul, too.

'This young man – name of Theo is it?'

Sam could not hide his astonishment. How on earth did she know? Bridie was gratified – it was good to surprise a man sometimes. Kept him on his toes – not but what she knew the superintendent was a happily married man. Lucky for some, she thought; whoever Mrs Jones was, she'd been blessed, to be sure. She'd been married herself once, and what a mistake that had been. Light-fingered Michael Rory O'Malley whose eyes of twinkling green had lured her away from common sense – she should have known. Michael, missing these twenty years. Dead, she supposed. Well, she had stopped hoping long ago.

'It is – do you know where he is?'

'I do – at my house – found him outside – been attacked – bleedin' from the head. In a shockin' state, Mr Jones – I sent for Mrs Feak, the nurse, you know her. Well, he's bandaged up now, but, she don't know – needs a doctor. When I heard you were lookin' I came straight here.'

'Was he coming to your house – to see one of the girls?'

'Yes, and no – in a way. It's a bit of a tale, Sam.'

At that moment Dickens came in to find out if there were any news. He was on his way to Mrs Moon's kind neighbour who was looking after Kip.

'Mrs O'Malley has found Theo Outfin – badly injured. Attacked, apparently. She was about to tell me what he was doing outside her house. This is Mr Dickens, Bridie.'

Dickens remembered Bridie who had offered Sam her company for the evening when they had come out of Bow Street station once. She was wearing yellow satin then, magnificently loud, revealing huge white shoulders. He remembered her mountainous progress through the jeering crowd. She could storm a town single-handed with a hearth broom, and carry it, he thought as he took off his hat with a flourish and bowed.

'An honour, Mrs O'Malley, your servant.'

Another gent, thought Bridie – a grand lookin' boy though not as well set up as Sam. Bit of a swell with his fancy waist-coat and brass buttons. And great eyes, to be sure, looking at her admiringly. She acknowledged him with a shake of her peacock feathers. Then her eyes widened.

'Mr Dickens, Sam? You mean, Mr Charles Dickens?' Sam nodded. 'Mr Dickens, the honour is mine. Well, I'll be blowed – I tell you, Mr Dickens, me and the girls we read all your numbers. Very fond of Sam Weller, I am – 'tis a shame there wasn't a young man about like that when I was in the market for a husband. Smart as paint, he is.'

'And on his behalf, Mrs O'Malley,' said Dickens in the manner of that smart young man, 'I'm wery grateful. An', I'm sure I hopes there's no harm in a young man takin' notice of a young 'ooman as is undeniably good-looking and well-conducted.' He bowed again.

'Get away with you, Mr Dickens – young indeed.' But she was pleased.

'Now, tell the tale, Bridie, before Mr Dickens declares his undying love – we ought to go as soon as we can.'

'One of my lodgers, Katie Fitzgerald – just a lodger, Sam – not, you know – she's a respectable girl – no family, but I knew them – he was a clerk in a bank but left nothing when he died. The mother followed soon after so Katie works as a seamstress in the theatre. Well, she met Theo Outfin. He came to visit her often. Look, Sam, I think you'll have to see for yourself. You'll understand when you do.'

The theatre, thought Dickens – a connection to the mask? They had not followed up that possibility. But Theo Outfin was involved with a young woman. And not Mattie Webb. Surely that was his trouble rather than murder. And yet he had been attacked. Had he been suspected by someone who knew the disfigured boy? Well, they would find out something soon enough. He saw that Sam was already in motion, detailing Rogers to find Oliver Wilde – he should try the apartment in Piccadilly. If not at home, Oliver would be at the Outfins, and if so, Rogers was to try to be discreet – to ask for Mr Wilde. They had to hope that the servant would fetch him without alerting the family. It would be better for the family if Oliver could get to know the story first.

Dickens and Jones walked with Bridie to her lodging house off Compton Street. It stood in a quiet court and there was an air of respectability about it. You might have thought it would be the residence of clerks, perhaps from the law courts or counting houses. The curtains were clean and the paintwork fresh. Bridie took them in and up the two flights of stairs where Katie Fitzgerald's room lay at the end of a corridor. Bridie knocked and the door was opened by Mrs Feak, the Sybil of Star Street. She recognised Sam and stood aside to let him in.

Theo Outfin lay on the narrow bed, his head bound with a bandage. His breathing was laboured. It was obvious that he was very ill. Seated at the side of the bed was a young, dark-haired girl who must be Katie Fitzgerald. She looked at them with fearful eyes. Looking at her, they understood what Bridie had meant. Katie Fitzgerald was pregnant, her belly swollen on a thin, girlish frame.

''E needs a doctor, Mr Jones. I can't do anything else for 'im – nasty 'ead wound, it is – a brick, I should think,' said Mrs Feak.

Bridie put in, 'She's right, Sam – I saw it last night – blood everywhere and I saw the brick. No money on him. Thief must have taken it.'

Katie Fitzgerald did not speak; her eyes were fixed on the figure on the bed, but there was no response when she touched him gently on the hand. Dickens looked at the pale face, the eyelids closed. He thought he understood the despair in Theo's face and the loneliness. What was he to do, a young man, well-connected with a father who had high hopes for his only son? And he had got himself into a mess from which there was no way of extricating himself. No wonder he had not confided in his sister or Oliver. He would have been terribly afraid and there was this girl who obviously loved him. She moved her left hand and he saw the ring there. He had married her and did not know what to do next. Not gambling but a wife to support. Well, he would be his own man when he was twenty-one and inherited his grandmother's money. But he could not be the murderer, surely. That would make no sense at all. Apart from sending for a doctor, what to do next? The truth, he thought. Mr and Mrs Outfin would have to know the truth and they must decide what to do.

Sam sent Mrs Feak for the doctor – she would know whom to call, and Theo must be taken to hospital; that was clear enough.

'Miss Fitzgerald.' He had seen the ring, too. 'You two are married?'

'Yes.'

'You know that Theo must be taken to hospital, and that his family must be told? You understand?'

She nodded. She looked weary and frightened. It was all too much. Dickens hoped that the Outfins would accept what was not to be mended. If Theo died, which he might, then they must, surely, take responsibility for this girl and her child. He thought of Mrs Outfin's good-natured face and Sophy's innocent one. They would not turn her away. Of Mr Outfin, he was not certain, but Mrs Outfin might be persuasive enough. They waited, listening to the sound of Theo Outfin's breathing. Katie Fitzgerald's eyes were fixed on him. At last, Mrs Feak returned with the doctor and Dickens and Jones went downstairs at the sound of an urgent knocking at the door which Dickens opened to find Rogers, Oliver Wilde and Mrs Outfin.

'Mrs Outfin insisted, Mr Dickens – I couldn't –' Oliver was flustered.

'Mr Dickens, I beg you, tell me, what has happened to Theo? How came he here?' Mrs Outfin came in, her face flushed with alarm. Dickens noted that Sam, discreet fellow, had vanished into the parlour with Bridie. Rogers had gone back to Bow Street.

'He was attacked here, robbed – the doctor is with him now.'

'What was he doing here? At this house? I must go up.'

What to tell her? She needed to be prepared for the sight of Katie Fitzgerald and the wedding ring. He could not just let it happen – the sight of Theo would be enough to distress her.

The doctor came down. He looked anxious. Mrs Outfin collected herself to speak to him, 'Doctor, I am the young man's mother. What are we to do?'

'He needs hospital care. I am going to arrange that now. There must be no delay – his condition is grave.'

'No, Doctor, he must be taken home – I will have a surgeon come to treat him there – Oliver, you must go home, inform Mr Outfin – a carriage must be brought and two of the servants. Tell Mr Outfin that Theo is badly hurt and that he must arrange for a surgeon to be at the house as soon as possible. Doctor, are you able to accompany Theo to our house?'

'I am – but, young man – you must hurry, please.'

Oliver left immediately and the doctor went back upstairs to his patient. Mrs Outfin made to follow. It had to be now. Dickens was impressed by her decisiveness.

'Mrs Outfin, before you go to see him, I must tell you –'

'What? What is the matter?' She saw his grave face.

'There is a young woman with Theo. She is his wife.'

'How can – I cannot believe it – he would not –' Then she stopped and he saw how she thought of the strangeness of her son during the last months, his distance from them, his seeming to have such cares, and her thought that he might be in bad company – and understanding dawned. 'So that is what was wrong. I thought – well, I do not know what his father will say – you are sure they are married?'

'The young woman says so – I have no reason to disbelieve her. What would a lie achieve?'

'What kind of a young woman is she? Living here? She cannot be –'

'Of your class? No, she is not, but she is a respectable girl. There is more, I am afraid.'

Mrs Outfin paled. This was bad enough. Surely Theo could not have been guilty of something other than this foolishness? She hardly dared think, remembering her husband's anger and fear of what his son might be involved in.

'Tell me.'

'The girl, Theo's wife –' he had to remind her – 'is expecting a child.'

Mrs Outfin put out her hand to grasp the bannister rail. She looked as if she had been struck. He waited for her to recover.

'O, God. What am I to tell his father? He will be –'

'I think you should go up to see Theo, Mrs Outfin. Get him home. His wife will be safe here until you can return to talk to her and find out more. She is very frightened and alone at the moment – she is afraid of what might happen to him, and, I imagine, very afraid of the future, and of Theo's family. She must know what you might think of such a marriage.'

He saw her think of the girl upstairs and he saw that she was, essentially, a woman of feeling who would be able to understand the plight of such a woman. He thought that she would accept what had happened, knowing that there was nothing to be done but to take practical steps to look after her son, his wife – and the child – however that might be accomplished.

'You are right, Mr Dickens. They are our responsibility. My husband will have to see that. I shall make sure he does.' She went upstairs.

Sam came out of Bridie's parlour. 'Sorry to leave you to it but I thought it might be better for her not to see me here – it might have complicated matters.'

'You were right. You heard, though.'

'I did – and I thought you did excellently. What you said about that poor girl was just the right thing to make her think. Bridie will take care of Katie until Mrs Outfin comes back. As she said, it is their responsibility and I think they will deal with it. Let us hope that Theo recovers. I can hardly believe he is our man after all this.'

'Nor I, thank goodness – the Outfins have enough to deal with as it is without our discovering that he is a murderer.'

Another knock at the door. Oliver Wilde came in with two of Mr Outfin's menservants.

'We need a stretcher, a board or something to carry him down,' said Sam. 'I'll ask Bridie. If one of you would come.' He went into the parlour and a few moments later, he and the servant appeared, carrying an old wooden door which would serve as a stretcher. The two men went upstairs with Oliver.

A few minutes later the doctor came down with Mrs Outfin and Oliver, then the two young men who carried Theo Outfin. They manoeuvred the board as carefully as they could. Dickens noticed that a pillow had been provided for his head and a blanket covered him. He had not woken up though he still breathed. At the top of the stairs Katie Fitzgerald stood in her dark gown, one hand on her swelling belly, and the other, with the glint of gold on it, held to her mouth. Her eyes seemed huge in her white face. Was she to lose him?

19

MATTIE WEBB'S SHAWL

Dickens and Jones watched the carriage turn the corner. Theo Outfin was safe, for the time being anyway. They could do no more for him nor for the frightened girl upstairs except to leave her with Bridie.

'I must go, Sam, and fetch Kip – he will be waiting and so will Mrs Morson at Shepherd's Bush. I will come back later.'

'And I must go to the Du Canes. If Theo Outfin did not take that shawl then someone else must have done – unless Mattie Webb simply lost it, which will leave us back where we started – in the dark.'

They went their separate ways, Dickens walking swiftly to Dulcimer Street where Kip waited for him. They would take a fly, the one-horse carriage, faster than a cab or the omnibus. Kip was waiting patiently at the little chandler's shop owned by Mrs Peplow, the neighbour who had looked after him. He had a little box – kind Mrs Peplow had taken away his scorched clothes. She had known that he should not smell the fire on them, that he should never wear them again to be reminded of that terrible night. God knows, she had thought,'e'd remember it well enough without the sickenin' reminder of flame and smoke every time he undressed. She had found him some good, if darned, clothes, some underclothes, a shirt, jacket and trousers, and a pair of stout boots someone had left for repair and never come back for. And she had put an extra shirt and trousers in the little box, along with some soap and a comb – she did not know exactly where Kip was to go, but she wanted him to have something. She didn't want him to look like a pauper.

Dickens opened the door to the neat shop, the cracked bell jangling as he entered, to see Kip waiting. He saw Kip looking forlorn, like a parcel no one wanted to claim. The boy looked up at him listlessly – poor lad, he thought, he has lost that spark which gave life to his eyes. He thought of Davey when he had found him in the streets – there was the same look of incomprehension in Kip's eyes. Nothing made sense. All that he had known and loved had been torn away in that sudden explosion of flame and sparks. But there was hope, even though Kip did not know it yet. Dickens thought of Davey who had been lost and found again – there would be no grandfather to come from the sea, but there would be Mrs Morson and James Bagster and Punch, the horse – and a donkey – and a garden, and by and by, Kip would be healed.

'Are you ready, Kip?' he asked. 'I am going to take you where you will be safe, near the country where there is a garden and fields, a horse and soon, a donkey to look after. Will you come with me?'

Mrs Peplow came out from the back of the shop with a bag of apples and some barley sugar.

'Goodbye, Kip – don't forget to come back and see us.' She knew he would not. Why should he ever want to see that burnt-out house again?

'Ta, Mrs Peplow – I won't forget yer. Thanks for the clothes and things.'

It was time to go. Dickens bade farewell to Mrs Peplow, promising that Kip would be cared for. She believed him, the well-dressed man who had unaccountably turned up to rescue the boy. Nice eyes – understandin', she thought. Somethin' special about 'im. Kip had said he was Mr Dickens. Well, she knew of *the* Mr Dickens, but it couldn't be 'im, course not, 'ow would Mrs Moon 'ave known that Mr Dickens? Lawyer, p'raps? Still, whoever, 'e was, it was good of 'im to find a place for Kip – she'd not 'ave left the boy on the streets, but better for 'im to be somewhere else, to try to forget what he had seen. 'E was a good boy – she had always thought so.

Kip, his box and Mr Dickens boarded the waiting fly which took them on to Oxford Street then to the Uxbridge Road and on to Shepherd's Bush. Kip looked with interest at the passing scenes, the traffic, the great white houses of Hyde Park Terrace and Connaught Place – he had never been out of St Giles's, out of the dark knots of alleys and brooding tenements that he had called home.

'Wot's in there?' he asked as the fly rolled past Kensington Gardens where he could see the mass of trees, black against the winter sky.

'It's called Kensington Gardens – a huge park, Kip, full of flowers and grass in the summer – you will go there some day, perhaps.'

'Ain't niver seen a park. Me and Tilly –' He stopped and Dickens saw the tears pooling in his eyes. What comfort could he give? None. Better for him to talk about her – not to be like poor mute Davey whose terrors might never be told.

'Tilly?' he said, gently.

'Miss 'er, and Ma, not Pa – 'e's better off. Sick, yer know. But why, Mr Dickens, why'd Tilly 'ave ter go?'

'I do not know, Kip, and that is the truth. None of us can know. It happens sometimes. We lose the people we love, and we have to go on without them – do the best we can.' He remembered Catherine's sister, Mary, who had died at seventeen and whose ring he still wore. The scar of her loss had never healed over – she had left a blank which could never be filled. But that was no help to the child seated next to him. 'You have to do the best you can, Kip. Think of your mother – she would want you to make the best of your life. All mothers want that. And, think, she and Tilly are safe now. Nothing can harm them again. They sleep well.'

'Nothing can 'arm them.' Kip repeated the words. 'They sleep well – are yer sure, Mr Dickens? Are yer sure?'

'I am. And I am sure that Tilly would want you to be as happy as you can.'

'I'll try, Mr Dickens.'

'It won't be easy, Kip – you will not forget them and you will be sad at times because you have lost them, but it will get better. I know it.'

They were silent then, Kip trying to understand Mr Dickens's words and Dickens thinking of the losses he himself had endured. Yet, he was still here, and life did bring good things – he was fortunate, indeed.

Kip remembered something. Somethin' fer Mr Dickens. 'Mr Dickens, Scrap asked me about a boy called Robin – did I know 'im – 'e sed you woz lookin' fer 'im or somesuch – can't hardly remember now. Important, Scrap sed.'

Dickens let it pass – no need to talk about murder just now. 'Did you know him?'

'Yer, 'e woz abaht, yer know – sed 'is ma woz poor so 'e did erran's an' that.'

'Who for – can you remember?' Probably just the stationer Sam had mentioned.

'Did some errands fer a French lady, 'e sed, she made 'ats – dunno where.'

But I do, thought Dickens, I do indeed. 'Did he say anything about her?'

'Dint like 'er, frightnin', 'e sed – dunno why – any 'elp ter yer?' Kip looked at him anxiously. He wanted to do something for him. Mr Dickens 'oo'd bin good to 'im. An' Tilly, too – he remembered the golden sovereign – could it 'ave burnt in the fire? 'E dint know – dint matter, anyways.

'A very great help, Kip, thank you.' Kip smiled properly for the first time that day.

They arrived at Lime Grove and the Home where Mrs Morson and James Bagster waited for the boy.

'Kip, is it?' said James Bagster, looking down at the boy who held on to his little box, looking round the kitchen with anxious eyes. Mrs Morson had made sure that the girls, as Dickens always called them, were not present. 'Would you like to meet the horse, Punch?'

Kip looked up to the man with the kind eyes. He felt the warm pressure of a firm hand on his shoulder. He looked at the lady who smiled at him and at Mr Dickens who nodded. It woz awright, he thought, and just a little of the ache for Tilly lessened.

Some people had it, thought Mrs Morson as she watched the tightness in the boy's eyes loosen – a kind of grace in them, a loving-kindness as natural as breathing. James Bagster had it. She remembered his goodness, his patience with poor, mute Davey and his quietness with Patience Brooke whose life had ended in a pool of blood on the steps out there. Still, no use remembering that now. And Charles had it – she saw how the boy trusted him, how he waited for Charles to tell him it would be all right.

'Yes, Kip, go and meet Punch – he will be glad of your company when Mr Bagster is busy. I will come back to see you. And remember what we talked about today. You will be brave, I know.'

Kip smiled and went out with James Bagster's hand on his shoulder. He would be safe.

'A good man, James – he will know what to say, how to comfort him.'

'And you, Charles, and you. What a story that was about the fire – how terrible to see that poor woman go into the flames.'

'I shall never forget it. Before my helpless sight – if only she had waited, known that Kip would live. But I did not know then. I knew why she had done it – there was nothing left.'

'She had no children to go on for – when my husband died in that desolate place in Brazil my only thought was to get my children to safety. If they had not needed me, I don't know that I might not have died there too.'

'Thank goodness you did not – who else would I have found to cope with Isabella Gordon and her cohorts?'

'But I could not in the end.'

'None of us could – no news of them, I suppose?'

'Not a word – I do wonder where they are now.'

'Together, I am certain. Sesina needed Isabella. Still, Jenny Ding has done well, and Lizzie Dagg – when you think what they were when they came. You have done well with them – and we cannot save them all.'

'Well, you have saved Kip and Davey. Captain Pierce writes that he is well though he does not speak yet – it is early days. I have hopes.'

'I, too. And now I must go.'

He told her that he could not stay longer – he must get back to London to see Sam. He would let her know when the inquest on the Moon family was to be held. Mrs Morson and James Bagster would accompany Kip, and the burial would be at Kensal Green where Dickens thought James, whose son-in-law was a gardener there, could take the boy. Dickens would pay for the funeral. She must let him know how Kip was and he would come as soon as he could.

'Meanwhile –'

'Yes, Charles, is there something else you wish me to do?' asked Mrs Morson.

'Get a donkey.'

'A donkey? Why on earth do I need a donkey?'

'Kip does – he had one – or knew one – I'm not sure which – as a child. Scrap seemed to think it important.' He smiled, ruefully, 'So I said there would be one – and one should never make promises one cannot keep.'

'Indeed, no – any particular kind? Colour?' She smiled back at him. It was so like him, busy as he was, to remember such a detail, something that might please this boy who had lost everything.

'Oh, I don't know – aren't they all the same? The ones I see seem all to be a kind of muddy brown.'

'Donkey brown, they call it.' They both laughed.

'Make sure it has a nice nature – you know what donkeys are, always objecting to go in any direction required of them. I knew a donkey once, by sight – we were not on speaking terms, but I thought he was – not to compromise the expression – a blackguard – taken in by the police, he was.'

'I am sure we can trust James to find a suitably decorous donkey – perhaps a country donkey will be less –'

'Inclined to criminality than a city fellow,' Dickens finished for her. They laughed together. 'Well, I must return to our investigations – a complicated case, this, but Kip told me something interesting, something I must tell Sam as soon as I can.'

He was back in Bow Street within the hour – Sam had returned from the Du Canes and was waiting to tell Dickens what he had found out about the shawl. Looking at his friend's face, he knew that there was news. Dickens told him first that Kip was safely stowed with James Bagster.

'But, there is more?'

'Yes, Kip remembered that Scrap had asked him about Robin Hart. Fortunately, he did not seem to know that he had been murdered. He seemed to think I was looking for him and I let him think that. But he told me that Robin had run errands for a French woman who made hats.'

'Did he now?'

'And, Robin did not like her – she frightened him, Kip said. I thought it was interesting.'

'It is – very – and you will find it more so when you hear what I found out at the Du Canes.'

'You saw Mattie Webb?'

'I did – she lost the shawl.'

'Not in the churchyard – that would be –'

'No, she lost it at the Du Canes – she was hurrying in late, she said, and it caught on a bush or something. She left it, intending to go back for it – she did not dare be any later but once she had reported to the housekeeper she knew she could retrieve it. However, when she went out again, it was gone.'

'So, we do not know who took it?'

'This is the interesting bit. I asked her if she recalled any visitors that day and she remembered because something unusual happened. Mademoiselle Victorine –' Dickens's eyes widened – 'was to deliver a hat for Mrs Du Cane. Yes, she is still the milliner for Mrs Du Cane.'

'She lied to us – well, at least she gave the impression that she had lost her wealthy clients.'

'She did. But, apparently, Mrs Du Cane kept her on because she liked the hats and was not put off by her manner; indeed Mattie feels that her mistress is such a great lady that she hardly notices Mademoiselle Victorine. Mrs Outfin was, it seems, of a more querulous disposition –'

'But you said "was to", the implication being that she did not arrive.' Sam waited while Dickens thought for a moment. He saw Dickens's face change – his expression showed the moment when he worked it out.

'Someone else came! Who?'

'Her brother.'

'But, she told us that he is dead! Another lie – then the shadowy figure that the neighbour believed was a possible lover does exist. But, why should she pretend that the young man was her brother. It makes no sense.'

'A footman took in the hat box – the young man told him that Mademoiselle Victorine was unwell and that he, her brother, had brought the hat because his sister had promised it that day.'

'Did you speak to the footman?'

'I did and I asked him if he could describe the young man. He was vague, as you can imagine. The encounter lasted no more than a minute or two – his impression was just of a youngish, slight man, rather nervous, he thought, anxious to be away. Could have been her brother.'

'If the brother were not dead,' observed Dickens gloomily.

'But, say he is not – say she lied because she knew – or suspected what he had done. She said he had died in Paris – perhaps that is where he is now.'

'Or, the lover – we need to know if the brother is dead – or even if she had a brother. She might be lying about that.'

'Then we must ask her – she must be made to tell us whom she sent to deliver that hat – we have to suppose that whoever he was, he took the shawl though what for I cannot imagine.'

'Perhaps he knew it was Victorine's work and wanted to return it to her.'

'Then, why was it in the churchyard?'

'Because she is his accomplice. It must be, Sam. Think about it – she befriends the children and he kills them. She lures them to him by some pretence – perhaps she sent Robin on an errand to give a message to someone at the churchyard or she took him there, promising some payment – I don't know, but she left Robin with him – the girls in the churchyard did not see anyone else with Robin. She left because she had done her part.'

'Motive?'

'Hers? She loved him – brother or lover – would do anything for him. And, remember what we thought about her – cold, indifferent, so closed up – but she has one loyalty, one obsession – him.'

'It doesn't matter for now – we can theorise all we like. It is more important that we question her. Now! I'll get Rogers. We will send him round the back of the house – the beat constables have been keeping an eye on the place but have not reported any man coming out. I didn't really believe in the young man – I was more concerned with Theo Outfin. Let us hope we are not too late.'

20

THE HOUSE OF QUIET

They hurried from Bow Street up to Short's Gardens then through Seven Dials to Crown Street where Dickens had followed Theo Outfin into the lanes where the Moons lived, and where they had lost him in the sudden surge of the crowds at the cry of 'fire'. He was glad that Theo was not now a serious suspect. Would he live? he wondered.

It was dark now and the streets were full, but he could not help scanning the faces, looking for that pinched countenance with the thick spectacles which had concealed, perhaps, the face of a woman who had been prepared to help a killer. He remembered what Rogers had said when they had first discussed the shawl – it could be a woman. He had reminded them of Mrs Manning – ''Ard as nails', Rogers had said.

And she was. Dickens had read all about the case of cold-blooded Maria Manning who had shot her lover, Patrick O'Connor, through the back of the head, having invited him to a meal. She had directed him to wash at the sink where a hole had been dug and quick lime bought in readiness to dispose of the body. When the shot did not kill Patrick O'Connor, Maria looked on while her husband Frederick had finished him off by battering his head with a crowbar – Maria had watched impassively. Then, according to some newspaper reports, she had sat down to dine on the goose which she had cooked for three. The body was in the hole by the sink. Greed and envy had been her motives – envy of

O'Connor's money – and she was caught trying to sell off some share certificates. The search for her and her husband had been relentless – an inspector and a sergeant had been sent to Paris, but in the end she was found in Edinburgh. Oh, indeed, a woman could be as ruthless as a man – more so in Maria Manning's case, perhaps.

They were at Rose Street, outside the house where no lamp burnt. They knew at once that she was not there. Rogers went round the back into the little alley to find the back door from which the neighbour had declared that she had seen a young man emerge. Perhaps she had, but he was not there now. A labouring man came by, his boots striking on the cobbles. He looked at the policeman curiously, but passed on without comment. Dickens and Jones came round from the front. They would go in. The yard door opened easily, but the back of the house was dark.

'Shall I force the door?' asked Rogers. The superintendent nodded. He did not expect to find her, but they had to be sure.

It was easy to wrench the door handle. They went in to a poky scullery where the only sound was a tap dripping into the white sink. It smelt of damp, a graveyard smell. A door led them into the room where they had first seen Mademoiselle Victorine. The hats were silent shapes in the darkness, but when Rogers turned on his lamp the feathers were stirring slightly, and Dickens was reminded again of birds perched, ready for flight. The table was neatly stacked with cloth, tailor's chalk and pins, and the scissors lay closed. There was an unfinished hat and a few artificial flowers which had been taken off it as though she was refashioning it. It was as if she had finished her work for the day. Dickens went over to look – had she left anything? There was a wooden box, its lid closed, a picture of the Eiffel Tower on it. What was inside? Papers? A letter? No, she would not leave anything like that. He opened it and saw something that made him take a quick breath.

'What is it?' Sam whispered, hearing that sudden sound of surprise.

Dickens held up something which caught the light. A hatpin, about four and a half inches long, glinting wickedly – a sharp point easy to slide into the vulnerable heart of a boy who had no idea that it would bring his death.

'Could this be what he used? It looks lethal enough.' He kept his voice low.

'It could – I don't know. We will have to ask the pathologist. We'll take it with us. Now, upstairs. Rogers, wait down here – just in case. She might come back, though I doubt it.'

They went into the hall and up the uncarpeted stairs, creeping as quietly as they could. There were two rooms, one with the door open. They went in to see a neatly made bed, a chair by it and a wash stand. No sign at all that anyone had used the room. Its emptiness was absolute. The door to the other room was closed. They listened. But there was no sound. The silence seemed to swell, filling the tiny landing. Dickens thought he could feel it wrapping round him like a shroud.

Sam stepped forward and grasped the door handle, turning it, suddenly impatient. She was not there. She was not, as Dickens had for a moment imagined, lying dead in her bed. The bed was identical to the other – a bed for one occupant, narrow, covered in a white counterpane with a single pillow at the head. Above the brass bedhead was a simple wooden crucifix. Had she prayed here? To whom? Not to God, surely – if she were what they thought, accomplice to a murderer.

They looked at the small chest of drawers with its small looking-glass on a stand. There was a hairbrush and a set of rosary beads hanging from the stand. And a few seashells collected in a little dish – odd, thought Dickens. Some kind of memento? The drawers revealed neatly folded underwear, stockings, a white blouse and handkerchiefs. There was a long cupboard. A grey dress hung there, moving slightly in the draught made when Sam opened the door. It was as if she were hanging there. Well, she might if they found her. That was the point. Where was she? Had she fled with her brother, her lover?

Sam looked under the bed. There was an empty travelling bag. Did that mean that she was coming back? Had she just gone out to buy her supper? Sam did not think so and Dickens agreed. The emptiness of the house had a finality about it. The silence inhabited it now; it had settled there, companion to the graveyard smell.

She had gone, they were sure, despite the clothes and the travelling bag. Where was she? And, in this teeming city, could they ever find her?

They went downstairs to the room where the hats were motionless now. They looked at the box and in the drawers of a press where she kept her materials for making the hats, flowers and ribbons, her thread and needles and her embroidery silks. The shawl? The one they had seen when they had first visited Mademoiselle Victorine. It was gone. Time to go. There was nothing here. One could imagine that she was dead, so still and empty the house was and so lacking in any personal effects – no pictures, no ornaments – nothing to say that a woman had made her home here. That was it, thought Dickens; she had existed here but not lived. Surely, there could be no lover. And the two single beds? Had the one in the first room been her brother's? But, again, he had had the impression that the room was unused – no trace of whoever had slept there – just that faint smell of damp.

They went out of the back door. Rogers was to stay and wait. Sam would send a man to repair the door so that no one could get in. They went round the front again and knocked at the neighbour's door to ask if she knew anything about Mademoiselle Victorine, where she might be. She did not, though her little knowing eyes were avid for information about her reclusive neighbour. They were about to walk away when Sam turned back to the woman standing on the doorstep.

'Mrs?'

'Twiss. Ada Twiss.'

'Do you know Mademoiselle's last name – her surname?'

'She did say when she first come – tryin' ter be pleasant, I suppose – dint take much notice so I don't know if I 'ave it right – it sounded strange ter me. Sholicker – some such – foreign, o' course,' she said, as though her neighbour had no right to such an unpronounceable name.

Well, she was French, thought Dickens, amused at her disapproval of all things foreign.

Sam asked, 'Did you ever see the young man again? The one you told the constable you'd seen coming from her yard?'

'No – pr'aps it was a customer though she didn't 'ave many o' those. Dunno 'oo 'e was. Yer lookin' fer 'im?'

'Not really - we were just interested to know if he had been seen again. But, as he has not, we will leave it. Thank you, Mrs Twiss. Good night.'

The two men walked away. She looked after them, puzzled – she wondered what they wanted with the French lady. But the tall man looked as if 'e wouldn't say any more and she wondered what the policeman was doin' in the alley. Tom 'ad seen him as he came 'ome. Still, foreigners – what could yer expect? Funny woman that Victorine whatshername – standoffish. But she 'ad seen that gent. She remembered now – Tom 'ad seen 'im again – night o' the fire down St Giles's – oh, well, too late now. Any'ow, they sed they wasn't interested. She went in to enjoy the fried fish and potatoes waiting on the hob. She want goin' to let 'er supper get cold – an' it would if she went chasin' arter 'em. Too bad. She closed the door.

Dickens and Jones walked down Crown Street. What now?

'The name?' asked Sam. 'Could you make anything of it? You speak French.'

'The "sh" sound ought to be a "J", the "ker" sound might be "Coeur" so I will hazard a guess at "Jolicoeur".'

Sam raised his eyebrows. 'Pretty heart? Never!'

'It is a French surname – I have heard it before – not very apt is it?'

'No, but it will have to do – why couldn't Mrs Twiss speak French? What's the matter with these people – if you have a French neighbour, you might at least pronounce her name correctly!' Sam laughed at himself and thought of sober-looking Mrs Twiss waltzing in Paris. 'She was more interested in her fried fish – smelt good, I thought. So, where is Mademoiselle Jolicoeur?'

They gazed around the crowded street. Where to look? She could be anywhere and there was no one to ask. That was the damnable thing, thought Sam. Suspects usually had convenient family, friends, work colleagues, acquaintances – someone who could lead them to him or her. There was a trail, most often. The murderer took shelter somewhere. Someone knew, had seen, could point the way. They would have found the giant eventually. But there was no one in this bustling place who could tell them where she was or where her brother was. Yes, a young man had been seen three times – four if you counted Mrs Twiss's sighting in the alley – once with Jemmy at Hungerford Market, once with Robin Hart in the graveyard and once at the Du Cane house but there was no trail. They had both vanished as if they had never been. Ghosts.

'Hidden from all human knowledge,' observed Dickens as though he had read Sam's thoughts.

'Yes, I was thinking how suspects usually have someone who knows them – someone who can point us to them but, in this case, nobody seems to know them – true, she had customers, true, the young man was seen but that is all. They had no friends, no family.'

'Did you notice the crucifix and the rosary?'

'I did – I thought what hypocrisy – if she is his accomplice, how can she be praying and telling her beads?'

'I wonder did she go to church – a Catholic church?'

'You mean someone might know her from there – know if there is a brother?'

'Yes – a priest, perhaps. I wonder if she has confessed – not that he would tell us, of course. It would, perhaps, be a Catholic church nearby – there is the Sardinia Chapel at Lincoln's Inn – we could try there.'

'Yes, she could walk there. Anywhere else?'

'There is a chapel in Warwick Street, Golden Square. I read about it when I was researching for *Barnaby Rudge* – it was attacked in the Gordon riots as was the Sardinia Chapel. I described how the vast mob poured into Lincoln's Inn Fields. It must have been a terrible sight – the crowd was making for Newgate. Fire everywhere. Yes, we could try there, too.'

They chose Lincoln's Inn and walked there from Crown Street to Castle Street, into Drury Lane and across to Parker Street where on the corner the crowds were pouring into the Mogul Saloon, a music hall. They pushed their way through the good-humoured throng, the flower sellers, the match girl, the man with his tray of jellied eels, and they caught the spicy smell of hot elder wine and the rich scent of gravy from the pieman who cried out, 'Pies, all 'ot, eel, beef, mutton – penny each, all 'ot.' They passed Whetstone Place where in the grimy alleys they had once found the body of a murdered man. It was quiet now in the precincts of Lincoln's Inn. The chapel was at the rear of number fifty-four, not far from Dickens's friend John Forster's home. But Dickens had never been into the church.

It was open though empty. Candlelight shivered in the dusk, showing them the marble dome from which a great silver lantern descended. By day, light would flood in to illuminate the marble columns and the great painting of the descent from the cross, but now there were shadows as moonlight like liquid mercury slipped in through the plain glass windows. It was a place redolent of ghosts and there was the faint, sweetish smell of incense that took him back to the churches of Italy, dream places, unreal, fantastic, solemn. Galleries rose up on either side, and underneath in deepest shadow were the confessional boxes. Had she come here? Had she whispered to a priest with a purple stole, the purple of repentance and healing? When Dickens thought about Jemmy and Robin and Mrs Hart and that poor disfigured boy, he could not imagine forgiveness for her or for her brother or whoever he was.

They stood silent, undecided, caught in the shadows, gazing up at the dark dome which seemed to be merged with the black sky outside. Footsteps. A priest came out of the shadows and looked at them enquiringly. Sam stepped forward.

'I am Superintendent Jones of Bow Street. I am looking for a woman named Mademoiselle Victorine Jolicoeur. She is missing from her home.' No need to mention murder, yet. 'I wondered, perhaps, if she is one of your congregation.'

'I do not know the name. It is unusual, I think. I know most of the people who worship here – I think I would know her.'

'She is thin, a very pale face – and she wears spectacles with thick lenses. I think you would remember her.'

'No, I do not know her. She may worship elsewhere – there is Our Lady of the Assumption in Golden Square. I am sorry I cannot help you. She is in some distress, you think?' His eyes were kind and concerned. Dickens thought it a pity she had not worshipped there.

'Possibly – we do not know. Thank you, anyway.'

The priest glided away on soundless feet, vanishing into the darkness near the altar. They turned away. They stood in the quiet shadow of the church; they could hear the city as if it were far away, not just round the corner waiting for them to enter its throbbing life and renew their search.

'So, we still don't know whether there is a brother.'

'Paris,' said Dickens. 'She said she came from Paris. I was thinking earlier about Mrs Manning and the search for her –'

'The police went to Paris, I remember – an inspector and a sergeant, but –'

'Jolicoeur – it is an unusual name – she said they had a shop.' Dickens was eager now. Sam saw his eyes light up. 'Let us suppose it was a milliner's shop – it must have been – or a dressmaker's – so we might find something about her and the brother, whether he is dead. She might have gone there – they might have fled – she knew we had the shawl. Perhaps she thought it was time to get out after the third murder. She thought we might come again; she told us about Mrs Outfin –'

'Yes, I can see that. Perhaps she thought that we would give up when we found out about Mrs Outfin's death, but she must have known that with the third murder we might come back. It does not matter what she thought, Charles. I agree that we might try to find out more about her – but Paris – I don't know –'

'I could go.'

Sam grinned. 'I expect you could – put a girdle round the earth in forty minutes.'

'Not quite, but it is possible – the night packet from Dover –'

'Tonight!'

'Well, tomorrow then – the eight o'clock express from London Bridge – eleven hours to Paris – a visit to the Police Prefecture with an introductory letter from Superintendent Jones of Bow Street which sets in motion the search for a milliner's shop called Jolicoeur – slap-up dinner at the Hotel Bristol – a steak, perhaps, a bottle of claret – or would you prefer roast fowl?' Sam opened his mouth to speak but Dickens rattled on. 'A splendid night's sleep on a feather mattress – with pillows – up with the lark – or the sparrow, the moineau, if you prefer – breakfast – hot rolls and coffee – collect the address from monsieur le gendarme – find the shop – hear the tale from some stout, lace-capped *madame* in black bombazine – *eh bien* – *voilà* – *nous revenons*!'

'If I am to come on this madcap voyage, why do you need a letter of introduction?' Sam's eyes twinkled.

'Poetic licence! Just keeping the story afloat.'

'I could write to the commissioner, you know, and ask the French police to find out about the family – we don't actually have to go.' Somehow Sam felt that this would not serve. Dickens was already there in his fancy, coaxing his imaginary madame to reveal all, in his fluent French.

'But, how long will it take? And, if the brother is there, will they take him into custody? Would it not be more – immediate – if we were there to explain all the details of the investigation, the grounds for suspicion? In short, Sam, let us stiffen our sinews, summon up the blood, the game's afoot – to Paris let us go!'

'It's a gamble – suppose –'

'Them as don't play can't win, Sam.'

The light in his eyes told Dickens that Sam was tempted. He would do it.

'I am persuaded – as much by your eloquence as by the grain of common sense in your argument – and, not least by that steak and claret you promise me. Tomorrow at half past seven, then, at London Bridge for the eight o'clock express. Now, I must return to Bow Street and give my instructions to Rogers who must remain on watch. He can send someone to enquire at the church in Warwick Street and he can make sure a watch is kept at Rose Street. I am not sure why, but I don't think she'll go back there.'

'Nor do I – something of the grave about the place. She has gone – to Paris, I bet.' He grinned again, sure that they would find the answer in Paris.

They parted at Drury Lane. Dickens felt buoyed up – it would be an adventure. He knew Paris, Citoyen de Paris, he had styled himself. Mind, he thought, perhaps the Hotel Bristol was a little too public. He and Sam should stay somewhere quieter; they needed to be secret, not to have Charles Dickens's readers swarming over them. They should be secret agents, sneaking in to the Prefecture, watching the milliner's shop like his detective Nadgett watching Jonas Chuzzlewit, the murderer. He thought about Sam. Though Sam had laughed about the madcap journey Dickens had seen the lines deepened on his forehead, expressive of the anxiety he felt that they might be wrong, that while they were absent, the murderer might strike again. He thought about the hatpin – was it really the murder weapon? If so, then it had been left behind. Surely that would mean that the killer had gone. For Sam's sake he hoped so.

He was right. Sam walked back to Bow Street. He had been carried away by Charles's enthusiasm, swept along by the vividness of the tale of the woman in black bombazine and lace. Now he wondered. Was it folly? Yet what else could they do? They had to know about the brother, if he were dead or not, and when he had died if it were so. And, perhaps they would find out more about the mysterious Mademoiselle Victorine. Rogers could be trusted to hold the fort. If, God forbid, there were another murder, he would know what to do – and they would be back as soon as possible. Well, Paris it would be.

21

MADAME RIGAUD

Dickens, always impatient to get on, always arriving early for coach or train, saw that Sam was before him on the platform at London Bridge Terminus. He was examining the carriages and passengers boarding – no doubt wondering if their quarry were bent on flight. Dickens watched him and wondered whether he had changed his mind, but he saw that Sam was carrying a travelling bag – he was coming, then. His heart lifted. Of course, he would have gone alone. Having conceived the idea that Paris would provide some answers, he could not bear to relinquish the idea. Delay to him was worse than drawn daggers, but to go without Sam would have lessened the thrill – the excitement of the chase. The case had been so slow, so uncertain that he needed to be in motion, to be doing. He had his own travelling bag wherein were packed two thick blankets and brandy – Dickens, the seasoned traveller, knew how cold it could be.

Sam's bag had been packed by Elizabeth who had reassured him that the madcap journey he had described to her was not folly. She had listened to his fears and had reached the conclusion that Dickens had, though not in the same wild flight of words. He felt better – and Rogers, solid and dependable, had promised to keep a twenty-four-hour watch on the house in Rose Street and to send Feak to the church in Golden Square. If they found any information then Rogers was to pursue it. Sam had also apprised Inspector Grove of his intentions and that equally dependable officer had assured him of his vigilance. The fears of the night before had receded, though he would not be wholly happy until he was back – perhaps with the murderer in handcuffs.

He saw Dickens approaching, looking at him anxiously. 'I was worried that you might change your mind. I saw how concerned you were last night. I wondered if you might think it too reckless a scheme.'

'You were right. I did have doubts but Rogers – and Elizabeth, of course – assured me that I should follow your lead. Rogers said, "You can trust, Mr Dickens, sir, 'e's got a nose for these things – could 'ave bin a detective." Praise, indeed. And here I am.'

'I am obliged to Mr Rogers, indeed I am.'

'I have told him that we intend to return tomorrow night.'

'You are sure?' asked Dickens, still anxious.

'I am – well, as sure as we can be in this case full of uncertainties.'

'No sign of them, I suppose.'

'I have watched as many as I could – I don't think Mademoiselle Victorine is here though I can't swear that our young man is not – short of apprehending every slim young man, I do not think I could do more than simply observe.'

They waited for as long as they could, scrutinising the passengers. They were as certain as they could be that Mademoiselle Victorine was not there. There were plenty of young men – it was impossible to say whether any one of them was the man they wanted. The descriptions were so vague.

The guard blew his whistle. Clouds of steam came from the gasping engine; there was a heaving, grinding and snorting as of a dragon stirring. A young man dashed to a carriage further down the train. They should be boarding but they watched. The young man's hat blew off and, as he bent down to pick it up, they saw his laughing face. He flourished the hat at someone waiting by the carriage door and leapt on. Not him. Not the face of a murderer. The whistle shrieked again. The dragon emitted another burst of steam. It was ready to move.

'First-cladge tickets,' said Dickens in the manner of Mrs Gamp. 'Sammy, why not go to Paris for a day, bring your constitootion up. Your mind is too strong for you and 'ere you are drove about like a brute animal – let us aboard this ingein.'

Sam laughed and allowed himself to be bustled aboard into a carriage occupied already by two other passengers, a man and a woman. The first-class carriage was comfortably furnished with cushioned seats and tables between. They had hardly sat down when the door was flung open and in came another passenger, a stout red-faced man with an infinity of luggage, no end of cloaks, plaids and pilot coats, and a brass-bound dressing case – enough for a trip to the North Pole. Dickens wondered if he had come aboard the wrong train. Perhaps an explorer who had lost his way. The man sank into the seat opposite and wiped his perspiring brow. He eyed them suspiciously, daring them to laugh at the pile of coats which had slipped to the floor. Dickens leant down to assist in the gathering up of the coats. The portly man nodded his thanks and took refuge in the furthest corner of the carriage where he wrapped himself up so tightly that he resembled nothing more than a very large baby in woollen swaddling clothes.

The two other passengers were now concealed behind their newspapers. Dickens settled back into his seat. 'Let's talk of graves, of worms, of epitaphs …' he murmured.

'Let us not for goodness' sake. I have Sam Weller in my pocket – I need cheering up.'

'It is worritted you are, Samivel, don't denige it – thank Evans I 'ave a nice bottle of stout in that there bag.'

Sam chuckled. Dickens's mouth had suddenly collapsed, and there was Mrs Gamp again, almost in the flesh, but he kept a straight face, 'Mrs Gamp is in the second-class carriage, I believe.'

'So she is. *Punch* for me, then.'

Behind the protective cover of his magazine, Dickens was able surreptitiously to observe their fellow travellers. Sam, looking up from *Pickwick Papers*, knew exactly what he was doing. The red-faced man wore an expression of comical irritation. He had not quite heard what they had said but he was sure it was not polite – who the devil was that man whose face seemed to be contorted into the most grotesque expressions? Vulgar brute. Thank goodness he was now reading his magazine. *Punch*, forsooth, full of silly jokes and impertinent sallies against respectable people.

The two other passengers at the far end of the carriage on the opposite side were as still as waxwork figures; the man held a newspaper in front of his face. What was he hiding? The woman had a large dark purple hat with a veil in front. Dickens looked. Yes, she was breathing. He could see the way the veil was sucked in slightly and swelled out again as she exhaled. Not a corpse then. He could not make out the features behind the grey veil, but he could tell she was too large to be Mademoiselle Victorine. Not that he had expected her to be found in a first-class compartment, but you never knew.

By a quarter after ten o'clock they were at Folkestone where they had twenty minutes' wait. The man with the red face, now more puce, unwrapped himself, suddenly alarmed that he might be left behind. He made what haste he could, encumbered as he was with his coats and his case. Dickens and Jones sat still, Sam imperturbably reading about Mr Pickwick's meeting with Sam Weller's father and his tribulations with the uncommon pleasant 'wider' whose change to a wife brought about a decidedly unpleasant transformation of her character. Dickens was reading his copy of *Punch* magazine, grinning to see a reference to Mr Dickens's friend Micawber in a satirical piece about debt. Puce glared at them. Idle rogues. Always laughing – no work to do, he supposed. What business had they to get in his way? Did they not know that the steamer was about to depart for Paris?

A genial station guard called out, 'Refreshments in the waiting room, ladies and gentlemen. No hurry, ladies and gentlemen, for Paris. No hurry whatever.'

The red-faced man's face turned puce again, a kind of mottled purple, as he struggled with the door handle. Perhaps he was deaf, thought Dickens. He did not dare grin – the man might have a seizure. The door opened and out went Puce with a deal of huffing and puffing. The waxworks followed with considerably more decorum, holding the silence they had kept for the last two hours or so. Dickens and Jones collected their bags and descended.

This was a chance to watch again – to make sure that she was not among the crowds that bore down on the refreshment room to eat their sausages, pork pies, jam tarts or cake. Dickens went into the buffet while Sam observed on the platform. Dickens chose a cup of tea and a jam tart, avoiding the cake which he knew always turned to sand in the mouth. The jam did taste like jam though it might have been raspberry-flavoured glue, and the pastry had that familiar cardboardish texture. Still, the tea was hot. He watched as he drank. The Frenchwomen seemed uncommonly elegant in their little hats and close-fitting travelling costumes or they were short and round, peering at the English refreshments suspiciously with little, shrewd black eyes. None resembled Mademoiselle Victorine, creeping like a snail. He recognised the cheerful young man who had almost lost his hat. He was part of a noisy group, off to taste the delights of Paris no doubt. He hoped they would enjoy themselves. Puce looked at them all disapprovingly while he chewed determinedly on a piece of cardboard. He had paid for it and he would damn well eat it. Dickens noticed the smear of jam on his cheek.

Dickens went out to swap places with Sam who went for his cup of tea. 'Avoid the jam tarts,' he said, 'and the cake, and the sandwiches – a sausage roll, perhaps, though I shouldn't think there's a sausage in it.' He pulled up his scarf, lowered his hat and put a pair of spectacles on his nose – the ones he had forgotten to give back to Zeb Scruggs. He watched the people coming and going but there was no sign of those they sought.

Sam came out and, seeing Dickens, wondered if he could see anything at all so muffled up was he. He caught the glint of spectacle lenses – he hoped Dickens could see through them. Dickens the actor, he thought. He could play any part you wanted. Comical, tragical, pastoral, historical.

Then it was down the pier and on to the waiting steamer for the two-hour crossing to Boulogne. The sea was calm and they stood on deck watching as England faded into the milky distance.

Another train took them to Paris through a landscape of fields, windmills, fortifications, canals, a river, a cathedral. They changed at Longeau then stopped at the little station of Creil for ten minutes. Dickens could not resist stepping out on to the deserted platform. No one got off the train. A priest in a long black robe got on. The station cat yawned. On they went.

It was barely eight o'clock, snowing in Paris and bitterly cold. They were in a hackney carriage rattling over the pavements of Paris. Sam's eyes were everywhere, looking at the crowds in the streets and the brightly lit shops and cafes, taking in the shimmering lamps, the trees, the theatres, the houses, all the brilliant life of the city aglow under the shining snow. He forgot for a moment why they were there, but soon they came to a halt outside the Prefecture where he must go in and state their business. Dickens stayed in the cab – no time for them to be distracted by recognition of the famous author. Sam glanced back to see him swathed in his scarf, peering through the spectacles into the snow.

After about twenty minutes Sam came out – his courteous opposite number of the Paris police force would find out if there were a milliner's or dressmaker's by the name of Jolicoeur – it was, he agreed, an unusual name. It should not be too difficult. If there were no shop, he would find out the families who bore that name, and if Monsieur Le Superintendent had not enough time then, he, Monsieur Le Prefect, would institute a search of all Paris if necessary. The murderer must be caught and his accomplice, even though she was a woman, must be brought to justice.

'Most obliging our French detective, Monsieur Dupin. If we cannot – what?'

'And this shall be a sign,' said Dickens.

'What sign?' Sam was baffled.

'Monsieur Dupin is or was, I should say, a detective – a private one, granted, but one who solved his cases. In Poe's book *The Murders in the Rue Morgue* … I met him –'

'Who?' Sam lost track.

'Poe – in America. Odd man. Died last month. Strangely, he was wearing someone else's clothes – a mystery. It sounded like something from one of his own tales. Still, I cannot help thinking that if we have your Monsieur Dupin on our side then we will not fail. So, let us screw our courage to the sticking point. A drum, a drum.'

The Hotel Bonjour was small and a little shabby. No matter, the food was good. Sam had his steak and potatoes as did Dickens, along with a bottle of good French wine and some creamy brie cheese. They talked of tomorrow, hoping that Monsieur Dupin would find the Jolicoeur shop; and of what they would do if Victorine were there. With Monsieur Dupin's support they would question her at the Prefecture and take her back to London. She was the key. She had to be. And if her brother were there then he must come too. The superintendent would arrest him on suspicion of murder.

The word sobered them again. Paris was lovely under the snow. The fire was warm and the food comforting and filling, yet always there was that dark thread of memory like a trail of blood. They thought of the dead boys.

'I hope he is here,' said Sam. 'Then I can stop thinking that he will do it again while I am not there.'

'I have thought about that; I do not honestly believe that she or he will go back to that house. We felt it, did we not? – its emptiness, the sense that it was abandoned. It almost seemed as if it had been deserted long before we got there. And there is the hat pin – surely that is the weapon.'

'It may well be,' said the practical Sam, 'but she will have had more than one hat pin. We cannot guarantee it.'

'And there is the third boy. No mask as far as you could tell – perhaps there was not one, perhaps that murder was different. It must have been a shock to see that poor, maimed face – suppose that murder was committed in a different spirit altogether, a moment of revulsion and horror.'

'You are trying to say that it may have stopped him in his tracks, that in a way it was a mistake, whereas the other murders were deliberate, the desire to end those lives – hatred, as you said before – hatred of their beauty.'

'That is it entirely. I do not believe he will do it again. They have gone.'

'To Paris?' Sam smiled. He knew how determined Dickens could be.

'I hope that they are here or that we find out something significant. And so to bed?'

Dickens felt suddenly exhausted after the bustle and rattle of the train, the heave and swell of the sea and the dashing about in the cab. Sam looked weary too. They should sleep now. Sam would go to the Prefecture early and come back for Dickens.

Dickens fell asleep almost at once. He felt the motion of the train lulling him into a dream. Theo Outfin was in the carriage with him, dressed as a woman – he looked like his sister, but Dickens could not understand why he should be wearing an obviously false moustache. Theo – for it was he – was holding up a large hatpin. It might have been meant for a giant. He leant forward as if to confide in Dickens who saw then that his face was horribly disfigured. In the dream, Theo pointed the hatpin at him. It came dangerously close, and Theo was laughing with a mouth that was a hole. The train entered a tunnel. There was no escape. Dickens tried the door of the carriage but it was locked. The darkness was suffocating; the train travelled faster and faster. Dickens rattled the door. He was frantic to escape. He was falling into the dark hole. Then they were out of the tunnel. Theo turned into the veiled woman from the train. Her face loomed over his, and when she lifted the veil it was made of cobwebs, and the face was Victorine's whose lenses were opaque so that he could not see her eyes, but the lenses grew larger and larger until there was nothing of her but great white eyes. The train shrieked like something demented.

He woke sweating and conscious of a pain in his chest. Indigestion, he thought. Damn that cheese or was it the jam tart? The prosaic thought steadied him. God, he had felt terror then. Horrible. All the clocks in Paris seemed to be striking. Three o'clock. He lit the candle by his bed and walked over to the window sheathed in thick heavy lace that smelt of dust and cigar smoke.

He looked out on to a white world silent under the glittering moon with its corona of ghostly green. '*Queen of shadows, risen to blanch the world in its white sheen.*' He whispered the words of Lamartine, the French poet whom he had met and liked. *Solitude*, the poem was called – how apt. The snow muffled every sound. It was as though he were alone in the city. He looked down and saw in the street a set of footprints, a woman's. He thought of Victorine's closed face. Solitude. Was she alone now in this soundless city, a shadow in the shadows?

The room was chill and he felt the twinge of indigestion. Lamartine was a vegetarian – he thought ruefully of that steak. Perhaps there was something in it – vegetarianism. Though Lamartine had looked a bit bloodless. Oh, well, too late now. He looked at the footprints again, and thought of some lonely woman with a pockmarked face and a torn dress, haunting the street like a gaunt cat. He shivered, watching the snowflakes hover and whirl in the still air. They came faster and soon the footprints were covered over. Whoever she was, she had gone now. He went back to bed.

They breakfasted early on the hot rolls and coffee which Dickens had promised, then Sam went out into the white street to find a cab. Dickens poured himself another cup. He was thinking of Poe's Dupin and his detecting methods. To observe attentively was the key. The analyst, as Poe called him, makes a host of observations and inferences from which he draws his conclusions. Poe had used the analogy of the whist player who observes every external thing from his opponents' glances at each other, at the cards in their hands, even to their method of holding their cards. By the end, he knows every throw of every card and can play his own with as much confidence as if he had seen his opponents' cards face up. Now, thought Dickens, I have read and observed. Theo Outfin's face for example was not the face of a murderer. Victorine's face, he had thought first – and the first impression was important – was closed, cold, secret. He had been right, she had a secret. He and Sam had observed that silent house, and he felt that this was where Dupin's method failed them. The bed – it did not look as if anyone had ever slept in it. And yet, the brother. If it were a story then they would have found a convenient tuft of hair just as Dupin had in Poe's *Murders in the Rue Morgue* – behold the orang-u-tan! He laughed – what a mad tale. Too improbable.

And he was puzzled by something else – something that did not fit, something he was trying to remember that he had noticed at the beginning, but whatever it was seemed irretrievable. He did not know into which pigeon-hole of his mind he had put it. He had an idea that it was connected with his dream of the night before, but all he had now was a confused impression of the train, Theo Outfin and Victorine merging into one and a terror of her huge, opaque lenses. The memory was like a shadow glimpsed out of the corner of the eye, but gone when one turned one's gaze. Damn.

Sam came back with a paper in his hand. An address?

'Success?'

'Yes, indeed. Monsieur Dupin consulted the department which keeps records of businesses, markets, shops etcetera and there is a shop – a few streets way from here, in fact – a milliner's which was owned by a Madame Jolicoeur, now taken over by Madame Manette. We will try there – someone might know about the Jolicoeur family. Monsieur Dupin has kindly provided a map, and he has provided a Sergeant de Ville to smooth our way.'

They collected their travelling bags from the room and paid the bill. They did not want to return to the hotel. If they could not find Victorine or her brother then they must return to London on the earliest possible train.

They went out to where the Sergeant de Ville waited. The snow had stopped falling but the streets were still white. There was a sense of unreality about the glittering scene; a hush everywhere as if the city were in a trance. A few passers-by walked carefully in the snow. Dickens noticed a beautiful woman with fur framing her face. She had a little dog on a lead; it was wearing a pretty little coat and looked at him as if to say, 'I know I'm a victim of fashion.' He grinned at it. Sheepish, he thought recalling a snippet from *Punch* lampooning canine fashions from Paris, especially the sight of dogs with sleeves *en gigot* – he always enjoyed puns however lame.

In a narrow, elegant street they found the tiny shop, very smart, the window bearing the legend in italic golden letters: *Les Plumes de Ma Tante.* In the window was one well-cut black and white striped dress and on a stand a neat black velvet hat bearing one emerald green feather. But what drew their attention was the black and green embroidered shawl draped over the shoulders of the papier-mâché mannequin. Victorine's work? On the snowy step outside sat a thin black cat waiting to go in. It was early but the sign on the door said 'Ouverte'. A tinny little bell rang as they entered preceded by the cat.

A young woman turned at their entrance, though for a moment she focused her attention on the cat.

'*Frou,*' she said. '*Tu viens – tu es restée hors toute la nuite – la creature sotte.*' The cat shook itself. She opened a little door in the counter through which Frou passed, just glancing back at them disdainfully. Not French. The young woman looked at them.

The sergeant explained that the gentlemen were from London – *Monsieur*, he indicated Sam, was a policeman in search of Mademoiselle Victorine Jolicoeur who was missing from her home. Could Madame tell them anything about her or Madame Jolicoeur who had once owned the shop?

Madame Manette looked troubled. She told them that Madame Jolicoeur was dead and her mother, Madame Rigaud, Madame Jolicoeur's sister, had taken over the shop. The name of the shop was a memory of Aunt Cecile.

Dickens asked in French if she could tell them anything about Mademoiselle Victorine. Madame Manette frowned.

She looked troubled again, saying that she thought they should speak to her mother who was here – she would tell them about Victorine. The sergeant stayed behind as they went through the little door and into the workroom at the back where there were hats in various stages of composition and some finished on their stands. They were reminded of Victorine's room. There was a similar deal table with scissors, tailor's chalk, cloth, feathers, lace and felt – as well as hatpins. The atmosphere was very different – it was alive – the cat on a wicker chair by the fire and a canary singing in its cage. A girl was seated at the table, needle and thread in hand. Madame Rigaud was exactly as Dickens had described, stout in her black bombazine and her lace.

Madame Manette explained to her mother about the gentlemen from London and their enquiries concerning Victorine. Dickens could not quite tell what she said – she spoke low and quickly, but he saw Madame Rigaud's frown at the mention of Victorine and her swift look at them. She was irritated, Dickens thought, rather than concerned. The young girl was sent to mind the shop.

Madame Rigaud spoke English sufficiently well for the conversation to be carried on in English. She told them that Victorine was her niece whose mother had died over five years ago. They learned that as far as she knew Victorine had gone to America. They had not heard from her for two years or more. They thought that she might get in touch when she was settled in America. Madame Rigaud's tone was brisk as if she wanted to tell the story and be done with it. No love lost there, thought Dickens.

'But she is missing from London,' Sam interrupted. Surely they had not found another Victorine Jolicoeur?

'She went to England at first – years ago.'

'And her brother?' asked Dickens.

Madame Rigaud looked baffled. 'You mean *son frère*?'

'*Oui, Madame* – her brother.'

'There was no brother. Victorine was an only child like Lucie here, my daughter.'

'Oh, we must have misunderstood. I am sorry, Madame, perhaps you could tell us why she went to England.'

Madame looked as if she did not wish to revisit the past. She looked at Dickens and Sam, and saw that the policeman from London would not be satisfied until she had told what she knew.

'Victorine had a child – a boy. This was more than ten years ago. November, the snow, it was thick as now – a difficult birth.' She stopped, frowning, her lips pursed as if the memory were an unpleasant taste in her mouth. They waited. 'The father – Michel – was already married. He went to England to escape his wife and we thought he would not come back. But when the boy was two he sent for them. He was in Brighton. They opened a shop – a hat shop. My sister gave them money – it was only right since Lucie was to have the Paris shop. But then her boy died when he was nine. She wrote to us –' she paused, searching for the words – 'that he – *il s'etait noyé* – you understand?'

Dickens nodded, 'He drowned.' He thought about the seashells they had seen and he pitied her. Perhaps he was wrong, perhaps she could not stop Michel, perhaps she was not his willing accomplice, but Michel was all she had left.

'Yes, but she did not say what had happened, only that she and Michel were going to America. *C'est tout* – we know nothing more.' Her tone was final and there was the unexpressed thought that Victorine's whereabouts were not her concern.

'What is the last name of the child's father?'

'Blandois.'

'Did she take his name? Were they married?'

'I do not know, monsieur. We did not ask.'

The atmosphere stiffened somehow. Madame wanted them to go and in truth there was nothing else to say. They could only apologise for disturbing them and assure them that perhaps a mistake had been made. Madame Rigaud did not look convinced, but Dickens had the impression that Victorine had passed out of their lives, and that she did not wish to know any more about her. That phrase '*C'est tout*' had meant more than just that it was all for now – it meant that was all she had to say. He had a feeling that when they heard about Victorine – he was sure they would – Madame would not want to be involved. They had not seen her for ten years or more. They did not want her back.

Dickens had a thought. 'The shawl in the window, Madame, who made it?'

'My daughter. Lucie is very skilled, the best embroiderer I have known.' She smiled and there was a little look of triumph in her shrewd eyes. Victorine was not as skilled as her daughter. No, Victorine was to be forgotten. Again, Dickens felt that twinge of pity.

The Sergeant de Ville understood that they wished to return to London as soon as possible. The superintendent presented his compliments to Monsieur Dupin for his assistance and they were left in the snowy street.

'Brighton?' asked Dickens.

'I imagine so – tomorrow first thing. For now, a cab to the station. Oh, that we had wings.'

'It is only ten o'clock now – we ought to catch the eleven o'clock train. We shall be in London tonight.'

'The Brighton express first thing tomorrow morning.'

22

A FACE IN A CROWD

They were in London by ten o'clock. Rogers had sent Feak to meet them, surmising that they could at best be on the eleven o'clock train from Paris – Feak's instructions were to wait until the last train came. And when he saw the superintendent he was to tell him straight off that there had been no developments. Rogers had seen quite clearly that the idea of another murder haunted his boss. He needed to know as soon as possible.

They saw Feak, whose words tumbled out before they had a chance to say anything.

'Mr Rogers, sir, says to tell you that nothin's 'appened – about the case, I mean. 'E said you'd wanter know immediately, sir.'

'Thank you Feak, I am obliged to you both.'

'Shall I get a cab, sir?'

'Yes, thank you. We will come with you.'

'Are you going to Bow Street?' asked Dickens as the cab drew up.

'Yes, I need to see Rogers about tomorrow. He will want to know what we have discovered and what we think about it. Will you go home?'

'Yes, I ought to. You can drop me at Broad Street. I'll get another cab from there.'

'Tomorrow?'

'Same scene, several hours later! I will meet you at half past seven at London Bridge Station once more – the Brighton Line.'

Dickens got out at Broad Street. As was his way, he decided to walk to Oxford Street at least – to stretch his legs and to think about what Sam would be telling Rogers. On the boat, they had sat in the most sheltered spot they could find on the deck where they could speak in private about what they had heard. It was clear that Victorine and Michel had not gone to America. And the reason that Victorine had not communicated with her aunt was obvious, too. However impossible it seemed, Victorine had a lover. They thought about Dickens's idea that she had only Michel left – though why no trace of him had been found at the house was difficult to fathom. Dickens wondered if they had parted at the death of the child and that he had, for some reason, contacted her. Perhaps she had rejected him, and that had pushed him to murder – revenge for the death of his own boy. But she must have known because she had gone. Had she gone with Michel or had she fled from him?

'The shawl?' Sam had asked.

'He could easily have had it.'

'But, surely, his appearance at the Du Canes suggests that they are in it together.'

'True,' Dickens had been forced to agree. 'You are right – but it seems incredible that she who had lost her own child should countenance the murder of children.'

'You said yourself that you saw her as capable of obsession – that she might do anything for her lover.'

'So I did.'

Dickens began again. 'Why did Michel say he was her brother when he went to the Du Canes – it seems an unnecessary lie, and why did she tell us about a brother?'

'She did not want us to know about Michel – remember we think he had killed already by then. And she may have thought that we knew something about a man seen at her house – covering her tracks.'

'True – but it troubles me and I do not know why.'

They had left it there to sit watching the cold rolling sea under a cloudy sky, wondering whether it was true that these two had worked together to murder children. They had been glad to see the pinpoints of light which told them that the coast of England was near. Paris in the glimmering snow seemed like a dream.

It still did, thought Dickens. London seemed grimy and too noisy after that hushed whiteness. He walked up the High Street passing the dark bulk of St Giles's on his left. Poor Robin and Mrs Hart, too. He thought of how her grief was slowly killing her. He had understood that – so had Georgiana Morson. But Victorine? Could she really be accomplice? Could their grief have so warped them?

In Oxford Street he saw the cheerful sight of a coffee stall, a large, brightly painted wheeled truck with polished tin cans for hot milk, coffee and tea. He thought about stopping for a coffee and a twopenny ham sandwich, but there was a crowd of flash men with their girls, loud as fishwives, though rather more colourful in their gaudy satins. One looked at him pro-vocatively, winking her eye. He smiled at her but walked on. As he passed another crowd shoving towards the stall, he had a fleeting impression of a familiar face – Sesina on the arm of a young man dressed as a toff with a top hat and silk scarf. The crowd closed in and she was gone. Well, well, he thought, Miss Sesina with a gentleman. He had a very good idea of how she was earning her living now. And Isabella Gordon, he wondered where she was.

23

THE MISSING

Brighton. They stared at the grey sea, cold as slate under a heavy sky, and at the long distance where sea and sky met, where the world curved. There was no wind, just a leadenness in the air. Over there beyond that far line was Paris. They could see the faint smudge that was the steamer on its way to France. They were not there, Victorine and the mysterious Michel. Nor were they here in Brighton or, at least Dickens and Jones had not found them. And even further across the wide, wide sea lay America to where the SS *Mediator* would sail from London to New York in two days' time on November 28th. Rogers was down at the Pool of London investigating the passenger list in case the two had decided to sail for America. They had done all they could.

They had checked every milliner's and dressmaker's establishment in the hope that one might be the former business of a Frenchwoman and her husband. The name was Jolicoeur or Blandois. No one had heard of them. The next step was to get the Brighton police to check the addresses of any French nationals living in Brighton. But they could not wait in Brighton. They would have to hope that the police would find something.

'They could have gone to Liverpool,' observed Dickens, contemplating the sea. 'To America from there.'

'They could. I looked at the sailings – the *America* sails on November 30th for New York and the *Cambria* to Boston on November 29th, in three days. So, it might be the train for Liverpool. However, they could have gone to Ireland. They could be anywhere.'

A breeze sprang up, whisking the sea into little waves. The sky seemed darker and suddenly they were cold. The sea was empty, iron grey now but steelier in the distance – no trace of the steamer. They could hear the husky rasp of the waves on the gravelly shore and then the hiss and suck as they receded. Shivering, they turned away.

Sam's face was suddenly bleak. 'I think we may have to accept that we will not find them.'

They walked away from the sea front up the Old Steine and past the Pavilion which on this grey, dying day seemed as improbable as some Eastern legend with its minarets and domes as if it had flown there on some magic carpet.

They waited on the platform for the train to take them back to London Bridge from where Sam went back to Bow Street and Dickens made his way home. He thought about Sam's despondent face. He had to agree. At the beginning they had been forced to be patient in their search for Scrap and Poll. They would have to be patient now. His cab took him along High Holborn and into High Street. He thought of Mrs Hart. He had time. It was just about five o'clock. He got out at St Giles's Church and made his way to Monmouth Street where he saw Zeb and Effie at the door of the shop. They were looking anxiously up and down the street.

They looked astonished to see him. Effie's face crumpled with distress and he could see the tears.

'She's gone, Mr Dickens.'

Effie did not have to say who.

'When?'

'I don't know – this afternoon sometime. I went shopping. Zeb was here in the shop. It was busy. I went to see Occy's wife for a cup of tea. I got back about half an hour ago. When I'd talked to Zeb I went upstairs and her door was open. It never was, never. She's gone. I thought she was gettin' better. That's why I went to Occy's. I thought she'd be all right. She had some soup about twelve o'clock – and she took something yesterday. She seemed a bit stronger – now I think –'

'She wanted to be a bit stronger so that she could go,' Dickens finished for her.

'That's it,' said Zeb.

'I feel it's my fault, Mr Dickens – I should have come back sooner.'

'I should've checked on her – I could've just popped upstairs. And the back door was open.' Zeb was as distressed as his wife.

'I do not think you could have prevented it – you would have to leave her sometime. She would have continued to take some food and when you went out or were busy she would have gone. Could she have gone home?'

'We thought of that. I just said to Zeb that we should try.'

'I will come with you.' They would have to see. Perhaps she would go home to where her boy's things were. Perhaps she thought that she would die there. The alternatives were too dreadful. To think of her wandering alone through these streets, he could hardly bear it. He saw from their faces that Zeb and Effie thought the same. And they did not know how long she had been gone.

They hurried to the mean tenement where she and Robin had lived in their one room. The landlady, Mrs Bookless – and she was, apart from her rent books – a blowsy, grimy vis-aged creature who smelt of gin, and worse, couldn't recall when she'd last seen 'er but they could look if they wanted. She'd better go with them. With some reluctance she gave them a key. Dickens insisted even though she protested that it want right. 'Oo were they, anyway? 'Ow did she know wot they were after? As if, thought Dickens, Mrs Hart had anything to steal. If she had, the landlady would have had it already. She just wanted to be in on it. Ghoul, he thought. Mrs Bookless had to give way. The gent was a bit frightening, she thought. Lawyer, pr'aps. Cheeky beggar. 'Er own 'ouse, too. 'Oo did he think 'e was? Eyes like steel, she thought, quailing a little before his fierce stare. She looked after them greedily. Best go in – she dint want no trouble.

They climbed the rickety stairs to the top of the house. Effie looked at Dickens. She was afraid of what they might find. So was he. They waited, listening. There was no sound but their own breathing. He heard Zeb just behind him on the top step draw in his breath as if in preparation for something terrible, then he heard the breath let out again raggedly. Effie seemed to breathe in short, anxious gasps. Dickens did not know if he were breathing at all.

'Shall we try the door, Mr Dickens?' Effie whispered. Her face seemed too white in the dark corridor.

Dickens reached out and turned the handle. The door was not locked. He and Effie stepped into the tiny room. The moon shone through a skylight in the roof, and they could make out a table, a couple of chairs and in the corner just the one bed. They hardly dared approach. Zeb, behind them, struck a match and lighted the candle in a saucer on the table. He held it up so that Effie and Dickens could see. The bed was empty.

'But she's been here,' said Effie. 'Look.'

Dickens saw that the blanket had been turned back as though someone had just risen. He noted the two pillows. They had shared this bed, he thought. And, he saw, too, the shabby brown bonnet simply left there on one pillow. Her face had rested on the pillow nearest the wall – that is where Robin had slept, he had no doubt. She had lain here. For how long? He did not know, but she had come because Robin had been here. She had wanted to be with him, and then she had gone, not knowing that she had left the hat there – or not caring.

He was angry suddenly. He turned and clattered down the stairs. Effie heard him hammering on the landlady's door. That fat-faced woman with her greedy, calculating eyes must have seen Mrs Hart – and she had let her go. The woman came to her door, angry at the noise. He saw the mouth open in the face which looked as if it were composed of dirty yeast, and he was seized with a desire to take her by the throat and shake her. Mrs Bookless stepped back, cowed, and closed her mouth.

'You saw her. When?' He shouted at her. Effie was astonished. Mr Dickens, so polite and quietly spoken usually. But, she could see why he was angry. This woman had not cared a farthing for poor Mrs Hart and Mr Dickens knew that. Well, you only had to read the books – you knew that he cared.

Mrs Bookless opened and closed her mouth. She tried to deny it by shaking her head.

'When?' He took a step towards her. She backed off and he felt his power over her, this fat, blowsy creature who had no doubt terrorised Mrs Hart for the rent. Mrs Bookless looked round, eyes darting. But there was nowhere to go.

'About two hours ago. 'Ow do I know?' She was sullen. 'I arsked 'er –'

'For her rent?' His voice was contemptuous. 'And you knew her son was dead, and you knew she had nothing. You must have seen the state she was in.'

'Gotter make me livin' – thought 'er friends mighter give 'er sumthink.' She looked at Effie who had appeared in the doorway by now.

'Yes, they did, far more than you could ever imagine. Well, I doubt she'll be back and you can examine your conscience on that matter – if you have one.' He turned and left her. Zeb was waiting in the hall and the three of them went out into the air. At least they could breathe.

Mrs Bookless's flesh ceased quivering. She was that put out. Nosy git. Lotter fuss about nothin' – none of 'is business wot she sed ter Mrs 'Art. Bleedin' cheek. She closed her front door and went back in to see what was left in the bottle. She'd 'ave a good look round termorrer - Mrs 'Art mighter left sumthink. She was entitled, want she?

In the street, they considered where to look. Effie said she would go to Mrs Feak's to ask if she knew anything. Zeb would fetch Occy – he could help search and he knew a lot of people. Someone might have seen her. Dickens would go to Crown Street and fetch Scrap. Then he had a thought.

'We should go to St Giles's where Robin was found.' He thought of Mrs Hart lying in the bed and he imagined her dragging her way to the churchyard to lie down on that cold tombstone where they had found him. He did not know if she knew which one it was but it did not matter – she might go there.

From Moor Street they turned up Crown Street, making their way to Denamrk Street and then to the church. They went through the resurrection gate into the silent graveyard where he and Sam had seen that poor boy. He remembered how he had imagined the gentleman who had drawn the innocent boy to his side only to stab him in the heart. He felt the anger flare up again. He had to be found – the man who had taken Jemmy's and Robin's lives and, he believed, Mrs Hart's. They spread out to search. But she was not here. The tombs were still under the impassive moon. The dead were quiet. No messages from the grave. Dickens went to look at the chalk mark on that old door. The blind eyes of that crude masked face could tell him nothing. Was it at all important? He did not know.

They were ready to go their separate ways. Messages would be left at the shop if there were news of her. Dickens said he would ask Scrap to search and then he would go to

Bow Street to tell the superintendent – they could leave a message there. When they looked at each other's faces they knew what the message would be. Two, three hours had gone. They would not find her alive.

At Bow Street, Rogers had reported that there were no names on the passenger list which indicated that Victorine and Michel would be sailing on the SS *Mediator*. Another blank.

'Will we be going to Liverpool then?' asked Rogers.

'I suppose so,' said Sam. Rogers noted the weariness in his tone. Brighton had been no good.

'Bit o' better news, sir. Mr Wilde left a message sayin' that Mr Outfin 'ad come round. Very weak but 'e'll live, doctor said.'

Sam's face brightened a little. 'That is good news.'

'Yer don't think now that 'e's our man?'

'No, I don't. I am glad about that anyway. Anything else happen?'

'I went to that church in Golden Square but no one knew anythin' about Mamselle Victorine. She muster gone some-where else – if she did go to church. An' I asked Stemp to keep lookin' for Tommy Titfer – 'e's bin missin' since that night Mr Dickens and Zeb went to Rats' Castle. No one's seen 'im for days. Stemp should be back soon.'

'We meant to ask Scrap to take you to that alley where he saw the giant. Perhaps he killed Titfer. We'll do that when Stemp gets back.'

Rogers went out, leaving the superintendent pondering. Stemp would do his best. Sam remembered his outrage when they had arrested Jonas Finger over the murder of a little girl. Stemp had found the child and Sam had seen the pity and revulsion in his eyes when they had noticed the bruises. Stemp had children of his own; he had hung on to the cursing, brawling brute of a man until Finger gave in. He wondered about Titfer, a low weasly sort with a mother and a brother. If he were dead then they would suffer. He would wait for Stemp then go home to Elizabeth, and try to forget for a while the hopelessness of the search for Victorine, and, if he could, the suffering – sometimes it could be overwhelming. You felt impotent against the black tide of misery.

He bent his head to his paperwork. Reports on the three dead boys. Inspector Harker had sent him word about the inquest on Jemmy. It had been short. Harker had passed on the newspaper article which reported that Inspector Harker and Constable Parker had presented themselves, and said they had the case in hand, and were sure if they had time they could procure important evidence, and that they had a clue already. The investigation was proceeding in association with Superintendent Jones of Bow Street who was also investigating two murders which had similarities to the murder of Jemmy. The man who had found the body gave his evidence, which was not much. After a brief consultation between the coroner and jury, it was decided that the inquiry should be adjourned. It would be the same for the other two. He had managed to put off the inquest on Robin, but time was running out – a verdict of wilful murder by person or persons unknown was what he dreaded. Not unknown, he thought – just unfound. He did not want to go chasing to Liverpool, but he would have to unless they materialised at Bow Street to confess to their hideous crimes – and that, he thought gloomily, was very unlikely.

He looked at the *Standard* to see if there were any more reports about the dead boys. There had been a couple of short paragraphs on the deaths of Robin and the disfigured boy – the latter report assumed that the boy had died in the fire. Today's front page was full of news from Europe and France, giving most space to the row between the Assembly and the President, Louis Napoleon. There was a long section on the commission to be established to improve the metropolitan water supply – about time, thought Sam. The newspapers had been full of the cholera epidemic which had raged all summer. Page two was interesting. They had reproduced a letter from Charles Dickens which had been first published in *The Times* in which he argued against executions in public. Sam had to agree. He had seen the Mannings hanged and felt the horror of the baying crowd. And he wondered whether it was right to take a human life. But then he had been in court to hear Mrs Manning's screaming denunciations of British justice. She was a liar and a callous, greedy murderess. He had not pitied her when he heard what she had done to Patrick O'Connor yet when he saw her hanging form, he had turned away, and now he had to catch the murderer of children – it was impossible to forgive that, he thought.

There was a knock at the door; Rogers came in with Stemp who looked as though he had something to tell.

'Sir, well, I don't know if it's any use – I 'aven't found Tommy Titfer – but I 'eard something by the way. Titfer was runnin' errands for a toff and some folk are sayin' that 'e, Titfer, was takin' boys to 'im. I thought we should see Fikey again – 'e might know more than 'e told you.'

'Well done, Stemp – good work.'

'Want us to bring him in?' Rogers was eager.

'I think we might pay him a visit.' This might be something – at least it was action. 'And I think we should go and see the boy, Scrap – he saw the giant dragging a body on the night Tommy Titfer disappeared. We need to find out if Titfer is alive or dead.'

Another knock on the door. Dickens and Scrap appeared. Something had happened.

'Mrs Hart has vanished. I just came to tell you. Occy and Zeb are searching. We went to her lodgings. She had been there but was gone. I fear the worst. Scrap says he will help me.'

'Stemp has just brought information about Tommy Titfer. We are just off to Fikey Chubb's shop. I need to borrow Scrap for a little while to show us where he saw the giant with the body. In the meantime, I'll let you have Feak to help. I'll need Rogers and Stemp at Chubb's but we will come back to you as soon as we can. Where do you want to meet Scrap?'

'At Zeb's. I'll go back there now. We have looked at St Giles's but she wasn't there – we will probably have another look. Scrap, we will see you at Zeb's in –'

'Half an hour. It won't take long will it, Scrap?'

'Nah, I remember where I seen 'im.'

They went out together through the usual crowd. Sam looked at Dickens. They remembered the night they had taken Mrs Hart to Zeb's and how the crowd had parted at their coming. Sam shook his head. He held Dickens back for a moment.

'Have you thought of the river?'

Dickens looked sombrely back at him. 'I have. I thought we might find her before –'

'And where, that's the question.'

'I know. Too many places to search. I will get back to Zeb's. Come, if you can.'

'I will.'

Scrap took the three policemen through the winding alleys to the ruined house where he had hidden in wait for Poll. They went through to the alley where Nat Boney's house was in darkness. No dogs barked. Business was bad, then, thought Scrap. Good. I wonder where all them dogs went. He pointed the way that the giant had gone and went on his way to meet Dickens at Zeb's shop.

The superintendent, Rogers and Stemp separated and began their search, looking in the yards and abandoned gardens. The giant would have left the body in an unused place, Sam thought. No use looking where there were lights and voices. It did not take long. In an overgrown garden where rats scuttled in the dark, and the air was filled with the stench of decay and death, Sam saw a shape lying in a heap of stinking refuse. He went nearer with his bull's-eye lantern held it up. The yellow light showed him the body, the terrible face where the rats had feasted, and he saw the red plume of hair. The stink of corruption rose at him so that he had to turn away, though everywhere the air was bitter. Death was in his nostrils, in his mouth, the taste of putrefaction thickening on his tongue like fur to choke him. He forced himself to look again. It was Tommy, no doubt. Poor devil – it was a terrible place to lie, forgotten, left like a piece of rubbish in a midden. Sam sent up a hasty prayer. Whatever he had done, he could not be left thus with no word said for him. Even the murderer on the gallows heard a prayer before the noose tightened.

He called out for Rogers and Stemp and heard their boots on the cobbles of the alley.

'Poor devil,' said Rogers when he saw the horror that was Tommy Titfer now. Stemp said nothing. He had heard what had been said about Titfer and the boys. He was implacable – the little rat deserved what he got. But he said nothing.

'Your rattle, Stemp. We need a couple of beat constables to deal with the body. They'll be able to get the mortuary van down here and take him away. We'll deal with it all tomorrow. We need to see Chubb, now.' Stemps's rattle summoned two constables to the alley and Sam gave his instructions. Stemp would wait with one of them while the other returned to the police station. Stemp would come to Fikey Chubb's as soon as he could.

Sam and Rogers picked their way through the weeds and rank grasses and made their way out through the abandoned house to which the garden had once belonged. The roof had fallen in as had the stairs and they could see the moon like a spectral face looking down at them. In the lantern light they could see shadows dancing on the crumbling walls, ghosts of those who had once lived, laughed, taken supper, and played the ruined piano that sat drunkenly in the corner. Guests might have come in through this space where the door had been. But they were all gone now, to their graves, perhaps. Well, at least they would not know of the terrible thing that had lain in the garden where lilac had bloomed and roses had come in the summer.

Fikey Chubb's shop was open. They went in; Sam closed the door with as loud a crash as he could make. The shop smelt of Fikey and something like rotten meat. Fikey popped up from behind his counter like a malignant gnome – not that he was particularly small – just ugly, thought Sam maliciously. Fikey had that effect on him.

'Wot the 'ell? Oh, it's you, Superintendent, no need to bring the bleedin' 'ouse down. It's a friggin' disgrace – persecution, I calls it. I'm a –'

'Spare me the catalogue of your virtues, Mr Chubb. I have heard it all before.'

Hearing the iron in the superintendent's voice, Fikey subsided, though the scowl on his face did not improve his looks.

'Tommy Titfer?'

'Not that agin – I told yer last time. Don't know where 'e is an' I don't bleedin' care.'

'Oh, we've just found him. Dead. Strangled by the looks of it.'

'Poor bleeder – that's wot comes o' keepin bad company.' Fikey's sudden access of piety almost made Sam laugh. He was incorrigible.

'I take it you do not refer to yourself. I thought he was a friend of yours.'

'Tommy – 'e 'ad no friends – acquaintances, mebbe –' Fikey was becoming loquacious. Sam only had to wait. 'An' a lot o' rogues, 'e mixed wiv – I'm tellin' yer, Mr Jones, a man's gotter watch 'oo 'e keeps company wiv these days.'

'Exactly what I was thinking myself. And as you know so much about him, perhaps you would care to tell me with whom Tommy consorted. I've got plenty of time.' Sam's voice was cool. Rogers wanted to laugh. Consorted, he thought, that'd fox Fikey. Sam moved to the counter.

Fikey looked uneasily at Rogers who stood at the door, idly fingering his truncheon. He looked backwards at the open door behind the counter. Bloody 'ell, there woz another of the bleeders there. Stemp had suddenly appeared.

'Wot yer talkin' abaht – consorted – don't know wot yer mean.'

'I mean who were these rogues? I am interested in a particular rogue – a toff, apparently, for whom Tommy Titfer ran errands.'

'Dunno nothin' abaht that.' Fikey did not sound at all convincing.

'You do, and as I say, we have all night.'

Fikey gave in. 'Oh, I 'eard a rumour – somethin' abaht boys – dint take much notice – not my line. Told yer last time.'

Sam smashed his truncheon on the counter so hard that Fikey fell backwards, his face suddenly sick in the greenish gaslight.

'And you did not think to tell me. About Tommy Titfer.' Sam's voice was menacing. 'You knew about those dead boys – I told you I wanted information. Another boy has been murdered. Your information might have prevented that. Accessory, we call it. You are implicated, Chubb. So, you had better tell me now.'

'I dunno 'oo it woz. Tommy sed 'e woz 'opin' to earn a bit – I wanted me money back wiv interest.'

'You would. Did Tommy tell you anything about the man – was he a foreigner?'

Fikey looked baffled. ''Oo sed 'e was foreign?'

'I am asking if Tommy said anything about the man being a foreigner – French, perhaps?'

'Nah, jest sed 'e woz a toff – Tommy thort 'e might make a bit – yer know. Then 'e disappeared, Tommy that is, so I dint think no more abaht it. 'Ow woz I ter know it woz important?'

Fikey was beginning to recover. Mr friggin' Superintendent couldn't pin anythin' on 'im. But then he looked at the super-intendent's face as hard as an axe gleaming dangerously in the green light. Bloody 'ell. 'E'd ave to give 'im somethink – Fikey Chubb, informer. Folk weren't goin' ter like it. But a man 'ad ter look arter number one.

'One thing. Tommy sed the toff asked if 'e could get drugs. Well, Tommy, 'e knew. There's a place round 'ere wot is a drugs den – opium. Little Chinaman. Yer might find yer toff there.'

We already have, thought Sam, remembering the young man sprawled on that disgusting cot, shouting his fears into the filthy room, and the Chinaman indifferent to it all, except the possibility of a new customer. But the toff had not been Michel Blandois. Damn. Fikey Chubb knew it – he saw the beginnings of a sly smile on Fikey's face. Time to wipe it off.

'We will certainly go there. I know the place you mean. I'll be certain to tell Mr Chinaman that you sent us – Mr Chubb, most obliging to the police – and does it for nothing, too.'

The beginnings of Fikey's smile vanished and reappeared momentarily on Sam's lips. Bastard. Sod 'im, bleedin' mind reader. 'Ow did 'e know Fikey was goin' ter ask for a fee? That was the trouble with Fikey – no self-knowledge. Out o' pocket and worse, known as a friggin' blower. Oh, shit. He thought of the Chinaman coming for him with a great curved what d'ya call it – scimitar – like self-knowledge, geography was not Fikey's strong point. He looked at Sam. Seeing the ghost of a smile, he realised something. They wouldn't arrest 'im – no, they'd bleedin' leave 'im to be cut in pieces by some yeller-faced snake 'oo'd laugh as 'e did it. Could 'e ask ter be arrested? What a friggin' joke.

Sam knew all that was in the grimy alleys of Fikey's mind. Let him sweat or rather not. He could smell the man again. He'd get Inspector Grove and a few constables to clear out that verminous opium den. He wouldn't mention Fikey – he could not have the man's murder on his conscience. Stemp wouldn't mind, he thought as he looked at his stony face behind the counter. Stemp had not moved during the colloquy with Fikey, but Sam had felt Rogers's desire to laugh. Stemp saw things in black and white. Fikey was a rat. If he were put down then so be it. My trouble is, he thought, I read too much. *Every man's death diminishes me, for I am involved in mankind.*

Fikey was looking at him, wondering what this hatchet-faced man was thinking. 'Ard as nails, he thought, the bleeder. Soddin' crushers – hang yer soon as look at yer.

'Well, Chubb – you have been most helpful, most public spirited. We must leave you in peace. I should put up your shutters if I were you. Dangerous times we live in.'

Fikey did not answer. Sarky git, he thought. They went out, leaving Fikey to worry about hordes of yellow-faced Chinamen brandishing their great curved knives. Sam thought with satisfaction that Fikey would not sleep that night. And, although he had not found Michel, Titfer had been found – the giant had more than likely killed him. He had seen the crushed throat – same as the labouring man. And he had been reminded to shut down the opium den. It was time to go to Zeb's to see if there were any news of Mrs Hart.

Dickens and Scrap were at Zeb's shop with Effie. Zeb and Occy were still searching, as was Feak who had had the bright idea of going for his mother. Mrs Feak was there too. She had not seen Mrs Hart, but they had looked in the yards and courts near Mrs Feak's house, and she had come to Zeb's in case they found her, in case she was needed. Good people, thought Sam, as the smell of Fikey Chubb dissolved.

'Mrs Feak, good evening,' he said. 'You have not seen her?'

'No, Mr Jones. I wonder how far she can 'ave gone. She ain't strong. She won't last out there in this cold night.'

They all thought of her waxen face and starved frame. If they did not find her tonight, she would die.

'Rogers and Stemp will help. Will you stay here with Effie?'

'I will.'

'Mr Dickens and I will go out again now. Scrap, perhaps you ought to go home. Mr Brim will be wondering where you are.'

''S'all right, Mr Jones,'e knows I'm wiv you. Shall I come with yer?'

'I'd like you to help Mr Rogers, if you will. They'll need you to do your usual listening and you can get into places they can't.'

Scrap looked puzzled and a little disappointed, but he accepted Sam's request and went off with Rogers and Stemp. Sam took Dickens by the arm and led him in the opposite direction.

'Where are we going?' asked Dickens.

'Waterloo Bridge – she might have jumped. We can ask the tollkeeper – he might have seen her or she might be hanging about there, waiting.'

'That is why you did not want Scrap with us.'

'Yes, I don't want him to see her if she has drowned. If he finds her with Rogers and Stemp, Rogers will keep him from the worst.'

They walked back to Bow Street and down into Wellington Street which led directly on to the bridge. *The Bridge of Sighs*, Thomas Hood called it in his poem, the bridge notorious for suicides, especially young women who had nothing left but the prospect of an unwanted child and the workhouse. All night the turnstile clicked, and the halfpennies were given over to the tollman who knew if one would not stop for the change what she might do.

Dickens and Jones looked about them but there was no sign of Mrs Hart. They paid their halfpence each to the toll-man. Dickens thought of him as Charon ferrying the damned across the Styx, though he was cheerful enough despite the cold, bundled up in his shawl. They went to stand and look down at the river. If she came this way, they could stop her.

Dickens looked down at the water boiling below, swirling under the arch, and he thought of Mrs Hart's unresisting body sucked down into the blackness – that portal of Eternity. But, as someone had once told him, you had to mind how you jumped – from the side of the bay was best and then, his informant said, you would tumble true into the stream under the arch. The same man had told him of the young woman who sprang out of a cab going at speed then ran along the pavement and jumped, of the young man who cried out cheerfully 'Here goes, Jack!' and was over in a minute. He looked down to the water stairs and saw there a figure simply standing. He nudged Sam whose eyes followed his pointing finger. But then the gleam of a lamp showed the outline of a man – not her.

They could wait all night, they could scour the stairs, the wharves, the piers, and they could never stop. Yet they might never find her. She might already be gone, thought Dickens, into that dark water, drifting with the tide. What dreadful silence down there under the swell, fathoms deep where bleached bones were gathered. This river, so broad and vast, so murky and silent seemed to him such an image of death in the midst of the great city's life. They stood silently, wondering and the words of Hood's poem with its insistent rhythm and rhymes sounded eerily in his head:

Mad from life's history,
Glad to death's mystery,
Swift to be hurl'd –

Anywhere, anywhere
Out of the world!

'Where is she? Living or dead, where is she?' he burst out. Sam shook his head.

'Time to go,' said Sam. 'You go home, Charles. I will collect Scrap and take him to Crown Street then I will go home. We can do no more for her.'

'You are right. We'll take a cab and I'll drop you off at St Giles's. Let me know tomorrow if there is news – about anything.'

'I will.'

They walked away to the nearest cab stand. Beneath the arch the black water rolled on, rushing and swishing as it hastened towards Blackfriars Bridge, thence to Southwark, under London Bridge, past the Tower and Traitor's Gate, through the Pool where the great ships waited, tethered like huge dragons, straining to be free, to spread their vast wings on the sea, past Cuckold's Point where the pirates hung, washed by the hurrying tide, down through Limehouse Reach, whirling into the West India Dock Basin, out again into Greenwich Reach and away, away to the wide, empty ocean.

24

FOUND

I have supp'd full with horrors, he thought, as he contemplated his desk where the morning's letters were waiting. Even Dickens, whose energy was prodigious, felt the relief of a respite from the search. Paris, Brighton, the search for Mrs Hart had left him weary.

He looked at the manuscript of *David Copperfield* on his desk. He knew where he was going with that. Little Em'ly would run away with Steerforth whom David had taken to Yarmouth, and Mr Peggotty would vow to search the world for her. Whereas, undoubtedly, life was messier than art. The omniscient narrator could place his characters where he would. The murderer would be caught, the criminal brought to justice. He had put Fagin in the condemned cell in Newgate; Sikes in a terrible irony had been hanged by his own rope as he attempted to escape. The missing would be found, restitution made and lovers could be united. But life, ah, life!

However, he reflected, even if they did not find Victorine and Michel, they had stopped them perhaps – not perhaps – almost certainly. And Mrs Hart? She was dead, he knew it. He thought of Kent in *King Lear* who begged that the king should pass: *He hates him that would upon the rack of this tough world stretch him out longer.* Racked with grief, she had felt so too. She was out of it now, somewhere.

He turned to his letters. One from Oliver Wilde giving him optimistic news of Theo who was awake though very weak.

He was to be taken to the country, to Kent – with his wife. They were to go to Mrs Outfin's brother-in-law. Her sister was married to a clergyman, the Reverend Sydney Farthing. Good people, Oliver wrote, who would look after them both and make no judgement on Katie Fitzgerald. Another letter came from Mrs Morson telling him that Kip, though quiet, had settled in. He could picture from her words the silent boy brushing and brushing the horse, the steady rhythm of his work giving him a kind of peace. The next was from Captain Pierce. Davey was well though he still did not speak. He played with the old white dog in the garden. Captain Pierce was to move to the country. The boy would be better out of London, away from the place that contained all his unspeakable memories, away from the streets where he wept when he saw a child begging, away from the brawling women and drunken men from whom he shrank in terror. A farm or smallholding, Captain Pierce had written, near the sea. A new life where there would be tranquillity and outdoor work. Good, thought Dickens. Two saved. Three and four if you counted Theo and his wife.

His son, Charley, came in to talk about the interview for Eton which would take place early in December. Dickens was proud of him – Charley with his cheerful, open face, fine-featured and handsome with large, bright eyes – not unwillingly to school. Charley who wore his heart on his sleeve. A child of uncommon capacity with remarkable natural talent, Dickens thought. Eton – he remembered someone asking his own father where his son had been educated. The reply was that he might be said to have educated himself. And so he had. But Charley would not. Those luminous eyes were clear, innocent as yet, and he would not be troubled by the presence of some small ghost beside him with blackened hands.

'Well, Charley, what do you think of our going down to Eton in a week or two? Do you like it?'

'I think so, Papa.'

'Mr King speaks highly of you, of your work on the Latin poets. He says you know your Virgil and Herodotus – I am proud of you, my boy.'

'Thank you, Papa.'

'And, afterwards shall we have a treat? What would please you best?'

'The Zoo at Regent's Park – there is the new reptile house which we have not seen yet – we could go, Papa, just we two.'

'So we could – it shall be as you desire.' Not as I desire, thought Dickens who did not care at all for reptiles – still, he could look the other way – and he was pleased that Charley should want a day alone with Papa.

Charley went off to school with Walter, and Dickens went up to the nursery to see Alfred, Francis, Sydney and the baby, Henry, who was now eleven months old. Henry was sitting on Georgina's knee, gazing solemnly at Alfred and Francis playing on the carpet with their horses and soldiers. Dickens picked him up and looked at the little face, grave as a judge's.

'Oh, Mr H,' he said, 'what shall you be?'

Sydney, aged two, was playing by himself with a model ship. The Ocean Spectre, Dickens called him. Perhaps a sailor's life for him. What would they all do, he mused, the Responsibilities? The girls would marry, he supposed. Heavens, what a thought. He could not imagine whom Katey would marry – Lucifer Box, he named her, for her fiery temper. Yet, she would be a beauty. And Mamie whom he called Mild Gloster, more equable than Katey – perhaps she would not marry. She might stay with her father to look after him in his old age – he grimaced at the thought of old age – *sans teeth, sans eyes, sans everything.* He hoped not. The girls were upstairs now. He ought to go and see with what delights they had decorated their room. He encouraged them in all their artistic pursuits, drawing, painting, music, dancing – Katey had talent, he thought.

But Sydney brought over his ship to show Papa and the other two, not to be outdone, came with their horses, and for an hour or so he gave himself over to being a father and a good-humoured one too, getting down on to the carpet to discipline the soldiers and the cavalry, preventing the outbreak of war when a ship ploughed into the troops to scatter them and Sydney crowed with laughter to see the soldiers fall. Then, back to his letters. At least half a dozen to write. That was a small bag compared to some days – and his letter to *The Times* on public hanging had brought plenty of epistles, preaching his wrong or his right.

Here's a knocking, indeed, he thought as he went on to the landing. Whoever it was must be in a hurry. John, his manservant, was before him and opened the door to reveal Constable Feak, his hand raised in the act of knocking again.

'You rang,' said Dickens. Feak looked mortified, his bony face suffused with red. Dickens could have bitten back the joke. 'Only my jest, Feak,' he said. Poor lad – too late, he had seen the bell.

'Oh, sorry, sir, it's just that Superintendent Jones sent me. Mrs Hart's been found – down at Arundel Stairs – drowned.'

'I'll come. John, fetch me a coat, will you? Who found her?'

'Zeb Scruggs an' Occy. After you an' Mr Jones went, we looked all over an' when we went back to Zeb's, me mam – Mrs Feak, that is, she said 'ad we thought of the river. Well, o' course they 'ad but they didn't wanter – yer know – think that she'd –'

'I understand. Thank you, John. Tell Miss Hogarth that I will be back at lunch time.'

He went with Feak to the waiting cab. Feak told him that Zeb and Occy had gone to the river. They had looked around the bridge and the stairs and had come to the same conclusion that Dickens and Jones had, that they could search all night and might never find her. They went home and agreed to try again this morning. They had asked the tollkeeper, they had looked at the pier and walked along the muddy shore upstream and down as far as they could. They had walked along the Strand as far as Arundel Pier where they had found her – or rather a dredgerman had.

From the top of the stairs, Dickens saw Sam, Rogers, Zeb and Occy and a stranger. They were all looking down at a figure stretched out on the mud at the foot of the stairs. He went down with Feak.

The stranger was speaking, 'She muster gone in 'bout five in the morning when the tide was in – she'd go in at the bottom of the stairs 'ere. Known it before.' A man who knew the river, judging by his muddy appearance, his oilskin cape and tarred sou'wester.

He was a dredgerman, a fisher up of coals, metals, ropes, bones – and sometimes bodies. Now his boat, a peculiar craft named a Peter boat with no stern but the same fore and aft, was tied up by the stairs. The dredgerman, Noah Hatch, a short, square, strongly built middle-aged man, was coming in to shore when Mrs Hart was caught up in the ropes of the dredging net. It was shallow enough for him to get in the water and drag her out.

Dickens looked down. Mrs Hart's face white as bone looked up at them, but her eyes were closed. Her threadbare dress was wet and muddy, and her dark hair was all pushed back from the face as if, thought Dickens, that had been the last action of her desperate hands. It streamed over the mud. Of course, she had left her bonnet behind. She was not bruised or broken. It was as though she had simply lain down in the water to die. He thought again of Ophelia who had drowned, too – pulled to a muddy death – and of her song of bonny sweet Robin.

'But why did the tide not take her?' he asked the dredgerman.

Noah Hatch's eyes were thoughtful and compassionate. 'Look, sir, see 'ow 'er skirt is caught on that chain there.

She went in, I reckon, closed 'er eyes, and she didn't know that the chain held 'er so that she rolled up and down on the swell of the tide. Wanted ter die, I suppose, just lay there till the cold took 'er. Knowed 'er, sir?' He looked at Dickens's sorrowful face.

'Yes, she had just lost her only son. She had nothing left to live for.'

They all looked down at the dead face. There was a kind of repose in it. Nothing could touch her now.

Dickens and Jones walked away, leaving Feak and Rogers to arrange for the body to be taken away. Occy and Zeb went ahead to break the news to Mrs Feak and Effie who were waiting at the shop. There was nothing more to say about Mrs Hart. They walked back to the Strand, up Charles Street and back to Bow Street.

'What will you do now?' asked Dickens.

'To Liverpool tomorrow. I need to find out if Victorine and Michel are on the passenger lists of the *Cambria* or the *America* though, God knows, I have such doubts. It must be done. I need to see for myself.'

'Do you want me to come? Barkiss is willin'– muffle me up in my shawl, provide me with a bottle of brandy and a sandwich – and I am yours to command.'

'You are a busy man, Charles – I should like your company above all things but –'

'But me no buts, nay, I am with thee – to the world's end, if we must. I never will desert Mr Micawber!'

Sam had to laugh and agree. 'Well then, it shall be so – and I will bring the brandy and little Miss Posy will provide the sandwiches of the rarest beef.'

'Ah, Posy – she is doing well?'

Posy was the little maidservant found selling a pitiful bunch of artificial flowers in the street. Dickens had rescued her and placed her with Sam and Elizabeth.

'She is – changed beyond recognition from that poor scrap of a creature you brought to us – getting on with her reading and writing. *The Finchley Manual of Industry* is her daily study as well as the society papers. And, she has grown a little.'

'Good – I shall come to see her as soon as I can.'

'When all this is over.'

'When, Harry, when?'

'Tomorrow, perhaps. I will meet you at Euston Station for the eight o'clock express.'

'Something will turn up – which I am, I may say, hourly expecting and in case of anything turning up, I shall be extremely happy if it should be in my power to improve your prospects. Farewell, Mr Jones, God bless you.'

With Mr Micawber's orotund rhetoric ringing in his ears, Sam went into the police station smiling. Dickens marched away whistling the College Hornpipe.

He went home to have lunch and to think about what he would discuss with John Forster, his closest friend – apart from Sam, he thought. He had a scheme for a new periodical magazine. His notion was a weekly journal to be priced at three halfpence or two pence. He wanted it to appeal to the imagination and represent common sense and humanity at the same time, to contribute to the entertainment of all classes of readers – Posy included, Rogers, Feak, Mrs Feak, Sam, Elizabeth, Sir Edward Bulwer-Lytton – the queen herself. The hardest workers were to be taught that their lot was not necessarily excluded from the sympathies and graces of the imagination. This was to be discussed with Forster tonight – and he needed to think of a title. *Mankind*, perhaps. No, *The Household Face* or better still, *The Household Voice* – yes, he rather thought the *Voice* was it.

He picked up his pen – time to answer the letters and to ponder the progress of David Copperfield. He thought again with sadness of the drowned figure of Mrs Hart and how he had thought of the river running to the wide ocean. He thought of the Yarmouth coast where storms raged and the wild wind whirled over the heaving sea.

25

DISGUISE

Household Words – that was it, a very pretty name. That would be the name for the new periodical – with thanks to Mr Shakespeare. He would have to send a note to John tomorrow. He thought of the title as he was walking along Chancery Lane after dining with John. All was settled about the new publication, and he was ready to make a general announcement of the intended adventure.

In the meantime, Liverpool. What if they were aboard the *Cambria*? He could imagine himself and Sam scouring the cabins. When news came that Maria Manning might be aboard the SS *Victoria*, a fast frigate had been despatched to catch the ship and apprehend the murderess – it had not been Maria Manning but a perfectly respectable American lady whose name was Rebecca Manning. He just hoped they would not put to sea before he and Sam could disembark – he had horrible memories of the sea voyage to America from Liverpool; the weather so violent, the ship flung on her side in the waves, beaten down, battered and crushed by the monstrous sea – no, he thought, let us find her before the ship sails.

He walked on to Oxford Street where he came again upon the busy coffee stall where he was sure he had glimpsed Sesina. He could not resist having a look. He waited a while, scanning the crowds which came and went. He felt he ought to buy a coffee. The stallholder gave him a look which seemed to accuse him of taking up valuable space if he were not going to buy anything. It was quite good, hot anyway. Along the street came a group very like the one he had seen the night before – yes, there was the young man, he was sure – the one with the scarf and, yes, there was Sesina, looking lively in her finery. He stayed where he was. They might see him.

The young man came first – tall, slender, elegant really in his flowing scarf. Sesina caught up with him and they approached near where Dickens was standing. He turned away to let them come in beside him. He felt the young man's touch as he pushed in to get near the coffee tins, steaming in the cold air. Dickens turned now and looked into the laughing amber eyes of – Isabella Gordon.

'Saw yer, Mr D – bet yer dint think it was me.'

He was astounded. He had thought she could not surprise him again. He thought of that forlorn figure trudging out of Urania Cottage wiping her eyes with her shawl, yet here she was, her impudence restored, standing there with all the aplomb of a well-dressed toff. He had been right about one thing – he had known that Isabella and Sesina would find each other. Sesina looked less pleased to see him. Isabella was relishing his astonishment.

'How do you come to be here and –'

'Dressed like this? Suits me, don't it?' She swept off her top hat and he saw that her red hair had been cut. She looked like a boy, a handsome one at that.

'It does, indeed. I should not have known you, though I recognised Miss Sesina here the other night.'

'An' yer come lookin' for us. We ain't comin' back.' Sesina was wary and suspicious. He had never liked her as much as he had Isabella whose wit and liveliness he had found attractive. Isabella was confident, her eyes sparkling still with the delight of his surprise.

'Got our own lives now, Mr D. Don't need no 'elp – sorry we made trouble for yer but the 'ome was not fer us – too quiet – too many rules – we wanted a bit o'life. An' not all of us needs a man. Yer thought we all wanted ter marry, Mr D, but you was wrong.'

'I did come looking, Isabella –'

'Don't use that name now – just Iz'll do.'

'Very well. I did come looking but not to bring you back – just to see if you were all right and I see that you are.'

'Come fer a drink – tell yer the story.'

How could he resist? Of course, he longed to know – it seemed impossible that she had transformed in such a few days.

'We'll take yer ter a place we know – promise yer'll like it. Not far from 'ere.'

Isabella led the way from Oxford Street into a network of lanes winding off Soho Square. They came to a pair of houses that looked as if they had been knocked into one. He knew what it was – one of the little private theatres, not quite a penny gaff, the kind which he had sometimes visited as a very young man working at the solicitor's in Gray's Inn. He had been to a theatre every night for three years and had thought of making the stage as his career. He even had an audition with George Bartley at Covent Garden – a swollen face had prevented him from attending.

Well, he thought, perhaps he might have ended his days in a place like this – though it was not the worst he had ever seen. He couldn't help laughing at the placards outside. 'Astounding!' they shrieked; 'Startling!' – I bet it is, he thought. 'Don't miss it!' Apparently, Mrs Fitzjohn was the star, 'a regular stunner' in the highwayman line. So, that was it. Isabella had taken her cue from the appearance of Mrs Fitzjohn in her garb as a highwayman.

They went in to find seats in a bar that had been set up in the area before the theatre proper. Dickens watched as Isabella strolled to the bar for all the world like a gentleman of fashion, even if the clothes were second-hand – from the wardrobe stock, he guessed. A woman's eyes followed her hungrily and the girl at the bar looked at her with obvious admiration. He saw Sesina frown. Isabella came back with their glasses of gin. She lounged back in her chair and to his amazement – yet again – she took out a cigar and lit it, blowing out the smoke before her narrowed eyes.

'Well, Mr D, 'ere we are – convincin', ain't I?'

'To the manner born, Mr Iz – I give you my compliments.' He raised his glass to them. 'Now, you promised me a story.'

'Yer won't give us away, will yer, Mr Dickens? Ain't no 'arm in wot we do.' Sesina did not trust him entirely. She remembered only too clearly his sternness when he had dismissed her. He could be frightening, she thought – his eyes could see right through yer an' 'e might think it want right. She wished Iz want so cocky.

'I certainly will not. I am curious, though. Tell me.'

'Remember Alice Drown, Mr D? Remember she walked out? Just vanished over the wall.'

'I remember Alice very well – met her once at the theatre.'

'Well, before she went, she said if we woz ever to do the same, she'd 'elp us out. She knew we wouldn't stay – told us she woz gettin' work in the theatre – the Victoria – well, we went there an' she give us lodgins for the night an' some money. Big 'eart 'as Alice. An' she told us about this place – sed we could get work. When I sees Mrs Fitzjohn, I knew I could do the same – be safer, I thought, if one of us was a man an' I'm the tallest, so. We does an act together, me an' Ses – yer sed she woz an actress.' She laughed, remembering the fireworks at the Home when she and Sesina had flounced and fomented rebellion much to the chagrin of Mrs Morson. Dickens laughed, too, though he was glad to think that they would trouble Georgiana no more.

'And?'

'We're 'appy, Mr D. We likes the excitement an' we don't need no men – yer know wot our lives woz like – it's a dangerous world fer women. I've 'ad a few beatins in my time, I told yer – an' 'oo'd wanter bring kids inter this life, eh? I can't remember my mother 'cept she woz always sick an' there woz too many kids. Yer can't love 'em all. Not for us. We likes our freedom – an' we wanter keep it.'

'An' we don't want no one takin' it away. Leave us be,' Sesina was fierce. 'I been in prison an' I ain't goin back and Iz neither. We done our time. We gotta chance now.' Sesina wanted to close the door on the past and throw away the key, but Isabella was enjoying her audience, crossing her legs in the narrow plaid trousers. He noted the bright waistcoat, the loosely tied cravat and the hair brushed to one side. By God, he thought, she has modelled herself on me! He did not know whether to be horrified or flattered, but he had to admit she made a very attractive young man. No wonder that woman had looked at her.

'I am not going to spoil your chance, I promise.'

'Yer see, Mr D, we belongs 'ere – backstage, we're all the same, all in it together – it's 'ard ter explain – it's our own world,' said Isabella.

Of course he understood; he had acted in enough plays to know exactly what she meant. He knew all the anticipation of waiting in the wings, the whispered comments on the condition of the house, the last-minute adjustments to the costume, the sense of exclusivity that comes with being backstage – everyone, he thought, wants to be someone else.

'Wanter see the show? Mrs Fitzjohn'll be on,' asked Isabella. 'Best seats?'

'Lead on.' Dickens was intrigued to see Mrs Fitzjohn and her highwayman act. They went in to the theatre which was crowded with cheering spectators in the pit and in the boxes, but there was a place for them. The crowd was generally of the rougher sort but good-humoured enough. He saw the occasional little group of toffs come for a taste of low life, and to ogle Mrs Fitzjohn in her breeches and her high boots. She came on stage in a coat of green velvet and a scarlet and gold tricorn hat. Great stampings and whistles greeted her – the star of the show – and she began by firing her pistols into the audience to great applause. There was a great deal of singing and shooting of Bow Street Runners; a docile horse was brought on, hardly suitable for Gentleman Jack. It looked as if it couldn't amble, never mind execute a gallop. A coach was brought on looking suspiciously like an old street cab and the coachman was shot dead. A lovely damsel fainted into Jack's arms and the highwayman helped himself to a few kisses and several bags of clinking coins. Then followed an interlude in which two young ladies in sailors' dresses performed the skipping hornpipe.

Dickens enjoyed it all despite its tawdriness and the shabbiness of the properties. He could imagine Isabella taking Mrs Fitzjohn's part – it was surely time for Mrs Fitzjohn to retire. Underneath the wig and paint he had an idea that she might be fifty. Isabella would relish the role of highwayman, especially the pistols, and Sesina would make a pert little damsel. Mrs Fitzjohn would deceive no one as to her sex, but Isabella – well, he had not known her until she spoke – she made a convincing young man in her disguise.

Disguise thou art a wickedness – so, indeed. The answer came to him as he sat there thinking about Isabella. He remembered now the figure passing him near St Giles's – a man with a woman's face. And he thought about Sophy Outfin dressed in boy's clothes – so like her brother, so like her brother. And Theo in his dream dressed as his sister.

'I cannot wait,' he whispered to Isabella. 'Forgive me, I must go at once. I hope we shall meet again.' He pressed a sovereign into her hand. 'Take care of yourselves. Goodnight.' Then he was gone.

He hurried back to Oxford Street to take a cab to Norfolk Street where he hoped Sam would be in. He must speak with him at once. He leapt into the nearest cab – it seemed so slow that he wondered if the horse were back to its real job after its stint in the theatre. He almost leapt out again to run all the way, but it had been another long day and it seemed an age since he had played with the boys on the carpet. Heavens, one of Alfred's wooden horses would be faster than this.

At length, the cab got him to Sam's house; there was a light downstairs which usually meant that Sam was home. He leant over the railings at the front of the house and tapped gently with his stick.

The door opened to show Sam. 'It is a bit early for the train, is it not?'

'We shall not be going to Liverpool, Sam; we must go to Brighton again.'

Sam let him in. He could tell that Dickens had something to impart – he saw how his eyes shone with triumph. He had found out something important or he had solved the mystery. They went into the parlour where Elizabeth was sitting sewing by the fire.

'Elizabeth, forgive me. I know it is late but –'

'You have news for Sam. May I stay?' She had seen the flash of light in his eyes. How alive he was, she thought, so full of vitality, his face now so clear and eager.

'Of course – you must stay. I shall want to know what you think of my ideas.' He wondered then – what if he were wrong? Well, let us see what the rational Sam thought – and Elizabeth – they would both provide a counterweight to his wild fancy – and it did seem a little wild now. But, no – he was sure he was right.

They sat before the fire after Sam had given him brandy and water.

'Now, tell us all. We are agog – if you have solved this case, I shall ask the commissioner to appoint you instantly in my place and I shall take up blacksmithing – what say you, Elizabeth, to the country life?'

'I say that if I do not hear what Charles has to say in the next second or two I shall expire, and you will be blacksmithing without a wife to wipe your fevered brow. Charles, please.'

'I have been to the theatre – well to what passes for one. I was taken thither by Isabella Gordon and Miss Sesina – as I foretold, they are together.'

'And this is important because –'

'Miss Isabella is in disguise – dressed as a man and a convincing one at that. We went to a show featuring Mrs Fitzjohn in high boots and breeches as a highwayman, and while I was watching I thought of a man I had seen in St Giles's – a man with a woman's face, and I thought of Miss Sophy Outfin dressed as her brother as Mrs Mapes described. My thoughts turned naturally to Mademoiselle Victorine and her brother –'

'Who never existed – we found out that in Paris.'

'But we never understood why she pretended to send her brother to the Du Canes –'

'Well, she would hardly send her lover, Michel.'

'Indeed not. But, think, Sam – no one ever saw them together – we believed her to be Michel's accomplice, and though the shawl was in the graveyard those two girls saw only a young man – or what they thought –' He broke off, seeing Sam's face register understanding. 'You see, don't you? There was no brother, there was no lover – only Victorine.'

'Disguised as a man – that is what you thought when you saw Isabella.'

'It was – she was so convincing. If I had not known her when she spoke to me I would have taken her for a young, attractive man.'

'But, Victorine – she was – I don't know what she was. Too slight, I suppose,' Sam was not entirely convinced. 'There was a case, years ago when I was a constable. A man called Bill Chapman appeared in court with a woman called Isabella Watson who was charged with assaulting her sister.

Bill Chapman was with Isabella, but it turned out that Bill Chapman was a woman.'

'There you are, then – it happens. It proves my theory.' Dickens was determined now. He had come thinking that Sam and Elizabeth might contradict him, but now that Sam seemed uncertain, he was sure.

Sam saw the familiar gleam in Dickens's eyes, but he, too, was determined to have his say. 'Not quite. My point is that Mary Chapman was like a man. She was chewing tobacco, she had the gait of a man, the voice of a man – she looked like a costermonger.'

'But you said yourself that you don't know what Victorine was. We said she was sexless. And the witnesses, Sam – Mrs Twiss saw a young man coming from her yard, Constable Green's witness at Hungerford Market said Jemmy was with a toff. The girls at St Giles's Churchyard saw a man. People see a person dressed in man's clothes – they don't look any closer. It's a man. They don't think that it could be a woman. Why would they?'

Sam didn't reply. Dickens and Elizabeth looked at him, but he seemed to be abstracted as though he were listening for something.

'Sam,' said Elizabeth, 'for goodness' sake, tell us what you think.'

Sam smiled back at them. 'I think I hear the sound of the hammer on the anvil!'

'You believe it?' Dickens wanted a definite answer.

'I do. You are right, Charles – it does make sense, but –'

'But me no buts – remember the footman at the Du Canes – he described a slight, young man –'

'Whom he was ready to believe was Victorine's brother because there was a resemblance – it could not have been Michel. It's impossible to believe that her lover resembled her. I was going to say, but why? Why would she dress as a man?'

'Yes, why? Surely, it would have been easier for a woman to lure the boys? Would they not have gone more readily with a woman if she asked them to do an errand for her?' asked Elizabeth.

'That's true, but whatever her reason, her disguise meant that we were looking for a young man – even when we went to her house, we had no thought that she was the murderer. Even when Rogers said it could have been a woman, we did not think of her. But, Charles, why must we go back to Brighton? We have been there and I have heard nothing from the Brighton police.'

'You remember what Madame Rigaud said about her son – he was born in November. I thought about it on the way here. The child must be buried in Brighton. Mrs Hart went back to her room where Robin lived with her – perhaps Victorine has gone to be with her son.'

'But Victorine is no Mrs Hart – she is a murderess.'

'But she is a mother who lost her only child,' said Elizabeth.

Sam looked at his wife. What could he say? She would, of course, think of the loss of the child – she had lost her only child too. He was silent, feeling her words as a rebuke. Dickens felt guilty – he had come here full of the excitement of his revelation, eager to discuss the crime in the abstract. He had not thought of where the discussion might lead.

'I am sorry, Elizabeth – it was thoughtless of me not to think –'

'No, no, it is quite different, but I was simply thinking of what she might have felt about her child's death. When Edith died, I thought I should go mad, but I had Sam – I was not criticising, Sam – do not think so. But, suppose she is mad, that the death of the child has somehow twisted her so that she does not understand herself what she has done.'

They stared into the flames, dying down now, all thinking of the losses they had borne. Dickens thought of the death of his sister Fanny in 1848 and her little crippled son who had died so soon after his mother. He thought of his sister-in-law, Mary, and the anguish he had felt then for the girl in whom he had felt a father's pride. It was the death of innocence, he had thought, the cruel, random taking away of a life of promise, of gentle youth and goodness. Yet, in the fight of life, it was necessary to hide our hearts in carrying on to discharge our duties and responsibilities, but then that could be done with the help of work to be carried out, the love of family, friends. Perhaps it could not be done without those things.

'Loneliness – that was the impression she gave – Sophy Outfin mentioned it and so did Mary Mapes. That house, Sam, when we went there, how empty it seemed.'

'I can see how that might warp her, but why kill those innocent boys? What had they done?' Sam found it difficult to pity her – three boys dead, three killed because she had lost one.

Elizabeth looked grave. She had felt a kind of pity when she thought of Victorine as a mother who had lost her only child, but then she thought of those dead boys and what had been done to Mrs Hart. Sam was right to remind them of the fact that she was a murderess.

'You are right, Sam,' she said, reading his thoughts in the set of his mouth. 'Whatever she felt does not excuse what she has done.'

'And we must find her. We cannot know that she will not do it again.'

'So, we will go to Brighton, find out where the child is buried – a Catholic church –'

'And we will wait, I suppose. I hope you are right. In the meantime, I'll telegraph to Liverpool. The police there can examine the passenger list for the *Cambria* and they can wait to see if she turns up, either as herself or as a young man. I'll give them all the names she might be using: Jolicoeur, Rigaud, Blandois. I need to be sure that I have covered that possibility.'

'I will go now – and I will see you at the station tomorrow. Goodnight, Elizabeth.'

Sam saw him out. Despite the possibility that they were close to a solution, neither felt at all satisfied. This was the worst part, thought Sam, knowing too well the consequences of their finding her.

'Goodnight, Charles.'

'Goodnight, Sam.'

They said no more. Dickens knew his friend's thoughts. Sam could never feel triumph in the catching of the murderer. Justice would be done, but like Dickens he would hate the jeering of the crowd at the death, the greedy desire to see the rope jerk and the body dangle. He walked away, subdued by the dark thoughts, the excitement of his sudden revelation dissipated. Why had she done it? Yes, he could imagine that she was mad, that her loneliness had warped her, but what had she thought about those boys she had killed? Why had she chosen them? They were the same age as her boy would have been, and he remembered Robin and the boy named Nose lying as if sleeping on the marble slab, and Jemmy. They had all looked alike, perhaps resembling her own son. Was that it? She thought she had found him and when she saw that each boy was not her son she killed him. And what would the law make of that?

A defence of insanity was possible under the law if it could be proved that the defendant was labouring under such a defect of reason that he or she did not know that the act committed was wrong. Poor Mary Lamb, who had written *Tales from Shakespeare* with her brother, Charles Lamb. She had murdered her mother. The verdict had been lunacy – her brother had taken care of her for the rest of his life. She had died only two years ago at the age of eighty-three. But this was different. There would be no one to take care of Mademoiselle Victorine, and her murders, unlike Mary Lamb's murder, were not in the heat of some crisis. Victorine had lured those boys. And – he remembered Kip's information – she had known Robin Hart, she must have known his mother and what the boy meant to her – yes, it might be a kind of madness, but it involved calculation, the desire to punish and, as he had said to Sam, the killer had hated.

He had been sure that she would not kill again, but when he thought of the hatred she had conceived, he was not sure – and the mask – that drawing – there was something horrible about it.

He walked on to York Gate to make his way to Devonshire Terrace. He paused by the church of St Marylebone, its whiteness silvered in the moonlight. It seemed somehow remote in its marbled quietness, its steeple with its Corinthian columns pointing into the heavens. The chaste stars looked down upon the darkened city, its mansions and its hovels wherein human lives passed in agony and desperate passion. *Is there no pity sitting in the heavens?* he thought.

26

FLOWERS ON A GRAVE

The eight o'clock express from London Bridge took them to Brighton in under two hours. The Brighton police had been informed on their first visit that Superintendent Jones of Bow Street was in pursuit of a murderer. They went straight to the police station where Sam explained that they needed to know where were the Catholic churches with burial places, and that he needed some men to watch each church. They should be looking this time either for a young, bespectacled woman or a young man. He explained that they believed the young woman to be the suspect, but that she might be disguised as a man. They believed that her child might be buried in a Catholic churchyard. They learned that there was only one Catholic church, St James's, which was in Kemptown – this would be undoubtedly where their suspect would have worshipped. However, it was not likely that the child was buried there – burials took place in the extension to the graveyard at St Nicholas's.

Superintendent Rook of the Brighton police seemed certain that the grave would be at St Nicholas's, though he would send two men to St James's. 'I will show you why I think you have come to the right place,' he said. 'There is something interesting at the churchyard which your Mademoiselle Victorine may have seen. You have to see for yourselves. It will strike you more forcibly if you do.'

They were intrigued, of course, but Sam trusted the solidly built superintendent whom he had met before. He was a serious-faced man, a forceful character whose experience demanded respect. He had served under Chief Constable Henry Solomon who had been murdered in 1844 in this very place, bludgeoned by one John Laurence. Solomon had been interviewing him about the matter of a stolen carpet. Laurence had seized the poker from near the fire and beaten him about the head – Solomon had died later from his terrible injuries. Sam knew of the case and the dreadful sensation it had caused. Superintendent Rook was not likely to trifle with them over the matter of murder.

Rain was beginning to fall as they made their way out of the station towards Church Hill where the church of St Nicholas was situated. Although Superintendent Rook explained that the new burial ground had opened in 1841, he took them first to the fourteenth-century church where they walked among the old graves until he stopped and pointed to a particular one – the tombstone erected to the memory of Phoebe Hessel. Reading the inscription, they understood what he meant. The words were astonishing:

In Memory of
PHOEBE HESSEL
Who was born at Stepney in the year 1713
She served for many Years
as a private soldier in the 5th Regt. of foot
in different parts of Europe
and in the Year 1745 *fought under the command*
of the DUKE of CUMBERLAND
at the Battle of Fontenoy
where she received a bayonet wound in her Arm
Her long life which commenced in the time of
QUEEN ANNE
Extended to the reign of
GEORGE IV

*by whose munificence she received comfort
and support in her latter Years
she died at Brighton where she had lived
December 12th 1821 Aged 108 Years*

'I see what you mean, Superintendent Rook,' Sam said. 'This is extraordinary. She was not discovered in all the years she served as a soldier?'

'Seventeen years and not even when she received her arm wound. She did let slip her identity to the wife of her commanding officer and then she was dismissed. An amazing woman – followed her soldier lover to the wars, apparently. I remember seeing her when I was a boy – couldn't believe anyone would be one hundred and eight.'

'And you think that Mademoiselle Victorine saw this, and that it gave her the idea for her disguise?' asked Dickens.

'Why not? She would have come here if her child was buried here – perhaps she remembered it – it is not something you would forget – all those years as a man.'

'It is so fantastic, it could be true. There are more things in heaven and earth, Sam.'

'Indeed there are. Now we must look at the church's records. We need to know if the child is here before we commence our vigil in this rain.'

They went into the ancient church to find the verger, a damp and ancient specimen, who, on the instruction of Superintendent Rook, showed them the volume in which were the records of burials in 1846. And there they found him – another lost boy whose death had brought about such suffering. Dickens thought of the innocent child, playing by the sea, perhaps carried away by the treacherous waves. Such a simple, bald statement: *Victor Blandois, Brighton November 26th, 1846, Age* 9. Sam heard Dickens's sharp intake of breath, and Dickens, turning to look at Sam, saw that he had the same thought.

'November 26th – today. She will come. I know it,' Dickens said.

They went across the road to the new burial ground and through its imposing archway. The place was still as death itself, cold and very melancholy in the dripping rain. She was there, a slight figure in her grey dress soaked into black by the slanting rain, bareheaded, heedless of the downpour, her sodden shawl hanging off her thin shoulders. They waited for five minutes, perhaps ten. Dickens did not know. It seemed an age, and all the while, the woman stood quite motionless. Time seemed to stand still. This was a terrible thing they had to do – to take her from that grave. Sam moved.

He walked across and touched her on the shoulder. She turned and knew the policeman who had come to her house. She did not speak, but knelt on the ground before the grave upon which she placed a little bunch of artificial flowers. Sam stood, his head bowed under the rain, and waited. Dickens and Superintendent Rook watched in silence. The rain fell steadily and they saw them through a misty haze as in a dream, the two figures, unmoving as if carved from stone. It was almost impossible to believe that the grieving figure was a woman who had killed children – but she had, thought Dickens. It was the only explanation.

A blackbird flew out of a tree, flinging its call across the silent graveyard. Sam bent to touch the woman again. She stood and turned to him, but she did not speak. Sam guided her towards the others, and she went before him, looking back from time to time at the grave where her son lay, and which she would never see again. Dickens saw how the rain blurred the thick lenses of the glasses. She could hardly see, but she showed no curiosity about the other two men. Superintendent Rook took off his oilskin, placed it round her unresisting shoulders, and he and Sam walked with her between them. Dickens came behind, and thus they went slowly back to the police station.

Once there, they placed her in a room with a fire burning. Superintendent Rook stayed to write down her confession – should she make one. She still did not speak. She was not afraid. What could the policemen do to her? It was all over. Why should she tell them? What was it to do with them?

Sam signalled to Dickens that he should sit at the other side of the table before her. Dickens understood that he was to question her. Sam stood by the mantelpiece so that he could see her. Dickens sat and looked at her. Victorine saw a man with a face of steel. His eyes looked into the very depths of her, cold, blue, hypnotising. She felt fear then. She did not want to speak, but he would make her, she knew it.

'Tell me about your boy.'

'He is dead, that is all.' Her voice was flat. It was as if she felt nothing now.

'What happened?' His face did not change and he continued to look at her, willing her to answer, using all his power. A certain implacable part of him surfaced like a half-hidden knife. She flinched as if she had seen the blade. He pitied her, but he did not let that interfere with his determination that she should answer.

'Tell me about it.'

'He drowned when he was nine.'

'And Michel?'

She was surprised then. How did they know about Michel? Not that it mattered. Michel. He was nothing to her. Only Victor had mattered. 'He went to America.'

'Why did you not go with him?'

'And leave Victor? Michel did not care. I went to London to please him, but he must go further away, he said. But I would not leave Victor – I could come to Brighton from London.'

'And the boys you found in London? What about them?'

She looked at him through the smeared lenses, but he could hardly see her eyes. He leant over and took them off and her eyes were suddenly larger. He saw for a moment that she might once have been attractive, that Michel might have found something there that she had hidden since Victor's death. Sam remembered saying that they would peel off the murderer's mask and the killer would know that he was caught. He almost wished that Dickens had not taken off those spectacles; she seemed somehow defenceless before them. But he saw that her eyes gave her away now.

She stared at Dickens. How she hated him. He knew everything. What did it matter? She would tell them, then. She would tell them about those boys, those boys who were nothing compared with her boy. And whose mothers did not care about them.

'Tell me about that first boy, Jemmy.'

'I had been to Madame Du Cane to fit a new hat. She was impatient to have it but it needed more work. She was not pleased. I went to the market at Hungerford and then I went to look at the river. The boy was there – he looked like Victor. I gave him some coins, a poor boy. He had no home, he said. I went back another day.'

'Why did you dress as a man?'

'It made me powerful. I could do as I wished. Madame Du Cane and Madame Outfin and, oh, yes, that girl, Miss Sophy, they thought I was nothing. They had everything, but I saw how spoilt they were, how selfish. Oh, I watched them in my disguise. I do not sleep – I went out at night. I was safe in my disguise. I could go anywhere. I saw them – that boy, I saw him in the alleys with that girl. A prostitute – and she was to have a child – she.' Her voice was hard with contempt. 'Oh, yes, they did not know what he did but I knew – behind their masks, they were nothing.'

'Jemmy?'

'I went back to the river – I asked him to come with me. I told him that my sister, Mademoiselle Victorine, would feed him – I thought he would come with me. I wanted him – I thought he was like Victor but he was not. He turned on me, accusing me – the words he used, vile, filthy words. Not Victor. He ran into the water and I dragged him out. Why should he live when my good boy was dead?'

'You drew a mask.'

'I did – they wore masks. Why not I? They would not find me. They would not know what it meant. No one would know.'

'What did it mean?'

'I could see – I must go home, but the eyes behind the mask, my eyes, they watched all – they could see the dead, and the living who found them and who would not understand.'

She closed her eyes then. They saw the terrible weariness in that pale, thin face – no, she did not sleep. Sam was reminded of the masks he had drawn, the blind eyes holding their secrets. He hoped she would not refuse to answer any more questions. He shifted purposely, making a noise with his feet as if he were stepping forward. Her eyes flew open and Dickens seized the moment.

'And the second boy, Robin?'

'He was a nice boy – at first. I gave him pennies. He was hungry. I would take him in – I would feed him. He always said he wanted to go home – how did his mother deserve a boy like that? She did not feed him. I saw him one night when I was out walking. I took him to the churchyard. I said my sister, Mamselle Victorine, wanted him to take something to a customer, and that she was waiting at the church. My sister would pay him, I said. But when I showed him the shawl he said it was his mother's shawl. He tried to take it. He talked only of his mother. And he said he did not like Mademoiselle

Victorine – she frightened him. He hated her, he said. But Victor loved me. That boy, his face when he said he hated me.'

Dickens thought of the boy leaning against the killer, submissive in her arms. Yes, he had been dead when those girls had seen them in St Giles's. She had pulled him to her and the pin had slid in. If they had come a minute or two before, Robin might have lived. No time to think. Move on before those eyes closed up again. They had to know it all.

'The shawl – where did you get it? You said it was Madame Outfin's.'

'I took it. It was at the Du Canes. Someone had thrown it away. They did not care about my work. I took what was mine.'

'There was another boy.'

'Not my boy. I made a mistake. I saw his face – he was a monster. Why should he live when my boy was dead?' Her eyes were cold. She was not afraid now. This man who thought he was so powerful. He was nothing.

He told her about Mrs Hart, how she had loved her son, how she had died for lack of Robin. But there was nothing. Dickens saw no remorse there, no pity. He had seen enough. Silently, he handed back her glasses. She put them on, her mask. Nothing now could pierce that impenetrable face. She was closed to them. She had told her tale.

They took her to London – to Newgate. And she spoke no more.

27

GALLOWS

A great many things took place in December. Charley had his interview for Eton and showed great intelligence in his knowledge of Virgil and Herodotus. Dickens wrote to Charley's tutor, Mr Jones, that he was inexpressibly delighted at the readiness with which Charley went through this ordeal with a stranger. Dickens kept Christmas in the usual way; on the twenty-fourth day of December he took his children to the toy shop in Holborn where they selected their Christmas presents; there was the pantomime with Mark Lemon and a country dance to end the old year. Kip flourished at Urania Cottage – a good-natured donkey with mild eyes had been bought and was Kip's special responsibility. James Bagster took him to his daughter's house at Kensal Green where he played with James's two grandchildren, and ate plum pudding for the first time in his life. Sam and Elizabeth entertained the Brim family – and Scrap, of course. The shop was closed and Mr Brim rested in the upstairs bedroom at Norfolk Street. Captain Pierce took Davey to live near the sea where the wind scoured the lanes and fields clean so that it was possible to breathe the clear air which dissolved some of the dark terrors of London, and eventually he forgot the nightmare city.

On December 29th Dickens sat in his study looking at the snow outside. The first page of the tenth instalment of *David Copperfield* was staring at him with what he called a blank aspect. He took up his quill to write a letter to his friend William de Cerjat in Lausanne. He told him that Little Em'ly must fall, but that he hoped to put the story before the thoughts of the people in a new way which might do some good, perhaps evoking sympathy for the seduced and ruined girl. He recalled the hanging of the Mannings: *the conduct of the people was so indescribably frightful that I felt for some time afterwards almost as if I were living in a city of devils. I feel, at this hour, as if I never could go near the place again...* And he felt the same about Newgate where Victorine Jolicoeur was imprisoned. She would surely hang in the New Year.

Newgate. Looming black, a stern slab of thick, cold stone, sombre as a fortress, where Mademoiselle Victorine waited in the condemned cell for the day of her execution. Dickens would not go. He could imagine it all too well, the narrow and obscure staircase leading to the dark passage in which a charcoal stove cast a lurid tint, and the massive door of the condemned cell. He could picture her in that stone dungeon with its scratched, hard bench, its iron candlestick which at night would cast flickering shadows on the wall until extinguished at ten o'clock by the two warders who kept guard over that slight, anonymous woman who had said nothing in her own defence, who had been found guilty, and who had listened impassively to the judge with the black silk on his head while he uttered the sombre words: *hanged by the neck until you are dead.* He could see in his mind's eye the Bible and the prayer book, and wondered if she had read them, or if she had made her confession to the black-robed priest from the Sardinian church. Dickens had remembered the kindness and concern in the priest's eyes, and had gone back there to enquire if the priest would visit her.

On the Sunday before the hanging, the gaol bell would summon the prisoners from their various wards to the chapel.

The condemned woman would be brought in to sit in the black pew from where she would stare at the pulpit and reading desk hung with black. The prison chaplain would ascend the pulpit. Dickens could imagine the words addressed to the unhappy prisoner doomed to die on the morrow, who must call upon Him who alone had the power of forgiveness, and who had said *though her sins were red as scarlet,* He would *make them white as snow.* He looked through the window at the white garden, at the thickening sky where snow gathered to fall silent and slow. He thought of Mrs Hart, Robin, Jemmy and Nose to be buried soon under the cold earth. He thought again of Victorine in Newgate.

He had written of the condemned man in that cell with its small high window barred with heavy iron, listening to the deep bell of St Paul's, counting the hours, seven, six, five left. He had written of how such a man might still hope for reprieve, and how in his restless sleep, he would dream of a happier past and wake to find that Time, inexorable, unstoppable, had marched grimly on, bringing the grey light of morning stealing into the cell. He did not think that Victorine would dream of a happier past. She would not sleep. She would lie awake, her eyes open in the darkness, and Mrs Hart, Robin, Jemmy and Nose would come to her then to watch her in silence, their eyes accusing and the boys would merge into one boy. And that boy would be Victor, streaming with water, his drowned eyes weeping, his grief for her a searing reproach. She would reach for him, but he would be gone. Then she would know what she had done. She would start from her uneasy bed. She would fumble for her spectacles, and see in that dank morning gloom that every object in the narrow cell was too frightfully real to admit of doubt – she would know that she was the condemned woman and that in two hours she would be dead.

And it all came to pass as he foretold. On a grimly freezing Monday morning when the bells of St Paul's and St Sepulchre's struck eight, the crowd was gathered, thick as flies, pushing and jostling for the best view. There was the black scaffold and the black chain with its hook to which would be attached the hempen rope that would encircle that fragile neck. Another bell rang out and the Debtor's Door opened to let out the solemn procession. First the chaplain intoning the words of the burial service: *The Lord giveth and the Lord taketh away.* Then Mademoiselle Victorine, so slight as to be almost weightless, her arms already pinioned. Then William Calcraft, sometime cobbler and pieman, hangman now for twenty years, paid a guinea a week and a guinea for each execution as well as the money he made from selling pieces of rope from executions. The short drop was his speciality and it could be an ugly business if the victim did not die soon – and Mademoiselle Victorine weighed nothing. He had measured her with his keen, cold eye. He'd have to be nifty, he thought, down the ladder to pull on her legs. Still, it made a decent show for the mob. Couldn't disappoint his public. He had hanged Mr and Mrs Manning before a crowd of, it was thought, thirty thousand or more. That day's crowd was no less guilty of the wickedness and levity against which Dickens had fulminated in his letter to *The Times.*

Mademoiselle Victorine walked steadily, betraying nothing of fear or sorrow – her eyes were lowered. Without her spectacles she could see very little, but she could hear the low growl of the crowd rising to a cacophony of shrieks and jeers. She was placed on the trapdoor, her head and face covered in a white cap and the noose placed round her neck.

Sam turned away – he had fulfilled his duty by being there, but he did not want to see to what end he had brought her. The horror of the crime almost faded from his mind when he looked upon the howling mob. The pity and horror, Dickens had said about the execution of the Mannings. He pitied her then and her victims, and poor Victor whom he had never known, but whose death had brought this. With these churning thoughts, he walked away, sick at heart.

EPILOGUE

In Paris, the hat shop was closed. Madame Regnier and Madame Manette had gone to the country for a little holiday. Apparently, Madame Manette was expecting her first child – it was well to be careful, Madame Rigaud had told her neighbour. The shop would open again in a few weeks. The girl would serve at the counter, and Madame Manette would sew quietly in the back room where the canary sang and Frou curled up by the fire. The child, a boy, was born in April. Spring, not winter. It was an easy birth.

In New York, Michel Blandois read an account of the hanging. He wondered if he might have prevented it all. He thought of a woman with soft curling brown hair framing her thin face and dreaming grey eyes that without spectacles could awake desire. He had loved her once. He thought of a winter's day by the sea and a child playing, running in and out of the water, his face glowing with life. He thought of how he had left him to talk to a Frenchman he knew, and how, when he had gone back to the shore, the laughing boy had gone, swept away by the drag of the tide. She had not forgiven him.

In the little apartment Michel lived with his new wife – she did not know that he was already married. It did not matter, Michel thought. His first wife would never know. The past was in France; the future was here in America, an empty slate on which he could write any version of his life that he wanted. The child cried and his mother hushed him, wrapping the beautifully embroidered shawl round him. He wished now he had not kept it. He had told Louisa that it had been his mother's – she had liked that. She was pretty with her short hair – when they needed money, she had sold her long black hair and now she looked like an attractive boy. Michel did not like it, but she said it would grow and she would be his Louisa again. She brought the child to him.

'He needs a name, Michel. He must be baptised soon. What shall we call him?'

'Victor,' he said.

In England, quicklime, white like crystallised snow, strewed the unmarked grave in the ground of Newgate. It was thought that quicklime would hasten the decomposition of the bodies, that it would eat the flesh and bones, and even the poor, twisted heart that had loved Victor. True snow fell softly on the grave where Victor lay, covering the pitiful, tattered flowers which would rot in the months to come, never to be replaced; it fell on the quiet grave wherein lay Mrs Hart and Robin, and it fell now on the grave of Jemmy and Nose, softening the harshness of the dark earth. Dickens and Jones stood there looking at the mounds of earth after the funerals for which Dickens and Sam had paid – not for these victims an unmarked pauper's grave, not for them the number scrawled in chalk on the cheap coffin which would split as it was lowered, not for them the crowded earthen vault. There would be a headstone for each pair, one inscribed with the names Jemmy Kidd and Joe Joram. Nose was all the name that poor disfigured face had possessed so Dickens had christened him, thereby blessing him with a name and a mother. Minnie Joram could be glimpsed by the reader of *David Copperfield*, dancing a little child in her arms, while another little fellow, Joe Joram, clung to her apron – a good mother. It was all he could do for that unknown, abandoned child. Someone, sometime, would pass by and wonder who they were, two boys in one grave – and pity, even if for a moment.

'*Their little lives, rounded with a sleep – sleep that shuts up sorrow's eye.*' There was comfort in Shakespeare's words, thought Sam, listening to the half-murmured phrases which were Dickens's epitaph for the dead. They walked away from the graveyard. Sam went home to the warmth of Norfolk Street and Elizabeth.

Dickens stood outside the door of number one Devonshire Terrace and looked up at one bright star shining, and thought of a story in which a child looked upon the star as on the home he was to go to. I hope it may be true, he thought as he opened the door to a tremendous rampaging and ravaging on the stairs down which several boys appeared to be tumbling all at once. Catherine stood at the top of the stairs, smiling down at the confusion of boys, Henry in her arms, and holding back Sydney who was longing to fling himself after the others. Georgina was at the bottom of the stairs, just in time to catch the plump and unpoetical Alfred Tennyson, aged four. Home. Magic word. He had come a long way from Hungerford Stairs.

HISTORICAL NOTE

In November 1849, Charles Dickens was writing *David Copperfield*. In the novel, young David is sent to work at the bottle factory owned by Murdstone and Grinby. As a twelve-year-old boy Dickens had worked at Warren's blacking factory at Hungerford Stairs; he never forgot the misery and humiliation of those days: 'Until old Hungerford Market was pulled down, until old Hungerford Stairs were destroyed, I never had the courage to go back to the place where my servitude began. I never saw it. I could not endure to go near it.'

Dickens married Catherine Hogarth in 1836; by 1849 they had eight children, the baby, Henry Fielding Dickens, being ten months old. Henry Fielding was the most successful of Dickens's children – he became a judge. Charley, the eldest son, did go to Eton in 1850; Sydney, whom Dickens presciently named 'Ocean Spectre', did go to sea. He died in 1872 and was buried at sea. Katey married Charles, the younger brother of Wilkie Collins, and Mamie stayed with her father until his death in 1870.

Dickens established the Home for Fallen Women with Angela Burdett-Coutts in 1847. He said that Georgiana Morson was the best matron he ever employed. Isabella Gordon and Anna-Maria Sesini were dismissed from the Home in 1849 for misconduct. I have imagined their subsequent history.

John Forster, Dickens's close friend, wrote the first biography of Dickens, and Mark Lemon, another close friend, was editor of *Punch* magazine.

Dickens met Edgar Allen Poe in 1842, and the French poet Lamartine in 1844 and 1847.

The periodical *Household Words* came out in March 1850. It was in this magazine that Dickens wrote his articles on the London police, including the anecdote *On Duty with Inspector Field*. The character of Superintendent Sam Jones of Bow Street is fictional, though his character does owe something to Inspector Field, particularly his authority over the criminals he and Dickens encounter. There is no evidence that Dickens was ever involved in a murder case, but he was interested in crime, and a recent biographer observed that he had a secret desire to be a detective. In this novel, and in the first of the Dickens and Jones mysteries, *The Murder of Patience Brooke*, I have imagined what might have happened if Dickens had been given the opportunity to investigate a murder.

ABOUT THE AUTHOR

J.C. Briggs taught English for many years in Hong Kong and Lancashire and now lives in Cumbria. *Death at Hungerford Stairs* is the second of the cases for Charles Dickens and Superintendent Jones.